SHERLOCK HOLMES AND THE TIME MACHINE

Book #4 from the Confidential Files of John H. Watson, M. D.

C.J. LUTTON

Edited by
JOANNA CAMPBELL SLAN

spot on publishing

*To Jeff, Debbie, Stuart, and Brenda (my wonderful sons, and daughters-in-laws)
— Thank you all for the love and support you've given me through my rough
time losing CJ and for putting up with all my texts, emails, and calls.
And to Sterling, Caleb, Matthew, and Steven — As I once wrote in a poem to
Steven, "Nana's Joys Are All Her Boys", so it was for CJ's love for his grandsons.
He adored you all.*

*Love,
Mom-Nana*

CONTENTS

OTHER BOOKS BY CJ LUTTON WITH
JOANNA CAMPBELL SLAN

Sherlock Holmes and the Giant Rat of Sumatra

Sherlock Holmes and the Father of Lies

Sherlock Holmes and the Nefarious Seafarers

Sherlock Holmes and the Time Machine

For more information and purchase links, go to:

http://www.booklaunch.io/joannaslan/thesherlockholmesstories

OUR GIFT TO YOU

Dr. John H. Watson has written a background report on the famous Diogenes Club. If you are interested in all aspects of Sherlock Holmes' world, this is a must-read! To claim your copy, go here —

https://BookHip.com/TNQTC.

Sherlock Holmes and the Time Machine: Book #2 from the Confidential Files of John H. Watson, M.D. by C.J. Lutton

Copyright © 2020 by the Estate of C. J. Lutton

C/o Joanna Campbell Slan

Spot On Publishing

9307 SE Olympus Street

Hobe Sound FL 33455 / USA

www.thesherlockstories.com

www.SpotOnPublishing.org

www.JoannaSlan.com

Revised 01/13/2020

Cover art: http://www.WickedSmartDesigns.com

Sherlock Holmes and the Time Machine: Book #2 from the Confidential Files of John H. Watson, M.D. by C.J. Lutton

ISBN: 979-8635407448

PUBLISHER'S NOTE

In keeping with Dr. John H. Watson's original notes, we have used British spellings throughout this manuscript.

PREFACE

June, 1897
London

When chronicling the many adventures Sherlock Holmes and I have shared together, my readers have grown to expect a tightly woven narrative replete with startling moments of brilliance and logic. Alas, this is not one of those cases.

From its outset, we were so thoroughly disadvantaged by the singularity of the case that our investigation was tantamount to a series of incomprehensible misjudgments and confusion.

You, the reader, must not infer that the above statements are construed as a criticism of my friend's capabilities. In point of fact, it was because of Sherlock Holmes' dogged determination and ability to instantly respond to the unexpected that this confounding case reached any resolution at all. As illustrated by his actions when pursuing the Father of Lies, Holmes' intellect is matched only by his courage. Once again, he has been called upon to yoke both strengths in order to safeguard the future of mankind.

After having forewarned you thus, I invite you to study these dramatic and somewhat dubious particulars and draw your own conclusions.

John H. Watson, M.D.

❦ I ❦

Under an already blistering morning sun, Sherlock Holmes and I found ourselves trudging back up the stairs to our flat, 221B Baker Street. We were exhausted after spending the better part of the previous evening and the early hours of this day at Westminster. Holmes had been called to an important conference relating to the upcoming Diamond Jubilee celebration of Queen Victoria, and I had agreed to go along as his amanuensis. Of course, Mycroft Holmes, Sherlock's brother, was there, too, as Mycroft is an essential part of the governing of our nation.

Given the Queen's extended mourning for her beloved husband, Prince Albert, and the pain caused by her rheumatism, HRH (Her Royal Highness) had decided that her son, the Prince of Wales, would represent her during the review of the Royal Navy to be held in Spithead, Portsmouth. Other members of the extended Royal Family and Her Majesty's royal guests would accompany Prince Albert Edward, known in the popular press as Bertie, to the port. Once there, the prince would review the Royal Navy.

Much was discussed in the way of preparations with a particular view to the safekeeping of the heir apparent to the realm, Prince Edward. Given that our monarch was the longest reigning sovereign since her grandfather, George III, the nation was more than happy to celebrate Queen Victoria's sixty years on the throne. Truly, she is considered the "Mother of the British Empire." All of us were mindful that with great crowds came great risk, and the need to protect the Royal Family was readily apparent. Accordingly, there was much to consider.

Our participation in the meeting ended only an hour ago when the Queen herself appointed Holmes as the Protector of the Realm. Specifically, she charged my friend with protecting her son and the Royal Family while they represented her interests in Portsmouth.

Rather than congratulating his brother, Mycroft Holmes' fleshy face scowled when the Queen announced the appointment. I was puzzled by Mycroft's disapproval. He'd never shown any sign that he was jealous of his younger brother. Although Sherlock and Mycroft both have often been asked to assist the Royal Family many times in the past, this particular task was one that my friend accepted only grudgingly. The concerns were indeed weighty, and the beastly heat had worn my friend's nerves to a frazzle. I am sure that Holmes noticed his brother's disapproval, but we lacked an opportunity to quiz him about his displeasure because Mycroft Holmes was still in conference with Her Majesty when we were dismissed from Windsor Castle.

I tried to discuss the matter with Holmes, but I was flummoxed at every turn. Holmes is typically impervious to such trivial matters as the weather. However, on this particular day, the climbing temperatures had worn his temper to a frazzle. Rather than irritate him further, I decided my worries could wait a day or two.

"Watson!" bellowed Holmes, as we burst into the flat. He dove upon the divan. "Draw the curtains and allow some shade to cool these infernal rooms. Get me a wet cloth to put over my eyes, won't you?"

Although his tendency to order me about can annoy me greatly, this time I did as asked, knowing that he was fighting one of his many migraines. Once he was situated, I stood at the open window and watched people as they gamely went about their business with stoop-shouldered determination under the scorching June sun. Since I had served in Afghanistan during the war, the oppressive heat was not as debilitating to me as it was to my friend.

It was under these most uncomfortable of circumstances that I found myself to be on the receiving end of one of my friend's most sudden foul moods.

"Watson, what must I do to earn your sympathy? Must I, with my last dying breath, with parched and blistered lips, beg you to do as I ask? Will you kindly draw the curtains and let me die in the cooling shadows? Please!"

"Holmes, you're impossible," was my peevish retort, as I snapped shut the curtains. "Everyone is suffering this weather, but you don't hear them caterwauling on about it."

"Most probably," Holmes groaned, "they are not howling in protest because their minds are too addled and parched to muster even the weakest cry. We will not be attending the Jubilee if this weather doesn't break. In fact, no one will."

Of course, I knew nothing would keep my friend from attending the Queen's Celebration. Protecting the Royals while they were at Portsmouth for the Jubilee was an incredible honour. And, of course, Holmes had given his word. The ferocity of his peevish complaining caused me to chuckle at the absurdity of his threat.

"Holmes!" I cried. "Is this the man who captured the notorious Villaggio?"

I was referring, of course, to the mysterious case of the Murdered Maestro. It was due to Holmes' renowned reputation, his insistence, and his unbridled admiration of the aging Francois Dulac that the doctors agreed to allow Holmes to observe the autopsy of the violinist. Holmes' keen interest in the macabre and his intimate knowledge of poisons led him to deduce that the maestro hadn't died of gastric fever. Of course, the doctors quickly confirmed that Holmes was right. Once Dulac's death was determined to be murder, Holmes was immediately on the case.

As it happened, Maestro Dulac's health had seemed frail and his limited income had been dwindling, so he entered into a financial arrangement with Villaggio, his longtime friend. Villaggio agreed to pay a monthly income of twenty pounds to the maestro for the rest of his life (*en viager*). In return, Dulac's grand apartments and their contents would become Villaggio's property when the maestro died.

Unfortunately for the schemer, Dulac lived longer than expected. What had seemed to be an ideal arrangement inevitably placed a financial strain on Villaggio. After growing more and more resentful and desperate, Villaggio hatched a deadly plan. He cleverly mixed arsenic with the violinist's bow resin. Thus, the maestro unwittingly inhaled the toxic dust when he performed his aptly called farewell tour.

If it hadn't been for Holmes love of the violin and his regard for the maestro, Villaggio would surely have gotten away with murder. When confronted with the evidence, Villaggio quickly confessed and the case was closed. Once again, Holmes had proven himself to be peerless when it came to solving crimes.

"How about a fire?" I asked laughingly, as I pointed to the hearth. "That's what you need. A crackling blaze to ward off the chill in your bones."

"You have a cruel streak running through your black heart, Watson. One that I've never seen in you before." Holmes disappeared into his room, shutting the door with a bang.

"Wake me when the furniture ceases to melt," he called, his voice barely discernible above the thrashing and clattering of drawers, books, and other whatnots being tossed about. As violent as his tantrum was, the sudden quiet of his room was equally violent to my ears. I worried that Holmes had hurt himself and went near his door to listen.

Of course, as was seemingly always the case of late, Holmes caught me snooping by suddenly jerking open his door. "Oh!" he said, surprised at my nearness. "Have today's papers arrived?"

"Why, no."

"Oh, well, never mind. The ink would most probably run off the newsprint from this blasted heat. You can go back to the task of being a Nellie Nettlesome." Holmes closed his door.

Once again I was assaulted by a fusillade of books slamming against the wood. Chuckling, I shook my head and walked to the window, tossing open the curtains to let the afternoon sunlight flood into our rooms. The air sparkled brilliantly, as tiny fireflies of dust flittered about the room, playing with the sun's rays. As each one was captured, it was unceremoniously carried to the sparse shadows and discarded, as the hunt continued for newer and brighter ones.

Looking about the flat, I was surprised by the amount of chaos two men can inflict on one abode, and made note to speak with Holmes about picking up after ourselves. Knowing full well that my surprisingly good humour would prove (as he put it) nettlesome, I whistled, "A Hot Time in the Old Town," a catchy little tune that I had heard at the Adelphi Theatre down on the Strand. Whistling shrilly and at times purposefully off-key, I went about the task of tidying up and annoying Holmes. I was rewarded with more cannon fire as my companion tossed another barrage of books at his door.

Whilst attempting to recall the lyrics of the song, I debated the merits of raising my voice an octave or two while standing at the threshold of Holmes' room.

A gentle rapping on our door interrupted my serenade. "That is probably Mrs. Hudson coming to evict us!" shouted Holmes from inside his sanctuary. "Now you've done it, Watson. Don't think the irony of your selected serenade has escaped me, either."

"Who's there?" I called, chortling and walking to the door.

"I've brought you the papers," Mrs. Hudson replied from the other side.

I opened the door and she said, "Good morning, Doctor. I see Mr. Holmes is at it again."

"I'm afraid so." I laughed, taking the newspapers from her.

She shook her head, clucked disapprovingly, and then left.

"Papers, Holmes! Do you want to read them? Or shall I use them for kindling?"

"Watson!"

I burst out laughing. That seemed to enrage my shut-in friend even further.

The door flew open and there stood Holmes in his brown kimono, a gift from a grateful diplomat. He pulled tightly on the sash and bounded out of his room, collapsing once more on the divan.

"Give them here," he ordered, snapping his fingers. "And didn't I ask you to draw the curtains? I declare, Watson! One would think that you rather enjoy my sufferings. For you seem to do everything possible to..."

My friend let his words dissolve into silence, as he began perusing the newspapers.

"Holmes, you're just being childish."

"Perhaps, but you still haven't shut the curtains."

Rather than quarrel on about it, I did as Holmes requested and drew the curtains. I sat in stewing silence whilst my companion consumed his daily fare of the tabloids.

"Tis a shame really," said Holmes, rousing me out of my self-pitying mood.

"What is?"

"That we are to be otherwise engaged this week attending the Queen's Jubilee in Portsmouth."

"Why do you say that, Holmes?"

"Because, Watson, the papers are rife with accusations and speculations." Holmes smiled wistfully, snapping the paper for emphasis.

"Meaning?"

"Meaning that London's criminal element have not gone on holiday. In fact, according to many of these stories, they're at their zenith. Because of the upcoming celebration, the police are stretched as thin as they've ever been, having nary a man to spare to investigate most of the rising crime.

"Why, look here," he continued, pointing to and reading one of the headlines, *Master Counterfeiter Still Eludes Police.*

I saw in my friend's eyes his longing to be in on the chase.

"Listen, Holmes," I began, attempting to ward off his growing bad mood, "your agreeing to protect the Prince and members of the Royal Family is an honour and a privilege. It's more than enough on your plate to satisfy your lust for adventure. When this assignment is over, I'm sure there will be more crimes for you to solve. I suggest that you forget the newspapers for now. Why don't you read the classifieds or the agony columns? They always seem to provide a diversion for you."

"Perhaps you're right. But still..."

"But nothing!" I interrupted. "Until this matter is over, you haven't the time to immerse yourself in another case."

Holmes eyed me curiously as I continued, "It does neither of us any good to have you sulking about our rooms. Protecting Queen and Country should be your sole endeavor for the time being. Crime will not disappear on you. Before long, you'll be complaining to me that there are too many cases for you to handle. It is always the way."

"Very well," sniffed my friend. "But mark my words. If after this is over, there are no crimes for me to solve, it will be you who gets the blame for my lot in life."

Holmes turned to the classifieds and was soon immersed in the hawking of the trivial. However, in very short order, he sat bolt upright.

"Halloa! Halloa! Halloa!" he cried. "Watson, you have no one to blame but yourself for this. It was at your suggestion that I distract myself with classifieds and the agonies."

"What are you talking about, Holmes?"

"Just this," he responded, smirking. "Read it yourself."

I took the paper from his hand and read the classified that had so excited him, "Mr. Holmes, you have been followed...tomorrow."

"Well?" asked my friend. I could tell he was intrigued.

"Well, what?"

"What do you make of it?"

"Nothing at all, but I'm sure that you have an opinion."

"Yes. And you do not?"

"No."

"Watson, you astound me. Aren't you the least curious as to its meaning?"

"No. I'm afraid not, Holmes," I said. Of course, I *was* extremely curious. Actually, it troubled me greatly, but rather than opine as to the classified's content or purpose, I chose to let my friend weave his own theories.

"Well, I for one find it curious," he said.

"Do tell." I argued the point, "Obviously, there's been a mistake. 'Mr. Holmes, you have been followed... tomorrow.' Of course that cannot be correct."

"Hmm, but what if it is? Then what?" Holmes smiled, content to be discussing a curiosity.

I pondered my friend's question for a moment. "All right," I said, finding a glimmer of an idea, "suppose it is precisely that. Then I would be safe in assuming that its author might well be a foreigner who is unfamiliar with our language."

Holmes' eyes sparkled as he listened to my theory. "And how, pray tell, did you arrive at this remarkable conclusion?"

"It's obvious," I said, confident in my logic. "The originator has used the wrong tense. Using the future tense, rather than the present, or most probably the past. Why, anyone with any schooling whatsoever would never have made such a blunder."

"Do go on," said my friend. "You hold me as a most attentive pupil, but I am confused about one thing—perhaps you can enlighten me. When does this mysterious foreigner of yours enter this little melodrama?"

"W-w-why..." I stammered, feeling my confidence wane and not liking the lilt in Holmes' voice.

"Enlighten me, please," he continued.

"Very well," I snapped. "If my reasoning is wrong, it is because of you. You're always going on about how I do not see anything, even if it's right in front of my face. But I've been round you long enough to learn a thing or two. As to the foreigner, I've found that such grammatical mistakes are common amongst foreigners as they attempt to master the Queen's English. One would be safe in assuming that the author of this puzzle is a foreigner." Satisfied with my reasoning, I leaned back and folded my arms across my chest smugly.

Holmes stared at me in amazement, shaking his head from side to side. "The future, present, and past tenses apply only to verbs. Since *tomorrow* is a noun, it has no tense, future, present, past, or otherwise. *Tomorrow* is precisely that, the day after today. But be that as it may, I understand what you are trying to say. Let's proceed with your hypothesis. Suppose the wrong word was used. Perhaps it should have been *yesterday*. Since we both know that neither of us left the flat during the day, the statement cannot have been based on fact. Then what purpose does it serve to use *yesterday*, when it can be so easily discredited? No! Yesterday is out of the question."

I let my arms fall to my sides as my friend feasted on my flawed logic.

"The next word would be *today*," he continued in a kinder tone, sensing my discomfort. "Of course, the same reasons would apply to *today* as to *yesterday*. We just now arrived back at Baker Street, directly from Westminster. Again, using *today* would make this an easily discounted statement. That leaves us with *tomorrow*. Yes, *tomorrow* was a carefully crafted choice of word. Its use immediately conveys a feeling that is ominous. I'm already suspicious of an event that has not yet occurred. I don't pretend to know its meaning, but I am suddenly alerted to its possibilities."

"All right," I huffed. "Have it your way. But suppose you don't leave the flat tomorrow? Where does that leave your precious logic?"

"Aha! That's the point, my friend. Unfortunately, there's an appointment that must be kept tomorrow. In fact, we'll be gone for most of the day."

"We? I have nothing scheduled for tomorrow."

"No, not you, old chum. I mean my brother Mycroft and me. We've made plans to catch a thief tomorrow. It's unavoidable, I'm afraid. But there is something else about this that intrigues me."

"And what is that?"

"There are very few people who know of my reading habits. How is it that this advertisement came to be placed in a newspaper that I always read?"

"Oh, Holmes. Once again you're sniffing at something that is purely innocent. People place these ads on the off-chance of having someone read them. Do you think everyone who places an advertisement knows the individual who will read or understand it? It's simply a matter of numbers. Perhaps you don't read the paper, but the chances are that someone you know does, and he or she will see your name and contact you. It's obvious."

"I suppose you're right." Holmes seemed disappointed that my logic had been studiously applied and could not be refuted.

"You mentioned that you're going out tomorrow," I started anew, not wanting my friend to fall into melancholy. "But what of the security preparations for the Jubilee?"

"There's more than enough time to—"

2

A knock on our door interrupted my friend, and Holmes absentmindedly crossed the room and opened it.

"Mr. Sherlock Holmes?" enquired our visitor, as I strolled over to join my friend and see who it was.

"I am he," answered Holmes, greeting our visitor. "And this is my friend and associate, Dr. Watson. Please come in and tell me what is so important that you are willing to run the risk of heat exhaustion."

I nodded to the man and eyed him curiously. He was a man of average height on a similar frame. He appeared to be nearing the end of his twenties or the early part of his thirties. He was nattily attired in a dark suit that draped his body comfortably. His hair, brown and nearer to black, was neatly barbered. As was his meticulously tended pencil-thin mustache that rested snugly above his lip. There was nothing singular about the man, and he could have easily been mistaken for a clerk or banker. In fact, the only things noticeable about him were his ample nose and sad, liquid eyes.

Our guest smiled sheepishly, daubing at his face with a handkerchief before sitting down in the proffered chair.

"It is extraordinarily gracious of you to receive me unannounced, Mr. Holmes," he began. "Especially with the added burden you have of protecting Prince Edward and the Royal Family. That is indeed an honour."

Holmes had been about to light his pipe. Now with tight-lipped anger, he quickly extinguished the match and stared at our visitor.

"Watson, see the gentleman out. I'll be receiving no visitors for the rest of the day. Good day, sir." My companion turned on his heel and abruptly retreated to his room, slamming the door behind him.

I rose from my chair, stunned by Holmes' rude behavior.

"I'm sorry, sir," I said, pitying the man and his failed endeavor. "But Mr. Holmes has pressing matters that must be attended to. I'm sure you understand." I moved towards the door, expecting the man to follow, but when I had turned back round, he was still sitting in the chair. Feeling my anger rise, I continued to be civil.

"Sir, I'm afraid you've caught Mr. Holmes at an incommodious time. Perhaps you would care to schedule another time for an appointment?"

"I'm sorry, Doctor, but it is urgent business that I am on. I must speak with you and Mr. Holmes directly. Your very lives depend on his agreeing to see me."

Because the visitor's posture did not suggest aggression, I felt little threat to my person, but I was unnerved by the sincerity and deliberateness of his tone. Given the sudden reemergence of Holmes from his room, it was obvious that our visitor's words had greatly affected my friend as well.

"How is it that you have knowledge of my appointment by the Queen?" Holmes queried, coming to stand directly in front of our visitor. "Whom do we have the pleasure of addressing?"

"I apologize. I'm afraid my social graces are most rudimentary at best. My name is Wells, sirs. Herbert Wells, and I have irrefutable information. If it is not acted upon immediately, you both will be murdered, and England will find herself under the most dire and dangerous of circumstances."

Holmes studied the man before him, weighing the caliber of this seemingly guileless individual named Herbert Wells.

"You haven't answered my first question, Mr. Wells," Holmes raised his voice accusingly. "How did you come upon this most secret information that I am protecting the Royal Family? This most assuredly is not something one would come by easily."

Wells rose from his chair and paced the floor in nervous agitation. He turned round, and having reached what appeared to be a difficult decision, sat back down.

"All right, Mr. Holmes," said Wells with resignation. "As impossible and implausible as it may sound, you must believe me when I tell you that I have read of your appointment in the newspapers."

"I don't know what your game is, sir," I argued, injecting myself into the conversation, "but the news of Mr. Holmes' appointment by the Queen is much too recent to be acquired as you stated. I can assure you that the matter is too sensitive for it to be made fodder for the public. It makes no sense, I say. Now out with it, man! What are you up to?"

Wells looked at Holmes beseechingly.

"Mr. Holmes, I am telling you the truth!" he cried. "I know of this information from the newspapers. It was reported in your obituary. Why won't you believe me?" he lamented, running his fingers through his hair.

"Mr. Wells," I said, as I noticed that Holmes had drawn a chair and now sat opposite our visitor. Studying our visitor more closely, I continued, "There are any number of flaws in your statement that can easily discredit you. First, Mr. Holmes and I, just a short while ago, have completed reading the newspapers. And I can assure you that there is no mention of Mr. Holmes' appointment. Second, the appointment is so recent that should the information have been found out, it would not have made today's editions. Third, and this is the most damning to your credibility, Mr. Holmes is at this very moment, sitting next to you. He's obviously very much alive. His obituary, indeed! Well, sir, what have you to say?"

Holmes glanced up at me and silently shook his head from side-to-side. I sat in my chair and waited expectantly.

Wells leaned forward in the chair with his elbows on his knees and continued to plow his fingers through his hair. Finally, heaving a heavy sigh, he spoke in a hoarse whisper.

"Sirs, I am at my wit's end regarding this affair. I know that my words are confounding, but you have only to hear me out to know that what I am telling you is the truth. May I continue?"

Holmes sat back in his chair and crossed his leg upon his knee. Reaching for another match, he lit his pipe. His eyes narrowed and he nodded once.

"You have read the classifieds?" asked our visitor, innocently.

Holmes' facial expression tightened, but he again just nodded.

"Hmm, yes, I see," Wells said. "That statement is also true. You will be followed tomorrow and might I add, you will be successful in the apprehension of the Viscount."

"Enough!" shouted Holmes, bolting from his chair. "Sir, my patience is at an end! You speak of things that you cannot possibly know!" My friend circled the room, stopping once to tap the tobacco from his pipe into the fireplace.

Startled by my friend's agitation, Wells collapsed back in his chair. "All right, Mr. Holmes," said he with great effort. "I can see that this is going badly. I am spinning a web of confusion from which I cannot extricate myself. At every turn, I am helplessly clouding the purpose of my visit. I have in my pocket an envelope. If I may, I would like to present it to you with the proviso that you will open it only in my presence at five thirty tomorrow afternoon. If after your reading of its contents you still do not believe me, then all I can say is the events are preordained and out of my control. But should you accept the contents as being factual... well...I will tell you of my plan. Agreed?"

Holmes nodded and offered his outstretched hand.

Coming out of his chair, Wells stood to pass my friend the envelope.

"Your word?" asked Wells.

"You have it." Holmes turned his back on the man, dismissing him with nary a glance.

Smiling sadly, Wells gazed at me and with a shrug of his shoulders, he exited our rooms.

3

It was some moments before Holmes reacted to our visitor's withdrawal. My friend turned away from the mantel and shook his head despondently. As was his habit, Holmes absent-mindedly filled his pipe and lit it again. "That man possesses information that is dangerous to me, Watson."

"I don't know, Holmes," I said. "His purpose is a mystery to me. Why did you react so violently when he made mention of a viscount?"

"Because no one but my brother and Lestrade are familiar with the case," he answered, drawing deeply on his pipe. "I haven't even told you."

"If it was to be a confidential matter," I reasoned, "then surely your brother would have kept it so. It's obvious to me that the information came from Lestrade's end. He's incapable of keeping a secret."

"Perhaps." Holmes glanced down at his hand as if seeing the envelope for the first time. He came to sit next to me on the sofa. Twirling the envelope in his hand and coming out of his melancholy, he asked, "What do you make of this?"

"What?" I said in return.

"Tell me what you see."

"An envelope."

"Yes, yes. But what else?" he queried impatiently, as he handed me the envelope.

"I see an ordinary envelope addressed to you. Nothing sinister, I would think."

"Ha!" he shouted scornfully. "Watson, will you never learn to observe things that are at the very least obvious?"

My friend went to the window and pinched back the curtains. He studied the street below for a few minutes before snapping the curtains shut again.

"Nothing," he remarked disappointedly, before shaking away his mood. "Ah, yes, the envelope. Tell me what is written on it."

I glanced down and read the words aloud, "Mr. Sherlock Holmes of Baker Street." I gazed up expectantly, but Holmes had drifted to another part of the flat, and he now draped himself over the arm of his chair at the chemical table. Covering his eyes with his arm, he asked, "What do you make of that curious mark on the top right corner?"

Again, I studied the envelope and noticed that a small numeral had been annotated. "The number one?"

"Yes. The number one." My friend slid off of his chair and came to stand beside me. "Does that not suggest that there will be another?"

"Perhaps. But it could simply have been a careless movement of the pen."

"Ah, Watson, what must have happened to you as a child to make you so dull-witted?"

"Holmes!" I shouted angrily.

"Oh, Watson, I mean no offence. It is just that there are times when it seems you have no imagination."

"Holmes, why bother talking to me, if I am so unimaginative?" I asked, not bothering to hide my anger. "As far as this blasted envelope is concerned, why not open it now?"

"Because I gave my word."

"That's all well and good, but I have not. Give it to me, and we can end this mystery once and for all."

"My word is our word in this instance. Dear me, Watson, but you do have a devious and cunning mind." Holmes stuffed the envelope away in the desk drawer.

"Suit yourself," I remarked, sulkily eyeing the drawer.

We spent the remainder of the day discussing the plans Holmes had made in providing for the safety of the Prince and the Royal entourage.

4

"Shall we go out and see what the world has to offer?" my friend smiled, after shrugging out of his kimono and dressing hurriedly.

"In this heat?" I feigned in mock horror. "Aren't you afraid that you'll melt?"

"Are you coming?" he asked as he grabbed one of his walking sticks. My quick friend was halfway down the stairs by the time I realised that he was gone. I rushed after him and found him outside, standing at the kerb while looking up and down Baker Street.

Though the temperature had gone noticeably cooler, it was nonetheless still hot and humid. The sweat quickly soaked me through. The shadows from the long day marched their slow and deliberate path across Baker Street and climbed the facades of the houses opposite us. Holmes eyed each developing shadow as it traveled from one building to another.

Having satisfied himself that nothing was amiss, we walked south to King and crossed east onto Blandford. My friend paused at the corner and as he had done before he gave the same exacting scrutiny to the buildings opposite us. Again finding nothing of note, we continued down Blandford till we reached the narrow Kendall Mews. We exited the opposite end onto George Street.

As we happened upon each passing pedestrian or carriage, Holmes would slow his gait, casting a wary eye upon the subject of his interest till they were well out of sight. At each new event, he shrugged his shoulders with obvious disappointment at not having attracted any skullduggery. We continued in this fashion until after a very circuitous route, we found ourselves outside the Criterion Restaurant. Walking inside, we found room at the long bar. Above the din of the crowded establishment, we spoke of trivial matters while waiting to be served.

Though the Criterion was teeming with the usual rabble of boisterous racing enthusiasts, the room was quite comfortable, as the air reflected off the white marble floor. Our drinks finally arrived, and Holmes steered the conversation to the singularity of the Criterion's patrons.

"Trials and tribulations," my friend observed casually.

"I beg your pardon?"

"Here, Watson. Look about you," he said, spreading his arms with a flourish. "There are many tales of woe, treachery, and duplicity woven into this seemingly innocent assemblage."

"I can easily entertain the tales of woe." I laughed. "Many of these chaps have lost their incomes by betting on three-legged horses. But treachery and duplicity?"

"It's a mathematical certainty that within any group comprising as little as three individuals," Holmes said, "there will be at least one of them that has committed, or is contemplating committing, an act that is illegal, unethical, or immoral."

"That is preposterous!" I contended, laughing out loud. "It's the result of your profession that you believe the worst of people. You cannot with any logic, prove it."

"Really? Would you care to wager?"

"All right, Holmes. A wager it is. The next drink is on the loser!" I accepted enthusiastically. "But just how would you go about proving your case?"

Holmes smiled thinly before drinking the last of his wine. His eyes dulled as he contemplated the rules for the wager.

"Without leaving this stool, I will point out a guilty man. In fact, he will run out of this place in such a hurry that even you will know that he is indeed guilty of something." My friend's eyes glowed with the prospect of demonstrating his prodigious skill at drawing inferences from close observation.

"I am not that gullible, Holmes," I countered, sniffing out his device. "Obviously, you have recognized someone that you have knowledge about. This ploy of yours will prove nothing."

"On the contrary, Watson," Holmes said. "I will let you set the guidelines of this experiment. Study all of the individuals within this establishment. Then select any three of them. Mind you, they do not have to be within the same group. And I will wager that at least one of these men will act as I have stated. Are you game?"

"A drink it is!" I replied, clapping my hands. "Any three you say?" I looked about the Criterion and its patrons with a discerning eye, before finally settling on the three most innocent appearing of them all.

"All right, Holmes, I have them. Now what?"

Holmes smiled. He turned round and whispered to the man waiting the bar, handing him three slips of paper. The barkeep gave Holmes an understanding nod, before glancing at me conspiratorially.

"Watson, please point out the three men that you have selected," Holmes said.

I did as instructed. The bartender came from behind the counter and visited them, one by one, being sure to hand each of them one of the slips of paper.

"Watch and learn." Holmes smiled, as the barkeep returned to his station.

The first of the three opened the note and glanced down at it. His head immediately swiveled on his neck as he searched about the room for the originator of the note. Without so much as a word, he ran out, nearly bowling over some of the startled patrons. The second of the three read his note, and he similarly paled before trotting out of the Criterion. The third had the most profound reaction. He fainted dead away! It took some moments of confusion before he composed himself with the assistance of those around him. He again studied the note.

After crumpling it in a tight ball, he let it drop to the floor and ran out of the bar as if he were on fire!

Holmes chuckled.

"Three out of three!" he exclaimed, still chortling. "The results surprise even me."

I sat stunned.

"What just happened here, Holmes?" I asked, surprised and confused. "What did those notes say that would make them act so precipitously?"

"Go and read it yourself," said Holmes. He pointed to the crumpled paper on the floor.

I stepped down from the stool and retrieved the note. Returning to stand next to my friend, I opened the balled up paper and read it aloud.

"'I know what you have done,'" it said and was signed, "Sherlock Holmes."

"Well, Watson? Do you concede that I have won the wager?"

"What?" I responded, in a daze. "Oh, yes, of course. But how did you know? I was the one that selected them. What did they do?"

"I have no idea." He laughed. "It would seem that everyone has something to hide, Watson. I merely relied on their own guilty hearts to choose what most offended their own sensibilities. A bottle of wine on my friend, Dr. Watson here," said my companion to the man behind the counter.

I shook my head in surrender.

The rest of the evening passed swiftly and uneventfully, and we made our way back to Baker Street.

"I'll already be out by the time you wake tomorrow," advised Holmes, standing in the doorway to his room, "so don't bother waiting breakfast for me."

"Be careful, Holmes."

My friend smiled sadly and nodded before pledging to meet back at 221B at precisely five fifteen the following afternoon. He bid me good night and shut the door to his room.

$$ \maltese \quad 5 \quad \maltese $$

I retired to my room and was fast asleep in a matter of minutes. The following morning, I groggily awoke with my nightshirt soaked in perspiration and clinging to my body. Even though it was many hours before noon, the sun was already blistering hot and slowly baking our rooms.

Peeling off my nightclothes, I decided to draw a cooling bath. As I waited for the tub to fill, I checked on Holmes. As he had indicated the night before, he had left early.

I returned to the now-filled tub and lowered myself into the cool water. As time wore on, I noticed that my fingers had wrinkled like prunes. I reluctantly stepped out of the tub. Refreshed, I dressed and rang for breakfast. After a while, I was browsing the morning papers over eggs and biscuits. Having consumed enough food for both Holmes and me, I pushed the breakfast plates to the side.

Sitting in the detritus of my morning meal, I replied to the correspondence that had accumulated over the past weeks. The day's heat seemed to have an enervating effect on my body and my spirit, so I took a quick nap.

It was late afternoon when Holmes' footfalls upon the stairs awakened me, as he took them two at a time. In a blur, he entered the room. I caught a glimpse of him and noticed he was caked in mud and grime. As I wondered what mischief he'd been up to, he disappeared into his room, slamming the door one more time.

"Won't be a moment, Watson!" called Holmes cheerily from inside his room. "My, what a marvelous hunt we had. I feel so alive and rejuvenated."

A glance at my watch told me that it was nearing a quarter to five. Having no other options, I sat back in my chair and waited for Holmes to make his entrance. A short while later, my friend exited his room looking none the worse for wear after his latest escapade. In fact, he positively glowed with excitement and anticipation. He was withdrawing his pocket watch when we heard a gentle knock on our door.

"Excellent!" cried my friend. "I do like punctuality!"

Holmes bounded across the floor with enthusiasm and swung open the door. Mr. Herbert Wells stood in our doorway, looking surprisingly more confident than he had on the previous day.

"Good afternoon, sir," he said to Holmes.

"Good afternoon, Mr. Wells," my friend responded solemnly while ushering the man into our rooms.

"Sir, I must ask whether or not you have opened the envelope that I gave you?" Wells took the same seat as yesterday.

"I have not. Would you care to examine it?" Holmes lifted an eyebrow.

Wells was nonplussed. "W-w-why, no, sir! You have given your word. If you would care to open it now..."

"Watson, please bring it here. It is in the drawer of the desk."

I did as he asked, handing my friend the mysterious article. Performing a last desultory inspection of the outside of the envelope, Holmes smiled thinly at Wells as he sliced through the fold on the flap with his pocketknife. Inverting it, he bowed it open and two items fell into the palm of his hand.

"B-b-before you examine the articles," Wells said nervously, "if you so desire, I will leave your flat and return when you have digested the information."

"That won't be necessary. Take a seat, sir," Holmes said.

Wells walked over to the divan and did as he was told.

Holmes walked over to the dining table and I followed. The two of us sat down on a pair of deeply cushioned chairs pulled up to the large mahogany table where we took our meals. My friend kept toying with the envelope's contents. The first item was a neatly folded page from a newspaper. The second was a similarly folded sheet of notepaper. Impulsively, with his fingertip Holmes brushed aside the newspaper and selected the note to be the first item to fall prey to his scrutiny. He carefully unfolded the note and let his eyes scan the page's text. Suddenly, he sat bolt upright with eyes wide. I noticed a slight tremor in his hands as he further studied the page.

"What is it, Holmes?" I asked, alarmed by his response to the contents of the envelope.

My friend didn't respond, but he did stare at the paper with a look of total disbelief.

"Holmes! What is it?" I pushed harder for an answer.

Acting as if he held a proclamation from the depths of hell, the great detective contemptuously tossed the paper aside. Wells, from his spot on the divan, jumped in shock, but he kept his place there safely out of Holmes' reach.

"Read it," Holmes commanded me.

I took the proffered page and brought it up to my eyes. It was nothing more than a detailed report on my friend's activities throughout the day. Not comprehending the import of what I had just read, I said, "I don't understand your reaction at all, Holmes. We were informed in the advertisement that you would be followed. Don't you see? Somehow, someone knew of your plans. It's obvious. It's all right here." I shook the note for emphasis, and then continued reading, but this time aloud. "You met and spoke with a man at... Oh, what's the use of reading it out loud? It's balderdash, that's what it is! It's as plain as your nose. You were observed doing this and that. Holmes, if it's this obvious to me, then surely..."

Storm clouds roiled across my friend's face, but I would not be deterred from exposing this fraud. "There's nothing to this. Not really. Someone had prior knowledge of your plans. This voyeur had people positioned to be in your vicinity and confront you at specific times of the day. For what purpose? I have no idea, but this entire affair smacks as a clever ruse to make you act a certain way. And I do not ascribe this matter to the whims of some gypsy fortuneteller or other such rot. It's chicanery, plain and simple."

I felt my blood rise at the very idea of someone testing my friend in such a manner, especially when he had a charge as important as the welfare of Prince Edward and other members of the Royal Family.

Holmes frowned, absently twirling the folded newspaper that lay pinned beneath his finger.

"Under normal circumstances I would agree with you, Watson. And I must say that your powers of deductive reasoning have grown immeasurably, but if you recall, I told you that I was to meet with my brother early today. No one could have foreseen that he would take a terrible spill this morning whilst attempting to get out of his tub. He badly sprained his ankle, but that did not happen till half-past seven. Yet you'll note that the next to the last item on the page refers to Mycroft walking with a pronounced limp of his right leg. It says he had to walk with the assistance of a cane. Nor can you account for Gregson's presence, as indicated. For the entire operation was planned with Inspector Lestrade. But he, too, suffered a calamitous event. His mother had passed on last evening, and he is probably at this very moment halfway to Doncaster to attend to his mother's affairs. Unless, of course, you're suggesting that both he and my brother are in on this, what did you call it? Ah yes, *chicanery*."

I strained forward as my friend pronounced each incredible word. "Then what are we facing here, Holmes?"

❦ 6 ❦

A sidelong look at Wells confirmed that our visitor was watching Holmes' reactions with an expression of sadness. In fact, I would have to admit that poor Wells looked to be on the verge of tears.

His only response was to glance down at his finger and at the newspaper that was pinned beneath it. Exhaling deeply, he unfolded what was the front page of the *Daily Mail*. The banner headline said it all:

Sherlock Holmes Captures Robber Viscount! Daring Plan Nearly the Death of the Great Detective!

Holmes read the words greedily, before handing the paper to me. I noticed that his skin had turned a milky white as the colour drained from him. The text went on to explain in gruesome detail the exploits of my friend, and how he had nearly lost his life whilst hanging from the iron rafters of Victoria Station with the villain in his grip. A photographer, who must be celebrating his good fortune, captured the entire scene at the very instant Holmes plucked the diving villain from the air. Holmes' quick action stopped the viscount from committing suicide once his plans had been found out.

(I must make note that this episode, though seemingly horrific by all written accounts, was a rather insignificant case. At some future time, I may decide to put the details before the public. But at this particular moment, I feel it my obligation to return to the case at hand and leave the details of the Robber Viscount for another day.)

Not knowing what else to do, I put the newspaper back on the table and glanced at Holmes, who was staring off into space. He must have felt my gaze.

"The date," he said. "Look at the date."

I glanced down, and to my horror, I realised what had so disturbed my friend. The dateline read: *Wednesday, the 23rd of June, 1897.*

That was tomorrow's date! My eyes blurred as the world seemed to tilt precariously, thanks to my great shock. I staggered to a chair.

Holmes continued, "And we cannot ignore the fact that we have had this information in our possession since yesterday. How can you explain the photograph, Watson?" His hand flittered toward the front page of the newspaper in silent surrender.

I could do nothing but shake my head in bewilderment.

Holmes mustered his composure and smiled weakly. "I believe you have another envelope for me, Mr. Wells?"

"Yes, sir." Our guest got up, handed the paper packet to Holmes, and calmly turned away. He resumed sitting on the sofa.

Holmes visibly trembled as he tore open the envelope and read the letter's contents. The tick of the mantel clock was the only sound. Wells and I suffered in silence. Finally, my old friend turned to face me. I had expected to see confusion etched upon his face, but I was surprised to see him smiling. "Read this, Watson, and tell me if this isn't going to be one of our most extraordinary cases," Holmes said, thrusting the note in my face.

My heart raced as I silently read the neatly penned letter.

Dear Mr. Holmes:

   I must apologise for my dramatics, but I assure you that my knowledge of things that have yet to occur are in all instances accurate and beyond reproach.

   I can safely assume that Dr. Watson is now reading this letter? Of course, I have no objection. (Excepting that the use of this information and the contents herein goes no further than his participation in assisting you.)

   You are my only hope in this matter! A crime has been committed, or should

I say will be committed, on Saturday, the 26th of June, 1897. The results of which are so profound as to bring England and all of Europe to WAR!

I felt the best way to make you understand the gravity of this horrific event, as well as the sincerity and honourable intent of the author of this letter, was to allow you to possess undeniable facts far in advance of the actual occurrences. I trust that I've succeeded in setting the stage and assuring you of my sincerity.

Tomorrow, you will purchase the Daily Mail, as well as any other newspapers you deem necessary and appropriate. You will verify that what you have read today (and have been the sole possessor of since a day previous) is factual in all accounts. Once you are satisfied, and if it is agreeable to you and Dr. Watson, I will visit you again with an associate of mine and we shall discuss this matter further.

Respectfully,

Herbert George Wells

❧ 7 ❧

Reader, you might at this point feel that I am betraying a confidence, as you will note from the words and tone of this incredible letter. Yet, I feel that it is far too important to exclude this important missive. After weighing my position as the chronicler of the great Sherlock Holmes, I have decided to include the letter from Mr. Wells within these pages. And yes, Mr. Wells has kindly given me his permission to do so. But I am getting ahead of myself.

"What balderdash!" I shouted, as I tossed aside the letter from Mr. Wells. "Surely you're not considering this? Are you, Holmes?"

Holmes stared at the paper and stooped to retrieve it from where it had landed on the carpet.

"I'll tell you this, Holmes. It smells of a trap," I continued to rail, my eyes blazing into our visitor's. "This is some sort of hoax. Seeing into the future? What rot!"

"What's the harm of our buying the papers tomorrow? If anything's amiss, then nothing is lost but the coins to purchase them," my friend said. "I would read most of them as a matter of habit anyway."

"Harrumph, it's just plain ridiculous! That's what it is! You mark my words." I lashed out.

"Good old Watson!" Holmes said in a soothing voice, before turning his gaze upon Wells.

"My good man," said Holmes, clearly enjoying the singularity of the circumstances. "I'm sure you'll understand that Watson and I have much to discuss. If you will call back round at say, at nine o'clock tomorrow morning, we will continue with what appears to be a lesson in the most abstract."

"Of course," our guest replied as he stood to leave. "Until nine then. Good evening, gentlemen."

"He's a madman, Holmes!" I shouted after Wells left us. "Why you are bothering with this matter is beyond me. But you will do as you always do — whatever you want. It's a hoax, I say!"

"We'll dine in tonight," Holmes said, as he ignored my churlishness.

We dined on cold mutton and potatoes. Over sherry, my companion regaled me with the details of the robber viscount.

During the various lulls in our conversation, I decided to broach the matter of the mysterious Mr. Wells, but at every turn, Holmes foiled my attempts. I had the uneasy sensation that I had recently heard of the man's name. But it was after one glass of sherry too many that I finally abandoned the problem. Inexplicably, I decided that I looked forward to being on another case with the great Sherlock Holmes, even though I knew it to be a farce.

8

I don't recall turning in for the night. However, as I awoke the
following day, if my pounding head was any barometer, then it
was entirely possible and plausible that I'd consumed considerably more than one glass of sherry too many. My suffocating hot room
was dark as pitch when I lay there contemplating getting up from my
bed. Rolling onto my side, I moved my hand moved along the night-
stand, feeling for the lamp. I turned on the gas and the room glowed
with promise. The exertion exhausted me, and I resumed my prone
position with a groan, crossing my arm over my eyes.

I heard Holmes moving about the flat and shut my eyes tighter,
wishing that his noisy feet would find a place to perch. Finally, unable
to stand the confines of my airless room, I trepidatiously swung my
legs over the side of the bed and used my feet to feel around the floor
for my slippers. It took some time for the realization to penetrate my
foggy brain that I had actually fallen asleep with my shoes on!

With halting movements, I pushed up from the bed and took my
first wobbly steps towards the washbasin on the side of the bureau.
After a few splashes of water on my face, I decided that there was
hope for me yet. That is, until I saw my reflection in the mirror. Never
have I laid eyes on such a bizarre countenance before. My face was

creased, and those crevices were made more pronounced by the dark bags under my eyes. My proud shock of greying hair was stringy and matted. Strands were pressed at converging angles against my forehead. In fact, I looked so rough that I was startled to sobriety in an instant and swore off the demonic pleasures of ales, brandies, and liqueurs for the hundredth time. I am sad to say that I have awoken under similar circumstances numerous times. My hands have had much practice in taking over for my addled brain. My nimble fingers knew their part in my restoration. With very little cognitive effort, I once again began to look and feel like a part of the human race. That's when I entered the main area. As I expected, he looked the perfect picture of health and gentlemanly comportment as he sat at the dining table perusing the papers. His constitution was truly remarkable, to say the least.

"Ah, Watson," said he, in a voice dripping with charm and sarcastic sympathy, "I feared you'd gone to meet your maker. I was about to take inventory of your belongings and sell them to the highest bidder. Thankfully, your presence has saved me from that laborious task, and I don't have to write you off. Not yet, at least. Although you do look a sorry sight."

My clever retort was but a feeble groan from a cotton-dry mouth. With a trembling hand, I reached for the pot of coffee and poured myself a cup. Blinking back the brightness of the sunlit room, I shuffled to my chair and sat down. Paying no heed to my friend's laughter, I sipped the steaming black liquid in embarrassed silence.

Though my mind begged the question, I feared the actual utterance of it. I finally asked, "Well?"

"They're exactly the same," came the reply, as he held the papers aloft. "I had the Irregulars buy papers from seven different stands. They are all identical to the one we saw last night."

I stared at my coffee cup in disgust. Holmes' ragtag group of errand runners had once again proved their worth and their loyalty to the man by buying papers from more than one stand. "Blast! What now?"

"We wait."

Any observant person would be familiar with Holmes' reliance on his powers of concentration, but most are unaware of his ability to wait. This habit oft proves useful as answers come to him, in one form or another. I highly recommend it. I put my empty cup on a side table and walked over to the window. While gazing out, a sudden burst of recognition roared into my brain.

"Of course!" I shouted. "Herbert Wells. Holmes, do you know who he is? He is H. G. Wells, the author. He wrote that terribly depressing story about some kind of time machine."

"I wondered how long it would take you to recall that," said Holmes, coming over to stand next to me. "I recognized his name immediately."

"Then why didn't you tell me?" I asked, as my face reddened with embarrassment. "Why was I forced to labour over his name? Never mind! Knowing who he is, you're still intent on going through with this?"

"Of course. I see no reason not to. Now let's not quarrel about it. Our guest has already arrived, and he brought some of his friends with him. By the looks of their load, I think they intend to move in with us."

I gazed down at the street below. Wells and a young man sagged under the weight of their burdens as they headed towards our building. Holmes ran to the door and opened it just as our visitors reached the top of the landing.

"Come in, won't you? Watson, lend a hand," said Holmes, relieving the author's strain by taking a number of cartons from him. I ran to assist the other young man who was breathing heavily from his exertion. Mr. Wells' associate was a curious specimen who stared out at the world from doleful eyes. His wildly flowing mane of hair sat high on his domed head. By my calculations, the newcomer could not have been much more than twenty years old, and yet there was something of an "old soul" about him that I, sadly, cannot find words to explain.

"Danke," he said with a shy smile.

I returned his grin with one of my own and carried the heavy cartons to the dining room table. After everyone had caught their breath, Mr. Wells introduced his companion.

"Mr. Sherlock Holmes? Dr. Watson?" Mr. Wells said. "May I

present my friend and associate, Herr Albert Einstein? Albert, this is Mr. Sherlock Holmes and Dr. John H. Watson."

We all stood to facilitate the introductions.

"I have read much about you, Herr Holmes," said Einstein, as he extended a hand for a greeting, "thanks to the efforts of your chronicler, Dr. Watson. And without going into detail, you will be pleased to know that you are both held in the highest esteem and studied by millions of students at universities around the world. Herr Holmes, you are regarded by the world's intelligentsia as the consummate logician."

Holmes and I took an immediate liking to the small man. He had a disheveled appearance. His eyes changed from sad to scampish as he studied his surroundings. Everything about him testified to his being a good-humoured sort of chap, and perhaps a bit off-center.

"Thank you," said Holmes, accepting his effusive praise as his due. "Take a seat, gentlemen." Holmes waved them toward the armchairs while he and I took the divan.

"Forgive my frankness, Mr. Holmes and Doctor Watson," Wells interrupted the pleasant mood, "but Albert and I possess irrefutable evidence that you are both to be assassinated at the Queen's Diamond Jubilee Celebration. I—"

"Mr. Wells," Holmes interrupted, "we have—and by we, I mean Watson and I—have been more than gracious and patient. We have played this game of yours without protest. I found it rather refreshing, but I am quickly tiring of it. If you have evidence, then out with it, man! We cannot act upon mere speculation. And thus far, we have been made to sit idly by.

"I would gather without too much effort, sir," Holmes continued, "that you are not the sort of gentleman that would normally associate with those whose lot in life is to bring harm and hardship upon the citizenry. Therefore, I must assume that you came upon this information quite by accident. If that is the case, perhaps you have made assumptions that are wildly speculative at best, and you have construed your information wrongly." My friend folded his arms across his chest and stared at Mr. Wells in a manner that most would find unsettling, to say the least.

"Ahh, if only that were the case," Wells said. "If it were so, I would gladly accept your opinion of me as being dull-witted and naïve. But I'm afraid the information we possess is deadly. If you do not act now, Mr. Holmes, both you and Dr. Watson most assuredly will be assassinated on the 26th of June."

"B-b-but that is three days from now," I stammered, rising from my spot on the couch.

"And you have proof of this?" Holmes asked, pulling me back down onto the divan.

"Yes, sir," the author replied. I heard real sadness in his voice.

$$\begin{array}{ccc} \maltese & 9 & \maltese \end{array}$$

"Let's have it then," Holmes commanded.

"Yes, of course," responded Wells. "But I will need your solemn promise that what you are about to see will go no further than this room. I have your word? Both of you?"

"My good man!" I said, unnerved by Wells' ominous warning. "Do you seriously expect us to entertain the unreasonableness of your request? We are to learn of the plots on our lives and you ask us to say nothing! Do nothing! That, sir, is out of the question!"

"Forgive me, Dr. Watson," Wells pleaded. "You have misunderstood my meaning. Of course I want you to act. What I mean to suggest is that you keep private the means by which you learn of the information."

The author eyed us expectantly, as quiet filled the room.

"Agreed," Holmes said and nodded, quieting my outburst before I could utter it.

"Dr. Watson," Einstein said, patting my arm with his hand, "it will all be made abundantly clear as we progress into this sordid affair. What we are asking is most reasonable. Perhaps, Herbert, I should discuss time with these good men, *ja?*"

"Yes," Wells replied.

"Excellent." Einstein smiled at us. He said, "Dr. Watson, you are a learned man." Einstein's heavy German accent changed the letter "w" to a "v" and made following his commentary rather difficult. I adjusted to his pattern of speech but I yearned to correct him when he called me "Vatson."

The young guest continued by asking me, "What do you know about time?"

Caught unawares, I answered flippantly, "There's never enough of it."

"Ah, Doctor, but you are wrong. I've discovered that there is time enough to do everything and anything. But that is not the answer I was looking for. What I should have asked you was, 'Do you consider time to be of the same import as sight, sound, smell and touch?'"

"No," I responded, seeing where he was leading. "Time is a creation of man. We measure our lives in spans of time. Time dictates when we eat, sleep, and wake. Time was created only to keep order."

"I see. Then, does time exist?" He cocked his head and studied me while waiting for my reaction.

"Of course."

"Hmmm, is it as real as this table or chair?" Again, his accent challenged my understanding. Einstein pronounced "this" as "dis." Most disconcerting.

"No, of course not. I've already stated that time is an intangible thing. It's nothing that you can touch, see, smell or hear." My voice rose defensively as I attempted to answer a confusing question.

"So, what you are saying, Doctor, is that time is all around us, yet we cannot see, touch, smell, or hear it? Then how do you know time exists?"

"Because by my watch," I said as I reached into my pocket and noted the time, "we have been here for fifteen minutes, and I am already tired of this nonsense."

"Excuse my manners, Doctor. I didn't mean to imply..." Einstein looked to Holmes beseechingly.

Holmes tugged at my sleeve. "It's all right, Watson. Einstein, perhaps it would be better if you would explain to us exactly what answer you are looking for. Obviously my associate's response is not to your liking."

"*Gut,*" he replied. "It has long been an accepted practice when teaching geometry that in order for anything to exist there has to be three spatial planes or dimensions. An object must have length, height and breadth. Is that not so?"

"Yes," Holmes responded, "but what has this to do with time?"

"Please, Herr Holmes, if you are to accept what we must tell you, you must first understand the laws of the universe."

Holmes sat back in his chair and nodded for Einstein to continue.

"*Danke.* In order for anything to exist, it must take up space. There must be a physical presence. In referring to an object in any meaningful way, you must note that all of the three dimensions or planes must be present and that they exist at right angles to each other. You cannot have length if there is no height and breadth. Each plane is recognized by the strict adherence of comparing one against another. No matter what plane you choose as your starting point."

Being attentive students, Holmes and I sat quietly, but a thought had occurred to me.

"What about music?" I began, feeling unsure of myself. "One can go to a concert and hear Brahms or Beethoven. There is nothing physical there. There's no height, length, or breadth, but the music exists nonetheless."

Einstein's eyes shone with delight. "Ah, Dr. Watson, but there are physicalities to music or notes! Of course, I'm referring to sound waves. A man by the name of Scott has invented a device that measures the acoustical attributes of sound by etching their presence or pattern onto smoked glass. It is called a phonautograph, but much more has been accomplished since then. So you see, Doctor, a note or sound can be seen. If it can be seen, then it follows that you are measuring the sound by the relationship of the three planes."

I sat back, absorbing Einstein's words.

"All right," Holmes chimed in, nodding his head. "We agree that in order for anything to exist, it must be referenced by the three dimensions that you've mentioned. I take it that you have another theory relating directly to the subject?"

C.J. LUTTON

"Yes, Herr Holmes, I do. But it is not a theory. It's factual, irrefutable." Einstein lifted a silver bowl from the table. "This bowl exists because it is durational. In other words, the three other planes cannot exist without time being its genesis. If I destroyed this bowl in your presence, so that not a single particle of it remained, we still know that it existed because we all saw it. What would be required to affirm that it existed is the ability to travel back into time, so we could observe the bowl before it was destroyed. So, time enters into the calculation. A plane or dimension that runs in another direction at right angles to the other three."

"A fourth dimension?" Holmes whistled in astonishment.

"*Ja,*" said Einstein, appreciatively, "A fourth dimension that can be visited at will."

"Preposterous!" I said, bolting from my seat, "It is against all conventionality. I've read Wells' book. It's his writer's imagination that has created such an implausible proposition. Traveling through time as if it were... As if it were... You make it sound as if one gets in a boat and travels a river. It's impossible. That's what it is. Impossible!"

The author seemed visibly deflated as he sat back dejectedly in the chair. Wells' associate rose and whispered in the author's ear.

"Albert has reminded me that time is running out," said the author. "Sadly, what I must show you will come as a shock. I was hoping to spare you, but alas, I've been unable to convince you of my sincerity."

Feeling sorry for the man, I rose to assist him out of his chair, but he angrily shrugged my hand away and opened a carton that sat on the table.

"Gentlemen," said Wells, "I must warn you this carton contains, quite literally, your futures. To be more precise, your futures on the 26th of June in the year of 1897. You may take it to heart, sirs, that should this event occur as it is written, and has already been witnessed by me on three days hence, you will both be dead."

I was greatly troubled by his words. I reached for Holmes' arm to steady myself and gazed into his face. My old friend was smiling. He considered Wells' words an opportunity to explore the unknown, and Holmes relished the possibilities.

"Are you prepared to peer into the future and see what it has in store for you?" asked Wells, intoning with a voice reminiscent of the soothsayers, sages, and prophets of my imagination when I was a fanciful youth.

Holmes glanced at me strangely, and then at Wells. Lastly, his eyes fell upon Einstein, and then the great detective smiled. "Let's be done with it!" said Holmes. "Let us see what the 'morrow brings!"

Moving round to the front of the carton, Holmes pushed Wells to the side, and gazed down into the box. His eyes widened with anticipation, as he slowly lowered his hands inside the container and removed a newspaper. It was the *Daily Chronicle*. After he scanned the headlines, he set it facedown next to him.

Holmes again lowered his hands into the box and withdrew a second newspaper. His brow knitted as he concentrated on the text of the articles in the *Daily Mail*. He continued on in this fashion without uttering a word, but as each successive newspaper was read and placed on top of the ones preceding it, it became plain, even to me, that the words were having a profound effect.

"Thank God, they're alive," Holmes whispered as perspiration dripped off the end of his nose.

"Who is alive?" I asked, reaching for one of the papers, only to have Holmes place his hand on top of mine.

"Watson, these are terrible words. Are you sure that you want to read them?"

I removed my friend's protective hand without responding and stared at the pile of newspapers, turning over the one on top. My knees sagged as I read the strident headline: *Sherlock Holmes & Doctor Watson Murdered!*

My eyes raced over the horrifying photographs of our lifeless bodies as we were "on display" at the feet of the police and inspectors.

My brain absorbed every numbing word and photograph of the other papers (each more graphic than the previous) in their depiction of our deaths. Finally, I became consumed by the finality of the conflagration of poisonous words. After a few minutes, I smiled weakly at my companion. Noticing the worry etched upon his face, I said, "I'm all right, Holmes."

"I know you are, old friend. It's just that I..." His words faded.

Mustering my courage, I went back to the papers and read them carefully.

The news article told of how, at the hands of assassins, we had made the ultimate sacrifice. In thwarting an attempt on the life of the Prince of Wales during the scheduled review of the Royal Navy, we were felled. However, our deaths were but a side note. The celebration of Queen Victoria's Diamond Jubilee had continued without us. The papers were dated the 27th of June, 1897. Our assassination had occurred on the previous day, Saturday the 26th. Only three days from now!

When I turned to Wells, I could see the sadness in his eyes. His overt emotion emphasized the reality of the words. It was all true. Holmes and I were going to be murdered on Saturday.

Having never before seen my death portrayed with such clarity, I didn't know what to expect of my emotions. My mood was startling and somewhat of a revelation to me: I was angry. I would have remarked on this, but I was drawn to silence by my companion's actions. While I had been mourning, my old friend had been comparing the various newspaper articles and taking furious notes.

Wells, Einstein and I were transfixed, as we watched the hunched-over figure of Holmes whistle, hum, and make a general racket while absorbing one horrifying story after another. Finally, with a snap of his fingers, he completed his task and turned to face us with a wickedly wide grin.

"Incredible!" he cried. "Simply incredible!" Holmes looked squarely at Wells. "I take it that you have a way?"

"A way what?" I asked, fearing the answer.

Holmes' face glowed as he said, "A way to travel into the future, of course."

Wells stared at Holmes and nodded. "I have done."

My feelings of anger vanished and were replaced with uncomprehending, incredulousness. "The future!" I shouted. "Have you gone mad, Holmes?"

"Steady, Watson," said the great detective soothingly, while patting me on the shoulder. "It's not as bad as all that."

"Not as bad as all that, you say!" I shouted, shrugging his hand off.

"Let me tell you something, Mr. Sherlock Holmes. I have been with you on many a bizarre case, but this one...this one... is just too much. Do you expect me to entertain that this man," I pointed to Wells, "has a machine that can fly through time? I most assuredly do not believe in such tomfoolery. What you are proposing is impossible, and you know it. I don't know what you expect to gain from this, Mr. Wells, but I will tell you this, you may have fooled my gullible friend here, but you will never convince me that this is not a hoax."

Before the last words of my tirade had left my lips, I knew them to be wrong. Somehow, H.G. Wells, the author, and his strange associate, Albert Einstein, had managed to corrupt the laws of nature, physics, and the remaining sciences by creating a machine that can travel through time.

❧ 10 ❧

"It's as easy as all that?" I asked, tossing out my last protestation. "We simply climb into this time machine of yours. Fly into the future and save ourselves?"

Holmes bobbed his head up and down excitedly and looked to Wells for confirmation.

"No," the author responded, and then seeing a crestfallen Holmes, he added, "Not exactly."

"I beg your pardon," Holmes' voice betrayed his disappointment. "Then of what use is the time machine? Are you saying that we're to be killed, and there's nothing that Watson and I can do about it?"

"No, Mr. Holmes, that is *precisely* what I am *not* saying! If you will listen carefully, I'll explain what is possible and what is not."

Einstein seated himself in an armchair. His face was solemn and still as he turned his attention to his colleague.

"Mr. Wells," Holmes said, while dragging me over to the divan. His gentle tone broke the suddenly sour mood, "you were about to explain?"

"Hmm, yes, Mr. Holmes, thank you. Where to begin? Dr. Watson, you've mentioned that you have read my book, I believe, but that you do not accept my premise as being factual. In truth, it is autobiographical."

"It is absurd!" I laughed, cruelly.

"Your response, sir, has been echoed by a multitude of others. I must admit it has made it all the more difficult to put my experiences in perspective." Wells' fingers drummed monotonously on the table. He stood beside the carton and shifted his weight from side to side. I could sympathize with his reaction to my criticism. No author easily accepts that his work has gone either unread or unappreciated.

"Very well," our guest continued, "my modest attempt at making a living as a writer was a novel called *The Time Machine*. The premise was the adventures of a man who had invented a machine that could travel through time. What is unknown to my readers, and that I am desperately trying to convince you of, is that I am that man. What everyone assumes to be a work of fiction, is in all actuality, a factual account of my journey." His eyes suddenly moistened and he was forced to draw a clean white linen handkerchief from his jacket pocket and wipe away the threatening tears.

"What I am loath to admit is that my utopian and idealistic vision of the future... Well, *that* vision was a work of fiction!" He brought his hand thundering down on the table. "As an observer, my naïveté is unsupportable when weighed against the vagaries of time and the whims of mankind. Especially when I, as that observer, lacked the acumen to alter things as they are or will be, without upsetting the delicate balance of time and nature. That is why we are here." He searched our eyes for understanding.

Unfortunately, I was incapable of accepting him at his word, knowing full well that the man was obviously as mad as a hatter.

"I'm not sure that I understand," said Holmes, eager to get to the point and to move off the starting block. "Our assassinations are less than three days from now. Are you proposing that Watson and I travel into the future and intercede, or not?"

"Of course not. Besides it is not as easy as all that, Mr. Holmes. You must solve your murders, of course, but—"

"Oh, is that all?" I snorted, interrupting Wells, "Then why didn't you say so? Holmes, we haven't a moment to waste. If we hurry, I'm sure that we can just make the three o'clock out of Victoria Station. I beg your pardon, that's the train to the past." My tirade was at its zenith, as I continued, "How can supposedly intelligent men, sitting round this table actually discuss—"

Ignoring my sardonic words, the author leaned forward and grasped my friend's hand. "Mr. Holmes, I beg you to listen. I have file upon file of information that is at your disposal. Including visual testimony of the, uh, event. Hopefully, it is more than sufficient."

"Visual what?" I asked, not understanding.

"We have photographs of the assassination," Wells said simply, as if this was an ordinary matter.

"We've already seen those horrible photographs in the papers here." I jerked my chin toward the scattered newspapers. "What good does—?"

"Watson," Holmes interrupted, "I believe Mr. Wells is speaking of something that is entirely different." He looked to the author for confirmation.

"Indeed, Mr. Holmes. You are quite correct. I am talking about something else entirely. Albert, is everything ready?"

"*Ja.*"

"Fine. Gentlemen, what Albert has in his hands are a series of sequential photographs, so arranged that as you flip through them you will see the assassinations as they happened. You will find these images extraordinary in both quality and content. I have been able to produce this graphic testimony by utilizing inventions that exist in the future. The twenty-first century to be exact. It is because of the very sensitive nature of my experimentation that I dare not reveal even to you what devices were used."

"This is all very interesting," Holmes observed impatiently, "but you were about to explain?"

"Of course, Mr. Holmes," Wells said, smiling. He seemed embarrassed. "Once again I have gone off topic."

"Go on," said Holmes, lighting his pipe and offering his tobacco to Einstein.

"*Danke,*" Einstein smiled, withdrawing a pipe from his pocket. The young man filled the bowl of his pipe and then lit it. The fact Holmes knew that our new friend was a pipe smoker was yet another example of the great detective's uncanny ability to make split-second observations that escaped other people.

"Gentlemen," said Wells, "I will not expose either of you to this horror, should you only take my word for it. Please be assured that I have more than enough material in those boxes over there for you to study. What I have brought along should both support my claims and set you on the trail of your murderers."

"We are not to travel?" queried Holmes, again showing his disappointment.

"Travel where?" I asked.

"Through time," came my friend's reply, and it set my blood racing.

"No," answered Wells. "As absurd as this may sound, there is not enough time. I'm sorry, Mr. Holmes, but that is a reality you must face. I am giving you an opportunity to solve a crime that—"

Holmes stared at the novelist with a look that would wilt most men. "Wells, I tire of your games. The lives of members of our Royal Family are at stake. I have given them my sworn oath that I shall protect them. If you care naught for my life and for that of my good friend, Dr. Watson, at least have a care for the people of this good realm!"

The soothing tones of Einstein attempted to reassure my friend. "Herr Holmes. You see before you two men who under any other circumstance would welcome your participation in this grand experiment, but as Herr Wells has stated, there is not ample time for you to absorb what all you must know in order to survive. I propose that you look at us as simply as clients of yours. Clients, I am sure, who offer you a most unique opportunity to exercise your brain to its fullest. And clients who can provide you with the smallest of details to assist in your investigation." The young man smiled in a manner filled with hope. His sincerity was on full display.

Holmes graciously accepted Einstein's words and nodded his compliance. "All right. Carry on."

"Fine," said Wells, coming into the conversation, "but before we go any further, I must explain how all of this came to light. That will give you a fuller picture of what we know. It will also assure you that you have everything you need to move forward accordingly. A previous associate of mine, a Mr. Philip A. Delphi, whom I have taken to calling Philadelphia, has gone missing. It's been nearly two weeks since I have last seen or heard from him, and—"

"Just a moment, Mr. Wells," Holmes held up a staying hand. "Watson, please take notes, if you will."

Of course, I did as asked. Serving as Holmes' scribe allows me to accurately jot down his words as they happen. It also provides both of us with a powerful memory aid. In short, I find it less of a hardship and more of an opportunity than one might think.

Holmes nodded to Wells. "Do go on, sir."

"Thank you," Wells said with a nod. "It has been his habit, since I have known him, which is going on nearly a year now, that Philadelphia would on occasion disappear for days on end without so much as a whisper of warning. So when he again did not show up for a synchronization study, I thought little of it."

"What sort of study?" I queried, pausing my pencil in mid-air.

This time it was Einstein who answered, "A synchronization study, Doctor. That is when we compare the machine's gyro-effects with the time destination's location."

"Albert," interjected the time machine inventor, casting a withering glare at his assistant, "please allow me to continue."

The young man shrugged and sat back, dejected.

"I discovered a discrepancy," Wells went on, unaffected by the growing tension in the room. "A dissimilar time destination that I myself had set to the exact coordinates the evening previous to Philadelphia's disappearance."

"A mistake, perhaps?" Holmes pressed.

"*Nein.* Your bro—" Einstein spoke again, before Wells' stony glare rendered him silent.

Again, Wells chose to ignore the question. Instead, he continued to plod doggedly along with his background report. "During a preliminary inspection, I discovered a new time destination still logged onto its gauge. There was only one explanation. Somehow, without my knowledge, the machine had visited the future. It was impossible, yet the reality of its occurrence was there, nonetheless."

"The date was the 27th of June?" asked Holmes, staring intently into the author's eyes.

Wells' face stiffened. "Y-y-yes. I'm afraid it was. I decided, and my associate Albert concurred, that we should investigate further. We needed to time travel to see what could be learned. Once we had seen what occurred on that particular date, we continued to visit upon the 26th of June, 1897, many more times. Each trip afforded us with a new direction of investigation. What I have for you are the results of our findings."

"So," I offered, feeling queasy, "someone went into the future, attempted to kill the Prince, and ended up killing us instead?"

"No, not exactly," Wells replied. "Time cannot be treated in that fashion."

"A matter of reconnaissance, perhaps?" asked Holmes, beginning to understand the intricacies of time.

"Precisely, Mr. Holmes!" cried the author, bobbing his head. "Now you've got it!"

"What?" I asked, feeling most distressed that I was not up to speed. "What is it?"

"If I understand what you are telling us," Holmes answered, sounding out his thoughts as he spoke, "one cannot affect something that has not yet occurred?"

"I must be thick, Holmes," I muttered. "What do you mean?"

"If I may?" Wells responded, taking up the task. "Dr. Watson, time as you understand it is broken down into three realms: past, present and future. That which has already occurred is the past. Nothing you can do will change what has previously happened. Agreed?"

I nodded and paced the room, trying to absorb all of the strange information coming my way.

"The present, though you assume to understand it, is much more complex. It's impossible to quantify it in any meaningful way," Holmes explained. His remark was meant for me, and he delivered it in a patronizing tone. He then turned his attention to Wells, "As you were saying?"

Wells beamed at Holmes. "I could not have explained it any better."

"Explained what?" I countered, piqued by my growing confusion, "Nothing has been explained!"

"I merely pointed out that your declaration is already in the past. It is something that cannot be undone," said Holmes, his eyes searching mine for understanding. Noting my noncommittal expression, he pressed on. "Let us suppose, Watson, that this is a pistol." He made use of his hand, in much the same way as would a child: he pointed his long finger straight out, folding the lower ones under and raising his thumb. "Bang!" he said loudly, pressing his finger against my temple.

In response, I plopped down into the swiveling chair next to Holmes' desk and said, "I don't get it."

"I've just shot you. I did this in the present, but the bullet is now firmly planted in your brain—and in the past. There is nothing either you or I can do to undo what has happened. Though we are—or shall I say, I am—living in the present, you are now a thing of the past. You are dead of a gunshot wound. I cannot resurrect you."

"Bravo, Mr. Holmes!" Wells applauded, seeming to enjoy my demise. I found it irritating beyond all sensibility, but before I could chastise the novelist, Wells turned the conversation back to seriousness.

"The best way to explain the present is that it's transitory. There's no man-made instruments that can precisely mark the present. The very moment a thought or action has occurred, it resides in the past. Do you understand?"

Vying for any position that would make me appear less than a dolt, I ignored his query, by injecting a question of my own. "Speaking of the past, if what you say is true, and you can travel through time, then it stands to reason that by going backwards and knowing what had previously occurred, you should be able to change history. Is that correct?"

At first blush, my words sounded confident, but they dwindled to an unsure query.

But the author visibly digested my words as if they were a sumptuous meal. Wells nodded to Einstein, who parried my logic with a question of his own.

"Suppose someone has the ability to go back in time?" Einstein jumped up and spun the desk chair I was occupying around in a dizzying circle. "If this person should happen upon his grandfather, as a youth. And, supposing this time traveler, not knowing that he has just come upon his own grandfather, has an altercation with this very man that results in his death. What do you think happens next?"

His grinning countenance filled my vision.

"But that's preposterous!" I shouted, pushing him away. "Why would I kill my own grandfather? What was the argument?"

I sat back, unable to draw upon a single word of civility and missing the point entirely. Both men looked to Holmes, expectantly. My friend's face grew pensive. The notion they were presenting had piqued his logical mind, and he was working out the answer. As the silence grew, all eyes were on him. All three of us waited for Holmes' response with growing anticipation. A sudden twinkle in my companion's eyes replaced his previously studious demeanor as he nibbled his lower lip and ran his finger over the bridge of his nose.

"Of course!" he exclaimed, slapping his leg. "Don't you see it, Watson? If you killed your grandfather, then your father couldn't be born! If your father was never born—"

The pieces of this confounded puzzle began to click into place. The enigmatic nature of time ripped away my earlier misconceptions and prejudices.

"Yes!" I shouted. At last I understood the direction we were heading. "I see it. If my father was never born, then I couldn't be born either. But if I could not have been born, then how was it possible for me to kill my own grandfather?"

My head ached, as I considered the impossible. Just a few moments ago, the room had seemed twenty degrees cooler than the outside world. Now it had suddenly become suffocatingly hot and humid.

"Do not trouble yourself, Dr. Watson," said Einstein. "Minds much more clever than ours have pondered this very same mystery."

"Confound it, man! Then what is the purpose of this exercise?" Holmes lashed out, "If what you've laid out is etched in stone, then all is lost. If we cannot go into the future, and act on the events. Or travel to the past, and similarly face the same restrictions, then what's the use of going anywhere at all?"

"Exactly my point," I added.

Wells leaned back deeper into his chair. His eyes shone as he explained his plan.

"Mr. Holmes, though your admirers are legion, I am perhaps your greatest devotee. I've followed your career with a keen interest, thanks in no small part to the efforts of Dr. Watson. My enthusiasm lies not in my fascination with the macabre or sensational, as many of your cases seem to suggest, but rather in the profound respect I harbor for any man who uses his brain to its fullest. Your powers of deductive reasoning and heuristic methods, as well as your ability to study and observe with a cold and calculating eye, are amongst the most trained that I've ever come upon. You see, Mr. Holmes, your brain has become an obsession of mine. I tell you all this not to buttress your already burgeoning reputation and well-deserved pride in your successes, but to make you understand that it is precisely because of these attributes of yours that we may succeed where I have previously never dared hope."

Wells gazed at us expectantly. Our expressions must have elicited satisfaction on his part for he nodded and continued, "What I am proposing may sound unreasonable, but I would like for you and Dr. Watson to witness your own murders by—"

"What?" I said, rising out of my chair. "You are out of your mind, sir. And you say you have no interest in the macabre? Ha! And you have just stated that we are not to travel through time. So how is it that we are—?"

At this point, my nerves had frayed to their limit. The prospect of revisiting my time on the battlefields of Afghanistan or my long days at the bedside of my dying wife, Mary, filled me with dread. To live through such misery once had scarred my psyche. Often I thought that what I had experienced was more than enough for any man to bear. What Wells was suggesting was that I could review such painful losses over and over again, ad infinitum. It was simply too much for me to stand. And yet this young pup and his erudite assistant spoke of such torture in a way that dismissed the pain that gnawed at my core.

"Let the man speak, Watson," Holmes said.

I stood glowering at my friend. After all that we had been through

—and all that Holmes knew I had suffered— I was amazed that he would entertain such folly.

"Hmm, yes," Wells said with a sniff of dismissal, piercing me with his disapproving eyes. "Mr. Holmes, I am offering you an unprecedented opportunity to apply all of your powers of deduction to seek out the criminals who will murder you. Do you understand?"

Intrigued by the idea, Holmes rose from his chair and paced the floor.

"Indubitably," he said. "We are to accept your word that all of this," and he pointed to the stacks of dossiers and papers, "is everything that can be gleaned from our deaths. And you are suggesting that we correlate what we already know with what we have here and determine who the assassin is? Is that right? Then using this knowledge, we will foil the culprit's plan before he has a chance to hatch it? Do I follow your logic correctly?"

Wells and Einstein sat in amazed silence, marveling at Holmes' succinct dissertation and immediate grasp of the problem. Whilst I, standing frozen to the floor, stared with mouth agape.

Holmes glanced my way. The corners of his mouth twitched. My good friend could barely contain his glee.

"What say you, Watson? Are you game? Think of it, man! We have an opportunity to utilize facts that have yet to occur. This will be our most interesting case to date!"

My friend's enthusiasm was readily accepted by a broadly smiling Wells and a delighted Einstein, but contrary to Holmes' demeanor, I believed that the entire affair was preposterous. A half-hearted mumble was my only response to Holmes' cajoling.

"What would Wells and Einstein think if they had known the truth about Holmes?" I asked myself, as I pondered a thought I would not dare to speak out loud.

I must at this time explain my meaning as to the use of the word "truth," and its application regarding my friend, Sherlock Holmes.

In the course of our many adventures, my friend would often display an outward appearance of giddy excitement when he's intellectually stimulated by a particular case or clue. What others might not realise is that this behavior was, and is, oft-times a facade. At certain times, deep within his grey eyes, I would happen upon a particular quirkiness (perhaps caused by a trick of light) that emerges at the outer edge of his iris. For lack of a better description, I can oft detect a shadow that bleeds into his pupils. As enthusiastic as he might appear on the outside, my friend's eyes can grow dim and dull. In fact, they can appear as lifeless as a porcelain doll's eyes of glass.

To the best of my recollection, my very first encounter with this disparity of expression that opposes the actuality of Holmes' mood was during Professor Moriarty's relentless pursuit of us at the Reichenbach Falls near Meiringen, Switzerland. Holmes was outwardly excited by the thrill of the hunt, and all of his actions dictated that this was so. But his eyes, which should have burned like coals, were dead in their expression. It was as if he had resigned himself to accept—no, embrace—the possibility of his own death.

I've never mentioned my observations to Holmes, because surely such a revelation would lead to a quarrel. But my recollection of the incident at Reichenbach and my friend's cold, unfeeling eyes are so vividly domiciled in my mind that I now know in an instant when such a disparity appears.

At this precise moment while meeting with H. G. Wells and Albert Einstein, I saw this very look emerge from deep within my friend's eyes.

I suppose, that had he been any other man, I most assuredly would have attempted to dissuade him from what he so excitedly coveted, a rendezvous with his own demise. But, pray remember, this is Sherlock Holmes! Even at his most vulnerable, he is still the most astute and inventive consulting detective in the world.

Let me not brush aside the other linchpin of my rationale. Yes, our lives were at risk, but we were not alone in facing peril. On our shoulders rested the weight of the realm. Holmes had made a solemn vow to our gracious Queen Victoria. By solving the riddle of our own preordained deaths, we would also be carrying out our sacred oaths as Englishmen. An oath I had taken when I entered Her Majesty's service years ago, and one that Holmes had sworn earlier this very day.

Therefore, I try not to judge myself too harshly. I did not cast aside my love for my friend even as he faced his own death with quiet determination. Instead, I chose to stand by him as he fulfilled his role as the world's most successful detective. Even if that role imperiled both of us! After all, Sherlock Holmes will always be as dear to me as a brother.

As all of this raced through my mind, Holmes' penetrating glare bore into my soul as he waited for my response. For just an instant, our eyes locked and the intensity ebbed, lifting the veil of my knowledge. A tiny flare of startled recognition shot along his face as he comprehended that I knew his true emotions. To my surprise, he grew serene and comfortable with our shared secret.

Unable and unwilling to disappoint my friend, I nodded my acceptance. I said, "There's no sense in waiting round to be killed. If there's something that we can do about it, then I'm game."

❧ 11 ❧

Holmes nodded at me appreciatively. "Watson, you're a rock." He turned to face Wells. "How do we go about this?"

The author smiled triumphantly and pounded the table. "Excellent! Take your seats. There's much to discuss. First, I must make it patently clear that the task you are about to undertake has never been attempted before. It's important that you understand that even though you are not actually going into the future, you will be seeing things that have not yet occurred. Is that understood?"

Seeing our nod of compliance, he tried to press on, but I, wanting to postpone the witnessing of our murders, asked a question. "Does this machine of yours—if it does exist—actually travel through the air? Wouldn't someone see it?"

"That's a very intelligent question, Dr. Watson," Wells said, sounding surprised, "But the time machine is not a carriage or any form of moveable conveyance in the usual sense. It cannot physically move as if it were Aladdin's magic carpet. It is anchored to one location. More to the point, it is tethered to the ground on which it now stands. Once the time machine has reached its time destination, the occupants or time travelers are free to roam the land. But they must return to the location where the time machine is physically located in order to come home to their point of origin. Timewise origin, that is."

Accepting his explanation without truly understanding it, I merely nodded for him to continue. But Holmes, on the other hand, was not at all bashful in seeking illumination. "Why doesn't the time machine move when it travels?"

Einstein took it upon himself to respond. "It's a matter of pure physics. Men of science at this particular moment now agree that time is only an additional dimension of space. In other words, time, as a dimension, moves with the other three planes simultaneously and does not exist solely on its own. It is virtually impossible to separate time from the remaining three dimensions."

Seeing that his words made the matter more confusing, Einstein paused to gather his thoughts. He rose from the sofa and rummaged through a carton resting on a side table. Finding what he was looking for, he turned to Wells expectantly. The author, appearing as similarly perplexed as we were, shrugged his shoulders.

Turning to face us, Einstein held an elastic band wrapped in his right hand and pulled it taut by spreading his fingers apart. In his left hand was a small sheet of notepaper. Grimacing with determination, he folded the paper lengthwise in half, then again, and again, until the paper was folded to a width of less than an inch. This he folded in half to a size of approximately three inches.

After he completed his handiwork, he walked back over to where we were sitting, and with great fanfare, he showed us what he'd done. The young man, obviously enjoying center stage, creased the paper down to half of its three-inch length and held it aloft between thumb and forefinger, so that it mimicked the letter V. Waving his creation in front of our eyes, he smiled mischievously.

"This," he said, while squeezing and then opening his fingers to compress and release the folded paper, "is the time machine." Flourishing the elastic which was so tightly wound between the thumb and forefinger of his right hand that it twanged with tension when he plucked it, he added, "And this item is time and the other three dimensions. Of course, the walls of this room are the walls of this room. Now, I place the time machine onto the four dimensions." He took the folded paper and draped its center crease over the elastic. That left both long legs of the V-shaped paper dangling.

"Watch closely," Einstein instructed as he strolled to the far wall. Once there, he pulled the legs of the folded paper toward his body. Once he had stretched the elastic band, he released it. The pent up energy sent the V-shaped piece of paper flying through the air. The paper crashed into the wall and fell to the floor.

"Point made!" Holmes said and laughed with delight. "A prodigiously complex scientific theory made simple enough so that even we understand. Isn't that so, Watson?"

"Whatever you say, Holmes," I replied, stooping to retrieve the paper and envisioning our brains crushed against the wall. "Whatever you say."

"Gentlemen," called out Wells, at last finding his composure and sounding very much like a barker at a sideshow attraction, "by viewing the gruesome crime, you will in effect, be visiting the future and witnessing your own deaths. Is there nothing I can say that will dissuade you from this horror?"

Feeling my stomach beginning to knot, I asked a logical question. "If what you say is true, and you saw our murders, then why don't you just tell us who the culprits are?"

"As many times as we've witnessed the crime, I'm afraid that we've been unable to deduce the criminals," Wells said, sounding dejected.

Holmes stared intently at the author. "From all written accounts, and, I might add, from what you have led us to believe, Watson and I died saving the lives of the Royals. That being the case, wouldn't you agree that this villain has shown a remarkable amount of incompetence? He failed miserably. Isn't that so?"

The author's face rumbled into a frothing storm, as he clenched his fists into balls of fury. Only with a monumental effort did he remain seated as he said, "That's right, Mr. Holmes. He failed. The assassin or assassins failed."

Holmes had already dismissed our guest, but a new thought caused him to steer the conversation away from the present mood. "You mentioned in your letter," Holmes said, turning his piercing eyes again onto Wells, "that England was at war?"

"Yes," Wells replied as he folded his hands in his lap. "After the attempt was made, our government believed that France and Germany were behind the scheme to attack the Royals. War was declared. All of Europe was engulfed in the conflagration. So you see, it's imperative that you succeed where we have failed."

Not liking Wells' words of impending doom, I sought refuge in the growing silence, but a new thought crept into my brain. I chose my words carefully. "You've stated that as far into the future as you've traveled, the identity of the assassin remains unknown. Am I correct?"

"Yes, yes. What of it?" Wells snorted.

"I may be dull, but is it possible to go back to the past to learn the identity of the man who tampered with the time machine? Surely, *he* is the man we're looking for."

"No matter where we've gone in time," answered Wells, his face a curious mixture of anger and pride, "the time machine carries not a hint of tampering. Except for the date destination. It's as if that unauthorized adjustment never happened."

Holmes must have wondered the same thing as I was proposing, because a tight grin lit up his face. He spat out, "It's all right, Watson. I'm sure Wells has thought of everything. If he says that we will find no signs of tampering, then I, for one, choose to take him at his word. I propose we forget about that for now and get started right away."

Holmes' tone and words seemed to have not been lost on Wells, as the novelist's face screwed up in fear. Noticing that he had achieved the desired effect, my friend shrugged, pulled me aside, and whispered, "Wait till we're clear of them, Watson." He nodded in the direction of our guests, "I have some thoughts on your observation. We'll talk later."

A sense of danger swept over me. Giving a glance toward Wells, I spoke to Holmes in a whisper, "It's just that I don't trust the man!"

With a troubled expression, my friend searched my face. My silence only led to his further frustration. In the end, he abandoned his queries with an observation of his own. "Watson, your counsel has always been a commodity more steadfast than the British pound sterling. I see no reason to question its value now. If you do not trust him, then that is good enough for me."

"All I ask, Holmes," I said, "is that you do not let down your guard."

"Thank you." My friend cupped my elbow, leading the way to the others. However sure his steps, he still seemed troubled. As if having made up his mind about some inner turmoil, Holmes' eyes glazed over into a dull nonchalance.

"We'd best proceed," Holmes said. "We don't want to be late for our own funeral."

12

Holmes' words sent a chilling reminder of our true purpose for being here and my stomach constricted in protest.

Wells sighed as he removed a stack of large photographs from the carton. To my great surprise, I saw that they were alive with brilliant colour.

"As you can see," Wells began, "these photographs have been glued together at the top. Much like a pad would be. All you have to do is grasp them from the bottom, like this, and riffle them quickly."

As an example, Wells let the photographs play through his fingers a number of times. There indeed appeared to be motion.

"Don't worry, Doctor. All will be well," Einstein said, upon seeing the colour drain from my face. "I have ways of knowing this. Ways that Herr Wells is not aware of. You must believe me when I say this."

Although he hadn't heard Einstein talking to me, Holmes did see my reaction to the moving photos. Holmes said, "Watson, if you would prefer—"

"Let's get it over with," I responded, a bit less graciously than I intended.

"Albert and I will leave you two alone, so you can view the pictures without embarrassment," said Wells, towing Einstein over to the sofa. "Let us know when you have finished."

"Thank you." Holmes offered a courtly nod of his head. "Are you ready, Watson?"

"Yes." I sat down next to my friend at the dining room table and sucked in my breath. Wells and Einstein seemed engrossed in a conversation of their own, and consequently, they paid us little or no attention. That gave the great detective and me a modicum of privacy. After I nodded for him to proceed, Holmes lifted the first pad of photographs and mimicked Wells' previous riffling actions. The picture came alive with motion.

"Amazing! Watson, do you believe what we are seeing?"

I sat in stunned silence, trying to comprehend what was before me. I could clearly see us in the moving pictures, as we waited for the Royal Family and the Queen's guests to arrive in the newly acquired Royal train with its six coach cars.

Holmes ran through the photographs over and over again, until there was nothing new to see. He then reached for the second pad of photographs and the scene continued. There we were, in the midst of a joyous celebration. We were accompanied by five other men whom I was not familiar with. Holmes seemed unfamiliar with them, too. A few seconds later, the Royal train thundered toward the quay. The colourful heraldic insignia on the engine brought a thrill of pride to swell in every heart. The English lion rampant on the left and the Scottish rearing unicorn on the right never looked so magnificent. Steam belched from the massive engine, as the crowd cheered the approaching locomotive.

A rush of air from the huge conveyance caused a swirling wash of papers and debris to be caught up and rain down on the happy gathering. The brakes squealed in protest as the engineer brought the train to a stop. The crowd went silent in anticipation, but once it was learned that the Queen wasn't inside, the tidelike current of the crowd changed, switched directions, and sought other interests. Holmes and I watched as the reviewing party from Windsor, including the Dowager Empress and the Duke of Connaught, stepped down and were escorted to the Royal yacht, The Victoria and Albert II.

Holmes pointed to the rotund figure of the Prince Edward as he waited on the steps of the coach. The remaining onlookers applauded wildly when they spotted the smiling face of the Prince of Wales. The Prince descended the steps, and our entourage stepped forward to greet him.

Suddenly, Prince Edward's eyes went wide with fright. Moving backwards hurriedly, he clambered up the steps and disappeared inside the coach.

The camera lens turned its focus onto Holmes and me. Each successive pad of photographs advanced the horror. The great detective's body suddenly lurched forward. In a desperate effort, his hands strained to reach behind his back and claw at something. At a point midway between Holmes' shoulder blades, a blotch of red blossomed on his coat. Holmes had been shot! He jerked to the right, sending his left hand flying to his side. As he twisted, he leaned to his left.

Another bullet caused his body to twist and twitch as it tore into his back. Holmes stumbled forward, nearly falling to his knees. He righted himself and wheeled round, arms flailing. His hands flew to his throat. He clutched at his neck to stem the flow of blood pouring out from another gaping wound. A final sickening puff of torn flesh and skull flew in the air, as the back of his head was blown off. His unseeing eyes rolled white as he crumpled to the ground.

So stricken by the horror of seeing Holmes' tragedy was I that I failed to see that I had already been felled by the brutal assassins. Off to one side, my body was sprawled in a heap with blood pooling beneath me.

Gasping for breath, I saw the tenor of the crowd change. At first, unaware of the carnage that had just occurred, the crowd pressed forward. The group swelled and swayed, hoping to catch a glimpse of the Prince. The outnumbered and unsuspecting police struggled to maintain order.

The confused crowd wheeled round, transforming itself into a tidal wave of panicked beasts. The police fought valiantly, but the fear and anger of the mob washed over them, and they were swallowed up and trampled.

No sooner would the crowd calm when something would cause

them to scatter and turn as a human wave in another direction. Curiously, the movement of the group reminded me of a murmuration of starlings. I thought of how they would take flight, and then the black-feathered cloud would head in one direction until a breeze or a swarm of insects would cause the group to roll in unison towards another direction.

"Watson, it was us!" said Holmes, snapping his fingers in my face.

"Of course, it was us," I said. "Don't you think I know that?"

"No, Watson," Holmes answered, looking down at me.

"What do you mean by, 'No, Watson?' Holmes, I saw what happened! It was—"

"I mean it wasn't the Royals they were after. *We* were the targets. Don't you see?"

I shook my head, struggling to ward off the gruesome slayings as they made their way back into my brain. My mind seemed unable to grasp the incongruity of it all. Just a few short moments ago, I had witnessed our murders. Yet, there I was with my friend. My friend who was very much alive. What's more, we were discussing the matter of our deaths. The fog in my head gradually lifted, and I gazed up at Holmes as he hovered over me.

"I'm sorry, old fellow," he muttered.

The scenes we had witnessed brought back long-buried memories of my time in Afghanistan. I thought I'd forgotten most of what had happened, but these photos had caused a wave of sentiment so visceral that every cell in my body was shaken. With effort, I said, "I cannot accept what I have just seen, Holmes. This is madness."

"By all written accounts," he continued, "you and I were called upon to take my brother's place because of his turned ankle. Consequently, we were gunned down just as the Royals' coach pulled even with us, and we stepped forward to escort them first from the train, and later to the Royal yacht."

I shuddered, recalling the horrible scene. Holmes droned on, "When questioned, all of the witnesses offered varying and somewhat contradictory accounts as to what had actually occurred. Of course, that is understandable and quite common in a case such as this. However, the one constant that resonated from every eyewitness, was the silence! Not one of the witnesses questioned heard the report of any gunfire. Surely, given the wounds we received, there must have been many shots fired. Then it would follow that someone would have heard them, but not a single witness stepped forward."

"Is it possible, Holmes? Can a pistol or rifle be fired without making a sound?"

My friend's face clouded with worry as he pondered my question. "I have heard of stranger things."

I assumed he was alluding to the time machine as well as a few of our other adventures. Although I knew he was right, I argued, "The witnesses were wrong about the noise. They must have been. There had to have been sounds from the shots. It's just that the confusion and jubilation of the arrival of the Royal Family drowned out any chance of someone hearing them."

"No. No matter how deafening the crowd, the people nearest the shooters would have heard the shots or, at the very least, seen something suspicious. The people farthest down the platform might not have heard them, but those standing nearest to us most assuredly would have. And, human nature being what it is, those who heard the shots would either fight or take flight. The panic would have been instantaneous.

"But that's not what the witnesses reported. All of the onlookers stated that they just saw us fall. We simply crumpled and went down. The spectators had no idea what had occurred. Not a single one of them! And you saw it yourself, it wasn't until we were already dead that the crowd suddenly reacted."

"I'm sorry, but I didn't watch the crowd. My attention was riveted on us."

"I know," my friend said, in a dispassionate voice. "But we are here now. We are still very much alive, and we know where and when our assassination is supposed to happen. Wells said that everything we need to ferret out the culprits is here in this room, now. All we have to do is to keep reviewing the photographs." His voice tapered off.

As we sat there, going over and over the images again, I came to realise that the human brain has a remarkable capacity to facilitate a dreadful defensive quality. After a half-dozen viewings, my mind was no longer repulsed by the horrors. In point of fact, I would opine that it was precisely because of the repetition of seeing our murders that my brain ceased to have any reaction at all. I sat there with a cold eye that failed to be prodded into fear, anger, or rebellion.

"What a horrible device this is," I said aloud. I tossed one of the packages of photos against the table, hard. "This invention will surely be the death of civilization because it allows one to watch distressing images over and over again. With each viewing a person becomes more and more desensitized to violence."

Holmes made reference to a most profound quotation from the New Testament. "Oh, death, where is thy sting? Oh grave, where is thy victory?"

"You, too?" I asked, startled by the revelation.

"Yes. I am able to judge the impact of repeated exposure to violence by watching your changing reaction."

"This invention," I said, "or whatever future contraption has these capabilities, will be the most corrupt tool of man ever made. Numbing the viewer into an acceptance of violence flies in the face of every advance made by civilization."

We sat in silence for some time, while Holmes revisited one particular set of photographs. "Watson," said the detective, pointing to a photograph of a man dressed in a long coat and wearing a hat that concealed most of his face. "I want your opinion of this man."

As Holmes flipped through the scene, the man walked exceedingly slowly. He stopped at a cluster of constables who were gathered a few feet to our rear. The officers, hearing the man speak, turned round, and snapped to attention as he produced what I took to be his credentials.

After a few seconds of discussion, the officers saluted and hurried away. The stranger stood alone for a moment, seemingly watching the retreat of the police constables. He then nodded to the men surrounding us and walked away.

Holmes stopped and looked at me. "Well?"

"A Chief Inspector, perhaps?"

"Perhaps. But I would wager that this mysterious person is Wells' man, Philadelphia. The description of Philadelphia matches this man perfectly. Also we must factor in the confusion with the time machine."

"Are you saying that the man in the pictures is the one who used the time machine? But how? Why?"

"There's no one else. Of course, it was him. As I said, I believe that this man is Philadelphia. Furthermore, I think Wells suspects that our assassin had to be Philadelphia as well. As to how and why we were targeted, I haven't a clue. But rest assured, I intend to find out." My friend's determined voice was reassuring and my sense of gloom lifted.

"I have seen enough of this," Holmes said matter-of-factly, as he gestured towards the pile of photographs. "I suggest that before we speak with Wells and Einstein, we delve into those cartons over there."

"What are we looking for?" I asked, hoping to keep the relief out of my voice. The idea of watching our grisly murders again was, to put it mildly, unsettling.

"I am hoping there will be a dossier marked 'witness statements' and that will be our starting point," Holmes explained.

❧ 13 ❧

There was indeed a dossier so annotated. Holmes and I found ourselves studying some of the most gruesome depictions of cold-blooded murder that we had ever encountered. But what was the most chilling aspect of this despicable crime, was that not one witness (out of the hundreds of onlookers recorded) made any mention whatsoever about hearing any reports of gunfire. It was as if we had been felled by magic bullets!

"Horrible," I said, snapping the last file shut.

"Remarkable, but I am troubled by this information," Holmes said, cocking his head to hear the sudden noise outside our door. "Watson? We have company. And unless I am wrong, we are to be interrupted by urgent business."

Holmes went to the door and opened it even before the visitor announced his presence. A young lad stood breathlessly in the door-way. He spoke loudly and clearly when he said, "I'm sorry, sir, but I must speak with Mr. Wells. It's important."

Upon hearing his name, Wells rose from the sofa and came to stand beside Holmes.

The young lad continued, "Mr. Wells, sir, I have an urgent and private message for you. It's about your experiment."

The author's face furrowed, as he led the boy out of our earshot and onto the landing. As the boy whispered, Wells' legs seemed to go rubbery beneath him, but he quickly regained his balance.

"Einstein!" Holmes called, his voice straining in pitch. "Come here! Hurry!"

Holmes and I stepped to one side, and Einstein came to stand next to Wells in the landing. Again hurried and whispered words were spoken. Einstein turned round to face us. He nodded goodbye to all of us with a tight-lipped grimace and followed the boy as the youngster bounded down the stairs.

Wells stood alone in the landing. As if muttering prayers, he kept his head bowed for some time. When he realized that we were watching him, he smiled weakly and trudged his way back into our flat. He looked about the rooms through unseeing eyes. Confusion and fear flashed across his face.

Holmes escorted Wells to the sofa. "What happened?" asked Holmes, as he sat down next to the man.

"I'm sorry, Mr. Holmes." Wells shook his head. Anger and bewilderment floated on his face, "but I am afraid my young friend, Albert, has been called away on an urgent matter. I do not wish to discuss it further."

"Hmm, yes. I see," said Holmes, clearly disappointed by the response. The great detective took a seat next to me on the sofa. "Never mind. We will proceed without him." My friend stared at the author with an unflinching eye. Finally, Wells was unable to withstand the scrutiny. He nervously rose and paced about the floor in slow circles.

"I couldn't help but hear you make mention, Mr. Holmes, that you confess to be troubled by the materials you and Dr. Watson were reviewing. Are they not sufficient to assist you in your investigation? I assure you that this is everything there is to possess on the matter."

"Oh no, sir!" Holmes disagreed. "There is more than enough. You have misunderstood my meaning. What I find most troubling is that you did not make mention that your associate, Philadelphia, is the one responsible for our assassinations. Surely, you have recognized him as the instigator. Is that not so?"

Holmes went over and stood directly in front of the author, blocking the path that Wells was tracing on the floor.

"Y-y-yes. I'm afraid it is," Wells stammered.

"May I ask why you have omitted such an important fact, sir?" Holmes' tone was neither accusatory nor harsh, but his words had clearly broken the man.

Wells raised his head. Slowly, he said, "Because, sir, I have failed. I have refused to see the obvious. I could not accept that I was so thoroughly duped into misjudging the man. Philadelphia had come to me with the highest of references, and was with me for nearly a year and I could not fathom his traitorous heart. I was so desperate and in need of an assistant that I failed to question his credentials. I should have known. But there you have it."

"Hmm, yes, I see." Holmes smiled thinly as he took a seat at the table. "But why did you not bring it to our attention? Surely his guilt is plain. And our having this information is most critical. If we are to succeed, that is. You do want us to succeed?"

Wells jumped as if he had been kicked.

"Of course!" he shouted angrily. "How can you ask such a question?"

"Because, sir," Holmes said, "you have yet to prove your allegiance."

"What more can I do, Mr. Holmes? I brought you everything there is!"

"The time machine?" Holmes snapped.

"Out of the question! You have all that you are going to receive!" With that, Wells once again paced the floor.

"I see," Holmes responded, his eyes following the author as he went back to marking off imaginary circles on our carpet.

"I'm sorry, sirs," said the author at long last, "but I have already risked and lost everything. I cannot, and they will not allow you..."

Wells seemed to be at his limit, but the author's reference to a mysterious "they" brought my friend to full alert.

"Suppose you tell me then, just who are *they*?" Holmes asked.

Wells ceased his nervous pacing and sat next to Holmes. Dropping his head into his hands, he sobbed quietly.

"Mr. Holmes, I do not know with whom to cast my lot. I have been betrayed so mightily that my instincts are now of questionable relevance. I have lost everything!"

"Come on now, Wells," I soothed, hoping to assuage his growing melancholy. "A man must not base his entire life's worth on his misjudgment of one disreputable character. We have all acted carelessly at one time or another. This man Philadelphia will get his due one day."

"Thank you, Doctor. If it were simply a matter of Philadelphia's betrayal then I would somehow survive the ordeal, but there are powerful forces at work." He paused, tugged at his collar, and blurted out, "Mr. Holmes, the time machine is gone!"

"What?" asked Holmes, rising from his chair and looming over the distraught author. "What are you trying to say?"

"Mr. Holmes," said Wells, "the absence of my friend Albert right this moment is due in part because of the actions of your brother, I believe that your brother, or someone in his employ, is responsible for the theft of the time machine."

❧ 14 ❧

If Wells' startling words had caught Holmes by surprise, he did not let on. Rather, his entire demeanor spoke of calm and quiet resolve. "I want you to listen to me very carefully, sir. I believe that your instincts are correct. If your time machine is missing, it is most probably the result of Mycroft's intervention. But that in no way dissuades me from moving forward. I will deal with my brother at an appropriate time. Right now, you must tell me everything there is to know about Philadelphia."

"Very well, Mr. Holmes, but I must make you aware of one other fact. It was on your brother's recommendation that Philadelphia came to be employed by me."

"Oh?" Holmes responded, "And how is it that you came to meet my brother? You do not strike me as one who would travel in Mycroft's circle."

"W-w-why, I've never met him, Mr. Holmes."

"My good man," I said, provoked by Wells' contrary statements, "you have leveled a most serious charge against Mycroft Holmes, and yet you say that you have never met him? I am at the very least, concerned with the incongruity of your remarks."

"Watson," Holmes interrupted me, "please allow Mr. Wells the opportunity to clarify this troubling declaration. Go on, sir."

"It's true, Mr. Holmes. I have never met your brother, but when Philadelphia arrived on my doorstep—and at a most propitious stage of my experimentation, I might add—he had in his possession a letter of introduction and recommendation. It was authored by your brother."

"I see. Would you by any chance still have this letter?" Holmes asked.

"I'm sorry to say, Mr. Holmes, but the answer is no. I looked for it recently and I believe Philadelphia stole it from me. I'd put it in my desk for safekeeping, and he knew that." Wells turned a brilliant shade of red. For an intelligent man, he had been very foolish indeed.

"I see," responded a disappointed Holmes. "Again, I do not mean to reflect poorly on your veracity, Mr. Wells, but how is it that your, uh, experimentation came to be known by my brother? After all, I wouldn't think that you had placed an advertisement in classified section of the papers."

"I don't know, Mr. Holmes, but Philadelphia appeared to possess a remarkable knowledge of the state of my progress thus far. That was the primary reason I gave such credibility to the letter he held. Also, I was in such desperate need of an assistant that I didn't think to question him about Mr. Mycroft Holmes' involvement. I simply took it as a matter of course, knowing the sort of work your brother does for our government."

"May I ask how young Einstein came to be in your employ?" Holmes pressed on.

"I see where you are going with this, Mr. Holmes, but his presence is above suspicion. I have known Albert for some years. We met at a symposium held in the Royal Greenwich Observatory where the theory of time was being discussed. I must admit that the motivation for my being there was purely economic, and my needs were such that I'm afraid I gained entry into the symposium by entering through an unlocked door and remained hidden in the shadows. I had hoped to gather enough research material for the novel that I was contemplating writing. Little did I suspect that the information I gleaned would set me a course for time travel.

"Albert had been an enthusiastic participant in the discussion. I saw that his theories regarding time travel were falling on deaf ears. He was roundly ridiculed for putting forth what the rest of the group called absurd notions and postulations. Albert, frustrated beyond words, separated himself from the group and came to sit a few rows in front of where I was hiding. I was sure that I had gone unobserved, so when Albert started speaking, I thought he was talking to himself. Venting his anger, so to speak."

"Go on," Holmes said, as he settled back in the cushions of the sofa and closed his eyes.

"But rather quickly, I realised that Albert was directing his words to me. He asked, 'And what have you learned from these great minds?' Believing that at any moment I would be accosted by these intellects and feeling that I had nothing to lose, I'm afraid I responded without censoring myself. I said, 'Great men are not always wise,' which is a quote from the Bible. It was amazing, Mr. Holmes. Albert burst out laughing. From that moment on, we've been the greatest of friends. He has taught me everything I know about time travel. Though he is junior to me, there's a quality to him that meshes well with my personality and my philosophy of life."

"Yes, I understand," Holmes responded. "My partnership with Dr. Watson here is much the same."

I felt my colour rise at my friend's good-humoured gibe, comparing me to Wells' youthful and inexperienced friend. At the same time, I had to admit that Holmes and I did *mesh well,* as Wells has put it.

"I believe you are correct in your opinion of Einstein," Holmes said, as he turned the conversation back to the seriousness it required. "How did Einstein come to be standing in your doorway? Was his appearance an act of Providence?"

"No," Wells replied with a flash of anger in his voice. "If the truth be known, it was I who contacted him. Albert didn't know that I was experimenting with his theory."

"His theory?" I asked.

"Yes. I told you that everything I know about time travel, I had gotten from Albert. He is the most brilliant of men."

"I see," said Holmes. "Can you provide us with any more information about this man, Philadelphia?"

"I'm afraid not. Except that in retrospect, he is most probably one of the most dangerous men I have ever encountered."

"Yes, of course, he is," Holmes said. I could not look at my friend when he confirmed Wells' suspicions because I was amazed and chagrined at Wells' childlike trust in other people. Holmes continued, "Is there anything else that you have kept from us?"

"No!" Wells fairly shouted. "I'm aware that my forthrightness has been lacking, but I assure you both there is nothing else."

"Very well. If there is nothing else, will you kindly excuse us? We have preparations to make."

"Of course," Wells replied, rising from the sofa. "My files?"

Holmes' stony silence and accompanying stare cowed Herbert G. Wells into silence.

"Of course," groaned the author, as he walked to the door.

"If you need to contact us, it's the Diogenes Club where we can be found. Good day, Mr. Wells." Holmes opened the door and ushered the man out.

❧ 15 ❧

No sooner had Wells exited than Holmes moved quickly across the room and ran to the window. He watched in silence as Wells disappeared round the corner.

"Hurry, Watson!" my friend commanded me, while whirling back round. "We have to pay a call."

"The Diogenes Club?" I asked, readying myself.

"Yes," said Holmes. "That queer little club is probably responsible for half the world's ills. A gentlemen's club. Ha!"

As Holmes waited for me to gather my things, he went over to the cartons that Wells had brought us and removed a dossier and the photographs. He quickly stuffed them into his valise.

"I'll hail us a cab. Hurry, will you? Pack an overnighter and conceal it under the landing downstairs, next to mine. When we return, we'll have no time to pack." Holmes spat out his orders to me before he rushed out of 221B, calling over his shoulder, "You'd best bring your revolver!"

I ran into my room and packed my bag. After checking to make sure my revolver was loaded, I slid it under my jacket. Before I left, I set my bag next to Holmes', as he had instructed me.

My friend was already seated in the cab when I climbed in.

"Regent's Circus, cabby, and hurry!" shouted Holmes as I settled in. With a crack of the cabby's whip, we were off. In very short order, we whisked down St. James to Pall Mall, passing the Carlton Club, and stopping at the kerb in front of the dreary facade of the Diogenes Club. After alighting the cab, Holmes gazed up at the imposing structure and eyed it suspiciously. He muttered under his breath, "Oh what tangled webs we weave."

We pushed through the entrance of the building. Immediately an attendant stepped forward, and upon recognizing my friend, the man nodded. Without a word, he led us to the Stranger's Room, and quickly retreated in search of Mycroft Holmes.

The Stranger's Room is where nonmembers are squired off to await an audience with England's "most unsociable and unclubbable" men. It's the sole area within the club where talking, though discouraged, is at least tolerated.

While waiting for Mycroft to appear, Holmes and I stood gazing through the window onto Pall Mall.

"Look!" Holmes said, jabbing his elbow into my side.

I followed his eyes and saw the man that I now knew to be Philadelphia lurking directly opposite the club in a doorway. Philadelphia was too deeply involved in a heated discussion with another man to pay us any heed. But we quickly backed away from the window and into the shadows, nevertheless.

"Do you know them?" Holmes asked his brother when Mycroft slipped in behind us. Placing his stout body between us, Mycroft stared at the two men. Then he nodded as recognition caused a scowl to form on his perspiring face.

"I know one of them. It is nice to see you too, brother," Mycroft said, turning away. A nod of the elder Holmes' head brought two beefy-looking men over to Mycroft's side. He quietly spoke to both of them. After they nodded once, they left without acknowledging our presence.

Sherlock and I returned to our positions at the window in time to see Mycroft's men run out of the Diogenes Club. They chased Philadelphia and his colleague down the street. After a while, Mycroft's men reappeared, panting and wiping sweat from their brows. Philadelphia and the other man were nowhere in sight. Embarrassed, the older of Mycroft's men glanced at us and shrugged his shoulders, pantomiming his disappointment. Mycroft stared down at them coldly. He dismissed his men on the street with a wave of his hand.

"Anything else?" Mycroft asked breathlessly, turning to us with a grimace on his face. The very act of standing was too much for his corpulent body to manage.

"Thanks to the incompetence of your men, I will not have the pleasure of interrogating those two suspects," snapped Holmes, not bothering to hide his disgust. "We must make do with talking to you alone."

Directing his small, porcine eyes in my direction, Mycroft pursed his lips. It was obvious he was weighing his brother's request for an interview with great care. Rather than answering Sherlock's request, Mycroft was troubled by my presence, and he didn't hesitate to show his concern. His glance my way made his disapproval of me obvious.

"As much as I desire your company, Sherlock," Mycroft said disdainfully, "I've other matters that are much more pressing at the moment. I cannot in good conscience leave these things unattended. You cannot presume that I will drop everything and pick up the gauntlet every time you find yourself involved in a trifling matter. Now, if you will both excuse me, I'll have someone escort you off the premises."

Mycroft's spiteful words and casually dismissive manner would send almost anyone into a blind fury. However, as Mycroft walked away, Holmes stayed where he was and smiled comfortably. When Mycroft arrived at the threshold of the Stranger's Room, Sherlock called out to his brother in a voice barely loud enough to be heard, "The time machine?"

❧ 16 ❧

Mycroft froze. The taunt had worked its magic, just as Sherlock had suspected it would. Mycroft spoke without turning around. "This way," he said and he continued his departure from the Stranger's Room.

Holmes shook his head and smiled broadly as we followed Mycroft through a maze of dark nooks and corridors. We passed scrupulously uninterested men whose only claim to the term "gentlemen" was a matter of the thickness of their wallets.

Finally, we stopped at the mahogany-paneled crawlspace beneath a set of stairs that led to the private rooms off the main floor.

Mycroft pressed his hand against a recessed panel. It sprang open, revealing a small black lever. Once he pulled it down, a muffled click was heard. The entire wall lowered into the floor. Mycroft waved us through. The panel hissed shut behind me as we descended wrought iron steps that took us down into the bowels of the Diogenes Club.

The walls were strung with electrical wiring. The lightbulbs glowed brightly, lighting our way to the bottom. There at the foot of the stairs, we were intercepted by another of Mycroft's men who guarded a mammoth beamed door. With a nod of acknowledgment at Mycroft, the man stepped aside and turned his back, thus allowing Mycroft the privacy he needed to access the gleaming tumblers.

But first, Mycroft reached into his vest pocket and removed a small card with a series of numbers written on it. After studying them, he returned the card to his vest. After each turn of the tumbler, a loud click could be heard. Suddenly, the door sprang open. As it silently swung on its axis, I noticed the thickness of the door to be at least eight inches. What I had mistakenly assumed to be a wooden door was in actuality a thick barricade with a solid core of iron. It was disguised to look like solid wood because its massive metal center had been concealed between two thin wooden panels.

Once through the portal, the door closed behind us with a resonating clang. We found ourselves standing in a large, eye-achingly bright room of cavernous proportions. The vaulted twenty-foot ceiling was painted a stark white with contrasting dark wooden beams dissecting the length and breadth of the expanse. Hundreds of canopied bulbs dangled from the black electrical cords, causing the entire subterranean structure to be awash in light. There was an ongoing murmur of hushed voices and the clattering of typewriters making incessant clicking and pinging noises, while both men and women toiled over their black machines.

Mycroft's surprisingly small feet led us through the outer ring of the floor and down a center aisle. On either side of us, a hive of activity and concentration ebbed and flowed as we strolled by each crowded cubicle. The murmur of hushed voices and clattering typewriters was surprisingly daunting. The true power of our government resided here. It was here that wars were planned and calculated. *Here!* Hidden from the citizens of the Realm, laws were compromised, deals were struck, and information was gathered. Ethics were set aside and rights were abused. All in the name of the Queen. I shuddered.

After traveling the length of this den of intrigue, we came again to the outside ring of cubbyholes. Mycroft turned left, then a sudden right, leading us into what appeared to be his very own glass-enclosed office. It was a small room, but by simply swiveling his head round, the elder Holmes brother could observe the comings and goings of his minions. It was all too easy to visualize Mycroft as a venomous spider, patiently biding his time and waiting for the telltale vibration traveling along strands of the web to tell him that prey was within his grasp.

On either side of the entranceway to Mycroft's office, a silent group of young boys stood vigil. Hoping, or perhaps dreading, the scrutiny of their master.

Being the last of our entourage to enter through the doorway, I had the opportunity to study the faces of the young boys as I passed them. Expecting to see polite, cherub-cheeked lads glowing with idealism and enthusiasm, I was saddened by their blank stares and lack of manners. Not a single one of them acknowledged my nods or simple words of encouragement.

"Do not take their lack of acknowledgment personally, Dr. Watson," Mycroft said as we took our seats.

I noticed that Mycroft had not bothered to close the glass door to his office. He continued talking to me. "Those lads didn't respond to you because they have been trained to ignore the unimportant."

"Unimportant?" I protested, while feeling stung by Mycroft's words. "When is it ever a good idea to ignore civility?"

"From the indelicate tone of your voice, Doctor, I would say now," Mycroft said.

"Gentlemen," Sherlock Holmes said, "we have matters other than manners and civility to discuss."

Mycroft directed fiery eyes at his brother. "Why have I been distracted from my duties, and who was that man outside the club?"

"Perhaps it is I who should be asking that question, dear brother."

"What does that mean?" Mycroft said. "I haven't the foggiest idea what you're getting at."

"You know very well that it would be impolitic of me to accept your declaration so readily. We've played this game far too many times for me to be so naïve. You recall of course, the incident with the one-eyed brewer?" Holmes' reference brought amusement to his brother's eyes, and they gleamed mischievously.

"Oh, come now, brother, you're not still carrying that little misunderstanding with you?" Mycroft said.

Holmes ignored his brother's taunt and stared in icy silence. A sliver of a smile curled the corners of his mouth as his eyes narrowed to mere slits.

Mycroft slouched in his chair, blotting the perspiration from his brow. Finally, he said, "Very well. Let's get down to brass tacks. I have much to attend to with the Jubilee Celebration only two days away. What is it that you require of me?"

"First, Philadelphia."

"A dreary little city in America. Certainly historically significant. What about it?" Mycroft sniffed.

"You know very well what I'm talking about," Holmes said in a rising voice. "You said that you recognized him."

"I recall saying no such thing."

"Holmes," I interrupted, as I suddenly understood the confusion. "I think Mycroft meant he did not recognize the other man. He wasn't talking about recognizing Philadelphia."

"Would you mind telling me what you are both talking about?" said Mycroft in exasperation.

Holmes grasped my point and quickly understood the confusion. "I'm sorry, Mycroft. This is my fault. Earlier, when I pointed out the two men to you, you said you recognized one of them."

"Yes, so I did. It was the taller of the two. An unsavory character known as Whisper. His true name is James French, and he's been a hang-about for nearly a month. Unfortunately, that's all the information I've been able to gather on him. It seems that prior to last month the man never existed, and I find that curious. Why do you ask?"

"We believe he's somehow involved in a case that Watson and I are currently investigating," Holmes replied.

"I'm sorry. I know nothing about the man." Mycroft shrugged and drummed his fingers on his desk for what seemed like a very long time. Finally, he said, "Perhaps it would be best that you tell me what you think you know. Of course, I'll neither confirm nor deny your theory. I'm sure you understand my position."

"As far as I'm concerned," said Sherlock Holmes in a tone devoid of emotion, "your position of neutrality is untenable. Somehow you've acquired the knowledge of time travel, if not an actual time machine itself. But what I cannot fathom is your reluctance to warn us. Were you just going to allow Watson and me to be assassinated?"

Mycroft said nothing.

His silence unnerved me.

"Let's go, Watson, we'll get no satisfaction here!" Sherlock Holmes rose from his chair.

"Sit down, brother," Mycroft barked. "Things are not what they seem."

"That may be so," said Sherlock Holmes, "but I assure you, dear brother, that had our positions been reversed, I most certainly would have warned you. In fact, I would have done so personally."

"What are you talking about?"

"Wells. How could you leave such an important task to a man such as he?"

"Wells!? What has he to do with this?" Mycroft was clearly alarmed by his brother's revelation. "Sherlock, I don't know what you are talking about." Sherlock persisted, "Are you telling me that you did not send Wells to warn us of the assassination?"

"Of course, I didn't. He is just an author of trifling fiction!" Mycroft bellowed.

Sherlock Holmes pondered his brother's words. "Be that as it may, why didn't you warn us that we were being targeted?"

"I was instructed—no, *ordered*—not to have any direct contact with you regarding this affair. No matter what."

I was incredulous at his response. "What kind of people do you work for? How can you support anything they do, when they would sacrifice the lives of two people so casually?"

"Ahh, Doctor, do not judge me or my associates too harshly. We all have to make compromises in our lives. If you—"

"What a load of nonsense!" I did not trust myself to add that Sherlock Holmes and I were two people who had devoted much of our lives to the service of our country. I glared at Mycroft. "Under the guise of security, you and your kind will justify anything. You either help us now, or at the first opportunity, I shall publish my findings so the entire world will see what scoundrels you and your associates are. How do you think the masses will react if I tell them that you and our government were willing to stand by while Sherlock Holmes and I were assassinated?"

Mycroft's face glowed crimson. "You cannot think that I would allow something like that to happen to you or my brother?"

Turning his blazing eyes on Sherlock, Mycroft added, "Surely you feel the same?"

"No, perhaps not, but I do question your methods." Holmes studied his brother coolly before adding, "If we are to survive this, then it's imperative that we have your complete cooperation."

"I will give you what I can," Mycroft huffed, as he adjusted his jacket over his copious midsection. "Tell me what you have found so far."

"Before I do, I have a number of questions. Do you or any other individual or group working with, above or under you, possess the time machine?"

"Yes."

"Why did you steal, uh, take it from Wells?" Sherlock continued.

Mycroft looked annoyed. "Wells doesn't understand the true capabilities of the time machine! The device belongs in the hands of those who realise its importance."

"And that would be the government?" Sherlock asked.

"I am the government!" Mycroft shouted.

"Of course, you are," Holmes responded without emotion. After all, he was stating a known fact. Distasteful in some ways, but still accurate.

❧ 17 ❧

"Sherlock, why are you being so polite?" I asked my friend. "If the positions were reversed, you could wager that your brother would not be so gracious. Let me prove it to you. Mycroft, did you witness our murders?"

Mycroft, seized by anger, reddened considerably.

"It's an easy enough question, Mycroft," I prodded him. "My question requires a simple yes or no answer. Nothing more and nothing less."

"Watson," Holmes said, "I believe Mycroft would have told us of the assassinations if he had been a witness."

"No," I replied evenly. "I don't think Mycroft would. But it is easy enough to settle this dispute. Well, sir, what is your answer? Did you or did you not witness our assassinations?"

"I'm sorry, Sherlock." Mycroft looked at his brother forlornly. "The doctor is correct. Yes, I witnessed the assassinations, but it's not what you think. You must understand..." Mycroft paused to glance at his watch. "This is neither the time nor the place to speak of such matters. Now, if you have no further questions, I have other matters requiring my attention. But—and I cannot emphasize this enough—things are not what they appear. However, I am honour-bound not to divulge the intricacies of this situation. I'm sure you understand."

It was obvious that my friend did *not* understand, for he chose instead to seek information regarding the time machine.

"How did you come to learn of the existence of the time machine?" Holmes sat rigidly in his chair. His posture made it apparent he was not ready to leave until he had answers.

Mycroft rocked back in his seat behind his desk. "We have many people."

"Albert Einstein?"

"Sadly, no. He refused to have anything to do with us."

Sherlock scoffed. "For a foreigner, the man displays remarkable good taste when it comes to assessing character—wouldn't you say, Mycroft? How did Philadelphia arrive at Wells' doorstep with a letter of introduction and a recommendation signed by you?"

Mycroft's eyes widened with surprise. "What's that you say? I never wrote such a letter!" His eyes darted to his staff members stationed outside his office. His expression changed from surprise to outright suspicion. A growing look of concern took over his face.

Sherlock Holmes, watching his brother's every gesture, nodded imperceptibly when Mycroft looked back at him. Mycroft managed a tight smile and returned the nod.

"Well, brother," Mycroft raised his voice. "If you have nothing else. I've a very busy schedule. I'm sure you understand."

"I understand this," Sherlock jumped out of his chair. "You are no longer my brother! Whatever our relationship was previously, that is all that you'll get from me! Live in your world, brother, and leave us out of it! Watson, we'd best leave this bureaucrat alone to do his dirty deeds. If you must, Mycroft, I can be reached at Baker Street. Do you understand?"

Mycroft nodded.

"Good day!" Holmes grabbed me by the arm, dragging me out of Mycroft's office. The suddenness of our departure caught Mycroft's people off guard. Even though they'd been trained not to respond, they couldn't help but take a few furtive glances at us as we pushed our way through the startled assemblage. In short order, Sherlock and I were striding through the Diogenes Club and headed outside.

"Perhaps in time you and your brother will reconcile your differences," I remarked, as Sherlock and I waited for a cab out on the kerb.

"What differences?" Sherlock asked me, whilst glancing back over his shoulder at the entrance to the Diogenes Club.

"What differences?" I asked. I was shocked by his indifference. "Why the very cavalier manner in which—"

Holmes interrupted my words with a nod of his head toward the club entrance. "Look there," he said.

One of the boys from Mycroft's staff came trotting out of the club's front door. After he spied us, he headed off in the other direction.

"Watch him," Holmes ordered me while keeping his back to the boy and thus allowing me to gaze over his shoulder. Holmes continued, "In time, that boy'll turn round to see what we're about. If your eyes meet, he'll act as if a thought had just occurred to him, and he'll hurry back inside the club. In a few minutes, another one will exit and most probably walk directly past us. Never making eye contact. He'll be the one who is most dangerous. He'll follow us by staying just ahead of us."

Just as Holmes had predicted, the boy stopped halfway down the street and then turned round. He noticed me looking at him, and at first appeared to be confused. Then, as if making up his mind, he walked back towards the Diogenes Club. Before entering, he stole another glance our way. Then he disappeared inside.

"Well?" Holmes asked, following the direction my eyes had taken.

"He's inside the club," I said.

"Keep your eyes on the doorway, another—"

"Here he comes!" I said excitedly. "It's the man with the bowler hat."

Holmes watched my eyes, tracking the direction of my gaze. Then he slowly turned away so that his back continued to face the man with the bowler hat just as he strolled by, giving nary a glance in our direction. The man continued down the street, pausing to cast an occasional look in a store window.

"That's our man," said Holmes, whistling for a cab. "We shall see more of him in the near future, I would guess."

"Fine," I said, whilst climbing into the cab, "Holmes, would you mind telling me what is going on? In the span of a few minutes, you have gone from disavowing your own brother to—"

"Disavowing my own brother?" asked Holmes, cutting off my observation. He rapped on the cab box. "Driver? 221B Baker Street and be quick about it!"

"You know very well what I'm talking about," I said, settling in my seat. "I'm tired of playing the fool. Just what actually happened between you and Mycroft anyway? There was an undercurrent there that I couldn't quite put my finger on, but it was there nonetheless."

"Watson, you astound me," Holmes said. As he settled in his seat, he turned to look back at our follower. The man in the bowler hat desperately sought to hail a cab of his own. Holmes continued, "I thought Mycroft and I were quite brilliant in our acting. Just what was it that actually gave us away?"

"I've had enough of this nonsense," I said, sliding further away from my friend and towards the door of the cab, putting distance between us. "If I am to die, then tell me so, right now. I cannot in good conscience sit by. I will go it alone if I must, but I will not sit still another minute without you telling me what is going on. Are we to be killed or not? And why are we going back to Baker Street?"

Holmes sat silently, listening to my tirade. Then he said, "To begin, I am not in the habit of guessing. I must have facts. To speculate, merely to mollify your curiosity, is tantamount to giving up on logic, and that I will not do. Now, as to our chances of survival, with my brother involved, I admit that our chances are greatly improved. That's all that I am prepared to say at this juncture, I'm afraid."

"Why are we returning to Baker Street?"

"To spring a trap. Have patience, Watson. All will be revealed when we get back to our flat. Ah, here we are now."

The cab pulled up at the kerb. After paying the driver, Holmes' eyes played over the area in search of the man in the bowler hat. We were disappointed that we didn't see him but there was no reason to linger on the street. So we entered the building and were greeted by our greatly agitated landlady, Mrs. Hudson.

"Mr. Holmes," she scolded, barring us from climbing the stairs, "in the future I'd appreciate being given ample notice when you are expecting such cumbersome deliveries. Why, so many men came and went! Their deplorable manners brought havoc to my house. Mind you, I understand that because of your profession you require certain liberties, but I should not be subjected to such confusion and mayhem!"

Holmes' eyes glowed devilishly.

"Mrs. Hudson, I cannot blame you for suspecting me of such callow indifference. I'm truly sorry, but it is Dr. Watson whom you should be cross with. I distinctly recall my mentioning to the good doctor that you were to be notified of the delivery. It was he, whose responsibility it was to inform you. As for his careless disregard of you and the other lodgers, I humbly ask that you accept our apologies."

Holmes put his hands on the flustered woman's shoulders and steered her to the side. Once she was no longer impeding his way, he immediately bounded up the stairs. His impetuous action left me to face the wrath of our landlady alone. My only option was to smile at her sheepishly.

"Don't worry, Doctor," she said with a smile. She whispered, "I know exactly what he's up to. Why I put up with him all these years is a mystery to me!"

"Thank you." I smiled at her, relieved that the kindly woman saw through Holmes' mendacity. She stepped aside, and I climbed the stairs.

"Mind you," she called out to me, "I will hold you responsible for his comportment from here on out."

"I'll be sure to convey your disappointment in him," I said, feeling soured by the responsibility.

"Holmes," I groused, entering our rooms, "Mrs. Hudson is very cross with the both of us. She said to tell you—"

I stopped as I noticed the tumult and havoc in our rooms. The place was now a tip! Not a stick of furniture had been left untouched or standing erect. In the midst of the overturned furnishings stood Holmes, wearing a thoughtful but placid expression on his face.

"What on earth happened here?" I demanded.

"I am not sure. Not yet, at least." My friend remained calm. He went over to the area where we had put the cartons delivered by Wells and Einstein. But the boxes of material were gone. In fact, everything was gone!

"They were thorough, I'll give them that," Holmes said in a dry manner.

"Who was?"

"Why, my brother's minions, of course. I thought as much."

"Do you mean to stand there and say that Mycroft is responsible for this mess? For what purpose?"

"To possess every scrap of information relating to the time machine."

A look of growing apprehension spoiled my friend's features. Heading out of the room, Sherlock Holmes called over his shoulder, "I'll be back in a second." He returned a short while later and dropped onto the floor the two bags we had secreted under the stairs earlier.

"Very careless of my brother," Holmes said, checking his valise and seeing that everything was where it should be. "Very careless, indeed. Watson, run to the window and see if our friend with the bowler hat is skulking about."

I went to the window and pinched back the curtains. "There he is, Holmes! He's standing in the doorway of the wine shop."

"Excellent," said Holmes, sidling up next to me. "It shouldn't be long now."

Unobserved, we continued to watch the man. As time wore on, the tenor of the activity below changed. The street suddenly teemed with a curious group of similarly attired men. Though they appeared casual in their manner, their actions seemed rehearsed and contrived. As they drew even with our inquisitive visitor, they suddenly set upon him. The man was quickly subdued and whisked away in a wagon that noisily clattered onto the street. In a matter of seconds, the street below returned to its normal pace.

❦ 18 ❧

"Well done!" said Holmes. But he quickly stepped away from the window and bit down on his pipe. "Watson? Your keen mind ferreted out Mycroft's duplicity in this scheme. To think that he had witnessed our murders, and yet he left it to a bumbling fool to warn us that we were in danger!"

"He's your brother, Holmes. He did emphasize that things are not as they seem, didn't he? However, I think the depiction of Wells as a bumbling fool is an unwarranted assertion. After all, the man has created an instrument that allows one to travel through time. That indicates a prodigious amount of imagination and scientific knowledge."

"Yes, I'll give you that. Pray remember, however, Wells is no longer in possession of that which he has created." Holmes paced the room. As he made his restless circles, the scent of his Arcadia mixture of pipe tobacco filled the air.

"I don't know, Holmes. You're seeking a place to rest blame, and no matter what you say, everything stops at the door of the Diogenes Club and your brother."

"Sadly, I must agree with you. But enough of this. I will deal with my brother and his club in due time. I suggest that we make our way to

Portsmouth today. We have two days before the celebration. The newspapers report that crowds are already gathering. I believe that's where we will find Philadelphia. Because of the failure of Mycroft's men to capture him, Philadelphia is aware that we're on to him. If I were he, I would set off for Portsmouth straightaway."

"Why? Surely he would run to ground now. He couldn't risk going through with his plan. The authorities will arrest him on sight."

"And what would the charges be? Murder in the future?"

"I don't know," I answered, "but a horrible thought just occurred to me. What if by our going to Portsmouth, we help fulfill the prophecy?"

"What do you mean?"

"I'm not sure. I don't understand everything about the theories of time, but what if, because of Wells' warning to us, the actions we take now are the cause of our own deaths? Perhaps our murders are the direct consequence of Wells' intervention and our participation in the investigation? For all we know, our arrival at Portsmouth has already been foretold, and Philadelphia could be lying in wait to grab us as soon as we get off the train."

Holmes studied me for a moment before responding. "I do not pretend to understand time travel, but your assumptions are remarkably astute. I congratulate you, Watson. Of course, we must take precautions. Now, come, it's time for us to leave."

Taking our bags, we were soon in a cab heading to Waterloo Station. The streets were a hive of general chaos and confusion, as tumultuous blistering oaths, epithets, and clamors vied for equality with the abrasives of clattering wheels, thunderous hooves, and neighing horses. Seemingly all of London was on the move. No doubt citizens were heading to Portsmouth to continue their celebration of the Queen's Diamond Jubilee.

Our progress ended abruptly two blocks from Waterloo Station. We came to a stop beside a winding column of carriages and cabs as they waited three abreast to disgorge their passengers at the station's entrance.

"We'll get out here, driver," Holmes called up, already opening the doors of the hansom.

Holmes tugged at my arm just as my shoes hit the sidewalk and pulled me away from the kerb. We backed away, with Holmes still clutching at the fabric of my sleeve, and in an instant, we were swallowed up in the humanity. There were more than a few startled faces and bruised shins caught in the rush of our purposeful gaits, as we rounded the corner and braced ourselves against the human tide.

With Holmes leading the way and taking the brunt of the onslaught, I followed at his heels in the calmer waters left by his wake. I glanced back over my shoulder and saw the empty wedge behind us immediately fill with pedestrians as the valuable commodity of space was reclaimed.

Holmes veered us towards an empty doorway. Comically disheveled, my companion pressed himself against the wall. Holmes said, "Have you ever seen the like before? Look at the masses of people!"

"No. And would you mind telling me where are we heading? The station is in the other direction."

"We're here," Holmes said, pointing to a doorway far down a soot- and filth-stained alley. The narrow passage was littered with dilapidated hovels sheltering questionable practices and business dealings. We stopped in front of a dented and rusting iron door that plainly suffered from years of neglect and disrepair. The jagged and broken bricks of the building's face were discoloured a chalky hue of whites and greys.

"Bunson's Theatrical Costumes?" I read aloud, glancing up at the weathered black-and-gold sign of the shop. "What is this place?"

"Using the vernacular of the day, it's another dimension," he responded, fishing a ring of keys out of his pocket and hunching over the tumbler.

Waiting for Holmes to find the proper key, my eyes played over the foul-smelling, rodent-filled middens of the back street. I watched with fascination as a skinny, flea-infested jagged-eared black-and-white cat lay in wait behind a mound of settled debris. Its one eye was keenly intent on keeping an equally emaciated rat within its view. The desperate feline flattened itself against the damp overflow of the clogged drain. Its body swayed back and forth as it made ready to pounce.

"Blast it all!" excoriated Holmes, sending the cat screeching into the air, as the rat successfully scurried away. "Too many lives! I lead too many lives!" Shaking the ring of keys, he began his search for the correct key anew.

My eyes went back to the cat, who sat staring at us with what I could only interpret as a look of anger on its matted and scarred face. The horde of rats were nowhere to be seen. After a while, the cat lost interest and limped away.

Understanding that we were the cause for the pitiable cat's failure to eat, I felt guilty. I shook off the nagging notion as the mental ramblings of a sentimental fool. It's a difficult life, I thought. For all creatures great and small.

Turning my mind back to the shop, I attempted to peer through the yellowed window. Every inch of glass held faded advertisements and old placards, excepting the lower right corner of the window. It was purposefully polished clean and absent of any printed matter. On a water-stained piece of dark velvet sat a wooden crate. On top of it was a gold-painted, plaster casting of an ancient Chinese dragon.

"Eureka!" shouted Holmes, holding up a rather plain-looking key. He inserted it in the lock and gave it a quick turn. The door creaked open. We walked cautiously into the shop, locking the door behind us.

As Holmes lit a lantern, a narrow thread of dusty light filtered into the mildewed and camphor-laden premises. One would naturally expect a sense of comfort from a glow of light when it is brought into a darkened room. However, the lone flame cast long bony fingers of shadows that clawed at the drab, faded costumes lining the center aisle. I, for one, found no refuge from the darkness.

Shuddering, I followed Holmes to the rear of the shop. I watched as he moved his hand along the wall behind a portrait of Queen Victoria. Finding a hidden release, Holmes pressed it. A wall panel clicked open. He smiled as he fussed with the lamp he had been holding. Suddenly the small room was aglow with light. Clearing away a stack of cartons, Holmes sat at a long table and faced the mirrored wall. He tapped the chair next to him, indicating that I should sit down, too.

"What are we doing here?" I asked, taking a seat.

"We are doing what is necessary, I'm afraid."

Holmes rummaged through the various glass jars and set a few of them aside. He then hefted a large black leather case onto the table and lay it flat, snapping open the catches and lifting the lid. Inside was a gruesome assortment of rubber noses and ears, moles and warts, scars and abrasions, as well as teeth, mustaches, beards, brows, and wigs.

Spinning me round in my chair, Holmes studied my face whilst pawing through the collection of facial and hair appendages. A selection from each category finally met his critical eye, and he set them aside.

"Put these on," he said, before tending to his own disguise.

Having countless times observed him applying his disguises, I knew how to prepare my face with the proper use of the spirit gum and contrivances. However, I did require his assistance in blending and feathering the makeup. When he had completed his own application, he turned his attentions to me.

Whilst he applied my pancake, I gazed up at Holmes and saw the face of a complete stranger. His transformation was so complete and masterly that had I not been seated here the entire time, I would never have known that it was Holmes whose dexterous fingers were disguising my face.

"Do not turn round," he said as I tried to view myself in the mirror. "I want it to be a surprise."

He draped a large cloth over the glass and then disappeared into a closet, only to return whilst carrying two mounds of bundled clothing.

"Here," he said, tossing me one of the bundles, "these will do nicely."

Untying the twine and separating the items, I recognized immediately the dark blue uniform of a constable.

"You must be joking!" I laughed as I pulled on trousers that were obviously meant for a man much heavier than myself.

I held the waist far out from my body and jammed my arms into the leg holes, flapping the fabric to emphasize the complete absurdity of it all. "Just look at this!"

"You're not finished yet." Holmes scurried about the small room, tossing aside a blur of clothes and fabrics till he found what he was looking for. Standing behind me, he wrapped a belt made of bulging cotton wadding around my waist. Next, he tied it so it wouldn't fall down. He ordered me to, "Pull the blouse and tunic over the belt and stuff any excess into the waistband."

I did as told and glanced down at my shoes, but I couldn't see them. I felt like a fool.

"Let me have a look at you." Holmes smiled, tugged, and adjusted my uniform. "Perfect! Watson, meet Constable Higgins." With a flourish, he whipped off the cloth covering the mirror.

❧ 19 ❧

The man staring back at me in the mirror's reflection was a ruddy-complected constable with a bulbous, pockmarked nose, and large ears. He was at least ten years my senior, and fifty pounds heavier than he should be. His handlebar mustache was broad and greying, and his bushy brows were arched and angry. The corners of his mouth turned down and a small scar stretched across his chin. Not to put too fine on a point on it, Constable Higgins was the cruelest-looking man that I had ever seen.

"No one to trifle with, eh, Holmes?" I remarked, watching the constable's lips move in the mirror.

"That is precisely the effect we are looking for," said the great detective. "And from now on, my name is Bounder. Call me Constable Bounder."

"Dash it all," I said. "Why must we go to such lengths?"

Constable Bounder, aka Sherlock Holmes, stared into the eyes of Constable Higgins, aka John Watson, in the mirror's reflection before responding to my rhetorical question. "We go to these lengths because Philadelphia knows what we look like. I am leaving nothing to chance. Philadelphia is a threat to us. What say we catch the train for Portsmouth?"

Before exiting the premises, Holmes turned the golden dragon away from the window. I eyed him curiously as he moved the statue.

"A signal," he replied to my unspoken query. "This is something that I had learned from a grateful and unusual character named Tseng Kuo. You've heard my mention of him a few months back."

He was referring, of course, to Tseng Kuo, the leader of one of the families belonging to the secret society of the Chinese Tongs.

"Every dwelling or establishment under his protection displays a certain icon or fetish," Holmes explained. "Of course, the icon's purpose is to let the opposing factions know that they are treading on protected territory and should they continue, it is at their own peril. I simply adapted the concept for my own purpose."

Because of the burdens placed on Holmes in his chosen profession, he probably has hundreds of these sanctuaries dotted throughout London.

"I must make you a list of my hideaways one of these days," Holmes said, reading my thoughts and locking the door behind us. I reflected that indeed, such a list might prove extremely useful.

The air pressed crushingly heavy upon my chest as we strode up the alley and out of its dank confines onto the main street. Falling in with the moving current of people, we were quickly carried downstream towards Waterloo Station and our destiny.

My mood had immediately soured, after being poked with shoulders, elbows, and canes. The exodus of London's citizenry carried me along in their impatient quest to see the Royal Family and join in the festivities celebrating the fiftieth anniversary of our Queen's ascension to the throne.

Holmes spotted our driver first. My friend nudged me with his elbow. Having reached my limit with the rudeness of the masses, I growled at Holmes in reply to his painful jab, "Not you, too!"

"No. Not me. Him." Holmes gestured with a nod of his head, pulling me out of the human tide.

Our driver stood at the kerb near the entrance to the station, scratching his head confusedly and searching in vain for an avenue of escape. Holmes pushed me towards the man.

"Tell him to move," Holmes instructed me. "Remember, you are a constable now. Inform him that he's a nuisance and a hazard because he's blocking the way. Get him to move his cab."

I pulled up on my trousers, tugged down on the dark blue tunic, and squared my hat. Once I had adjusted the chin strap, I felt more in character. Then I walked straight up to the man.

"Come on! Move along!" I barked gruffly, jabbing the driver in the ribs with my baton. "Is it the Queen herself that you're lookin' for? Come on, man! Away with you and your foul-smellin' horse. Move it before I get riled and bring you an' your beast in for creating a hazard!"

I pressed the baton deeper into his ribs.

"Hey, watch out there! All right, all right," he winced, backing as far from me as his seat would allow. "I'm off! Where was ya when this mess started, anyways? Tell me dat! Most likely razzin' some innocent bloke, I imagine."

I moved a step closer to the driver and raised the baton threateningly.

He threw up his arms to save his face from the blows he expected to follow. "Here, there's no need to be brutalizin' the honest folk," he whined. "The whole world's gone dizzy. That's what it has done! I'm goin'. But I tell ya this, that's no way to be actin'. That's for sure." So saying, he climbed onto the hansom, snapped the horse to attention with his whip, and drove away from the kerb.

Holmes had watched the entire encounter as he leaned against the wall. His eyes twinkled with mirth. Other people who witnessed the scene afforded me a wide berth as they scurried into the station. I walked back to Holmes' side with a swagger in my step.

"Bravo, Higgins! Bravo! A most compelling and tantalizing performance." Holmes raised his hands and applauded me.

Feeling confident about the success of our disguises, we sauntered into the nearby train station. Immediately we fell prey to the press of humanity that filled every inch of space inside.

"We'll never catch a train in this place," I shouted over the din.

✨ 20 ✨

"This way!" Holmes responded, weaving his way through the throng. As I watched, he jutted and jabbed his pointy elbows into some of the more recalcitrant human barricades. I followed in his wake.

We traveled the entire length of the train in search of a place to climb aboard, but to no avail. People vied for every possible handhold, hanging onto the outside of the coaches with grips that were precarious at best. Holmes stopped at the side of the Southwest Railway Company's massive steam engine and gazed up into the cab.

Turning back to me, he shouted, "Wait here, Higgins!"

As I watched, Holmes climbed up the ladder and into the engine. He spoke briefly with the engineer. After jumping down, Holmes came over and shouted into my ear. "I informed the engineer that we're on special detail, and we've orders to ride up front with him. I also told him that trouble is expected farther up the line." My friend marveled as he spoke, "The engineer actually thanked us for protecting his train. Can you imagine that? Come, Watson, climb aboard. And don't let your naturally endearing charm and personality creep into your disguise. You're the infamous Constable Higgins. Remember that!" He winked good-humouredly and pushed me up the ladder.

After the perfunctory introductions with the engineer and coal shoveler were out of the way and we were settled in, the whistle sounded. It was a little past eight o'clock when the train inched out of the station, plowing its way through a curtain of steam and smoke. Before long, we raced along the rails with the wind whipping round us. With effort, I managed to position my body so that the air rushing by spared me from the worst of the merciless heat produced by the engine and the hot summer sun. The clacking rhythm of the wheels encouraged my mind to roam freely. My thoughts were occasionally interrupted by the crunch of the tender's shovel digging into the black coal, before rattling it off the blade and into the furnace.

We hurtled along down the line. As we traveled, we waved at the thousands of people on the roads heading for Portsmouth. Morbidly, I wondered if any of these citizens were also our potential assassins. Shaking the thought out of my head, I glanced over at Holmes. He was immersed in reading the notes he'd taken when we first encountered Wells and subsequently were treated to the newspaper accounts of our deaths.

The sky was a water-laden palette of mouse grey and sepia. It held the sun an invisible hostage, as the heated air of our destination thickened in our lungs.

Nearing the station and hearing the boisterous revelry of England's citizens, Holmes put away his notes and caught me looking at him intently. His eyes were wide with nervous anticipation. As were mine, I'm sure.

Even before we came to a stop, other riders leaped down onto the platform. Immediately those passengers were set upon by hawkers peddling their tacky and exorbitantly priced souvenirs. Brutishly vying for the attention and sympathy of the new arrivals, they cajoled, coddled, and ofttimes threatened the wary and weary subjects, in an attempt to separate them from their money.

The reversing wheels protested with squeals before we came to a crawling stop. The engineer rammed the heavy levers forward and turned the steam regulators to their closed positions. Somewhere deep within the blackened bowels of the colossus, steam hammered to escape. In rapid staccato bursts of pent-up anger, the scalding vapors echoed and spewed out. *Puhpuh-puh-puh-puh*! A final and dramatic *woosh* proclaimed that another successful journey had been completed.

❧ 2 1 ❧

Holmes and I said farewell to the crew. We climbed down
from the engine and quickly melted into the crowd.

"It's impossible to think in here!" Holmes shouted,
leading me away and out of the station. "This is no good!"

He pushed me into a doorway while he scanned the faces of the
passersby. Clearly, his mind was in turmoil when he impatiently pulled
me away from the door and prodded me down the street towards the
harbour and the Royal Quay. In exasperation, Holmes said, "Though I
don't expect anything to come of it, we'll have to separate. We'll meet
at the harbour. Keep your eyes and ears alert for anything out of the
ordinary."

"Out of the ordinary?" I pitched my voice high and loud to get his
attention. "This whole affair is out of the ordinary. What do I look for?
Where do I begin?"

Holmes looked around and shook his head. "I am grasping at
straws. I never expected such commotion. Not this far away from
London. All we can do is try. Now, go! Just follow the lemmings."

He pushed me toward the kerb. I was forced to fight the crowd as I
crossed the street. By the time I had reached the other side, Holmes

was already out of sight. All I could do was head to the harbour and hope that I would meet up again with my friend.

Steady, old fellow, I told myself as I tried to sort out the task that lay before me. My uniform proved an asset in my efforts. As I pushed my way along, members of the milling crowd cleared a path.

The harbour was only a short distance away, but the trek seemed interminable. By the time I finally arrived at our prearranged destination, I was in desperate straits. My head swiveled this way and that, while trying to spot Philadelphia or the man in the bowler hat. The dense crowd made any such reconnaissance impossible. I worried that I would not be able to meet up again with Holmes.

My fears were put to rest as I heard my friend's voice coming from behind me. "I know," Holmes said as though he'd read my mind. He stepped out from the shadow of a column. "I had no luck, either."

I was delighted to see him. "Holmes!" I shouted

"Bounder. My name is Constable Bounder," Holmes corrected my lapse. "Nothing's amiss. Yet everything is. This is more than even I can comprehend. Although we do have an advantage with these disguises. We should be able to walk about freely as we search for the assassins. No one will question our motives. It is not an ideal position to be in, but it is all that we have, I'm afraid."

The hollow promise of his own words depressed me. He reached into his tunic, withdrew his notepad, and studied it in silence. His eyes would occasionally lift, and he'd fix his gaze on a particular individual for a moment before turning back to his notes. This continued for some time before he snapped the pad shut and put it back beneath his tunic.

Holmes shook his head and stuffed his hands deep into his pockets. He murmured, "What do we do? Where do we go? We can't stand here all day. We need to find someplace where we can perch and observe the comings and goings out of sight. Any suggestions?"

"No," I answered truthfully.

"We must choose a direction, even if it's only to get away from this madhouse."

My shoulders must have drooped with the impossibility of our task because Holmes tried to bolster my confidence. "See here, Constable

Higgins. Stand tall. We still have time to sniff out the fiends. However, right now I want you to think obliquely."

"What do you mean?"

"It's just possible that our assassins, if they are here, will act contrary to the crowd. Look for people who are going opposite the surge. Or even standing around. Our assassins will attempt to become invisible threads in the fabric of the crowd. They will do their best to look ordinary and appropriate. That will make them nearly impossible to detect."

"You mean they'll do as we have done?"

Holmes' eyes went wide. "Perhaps."

Although the celebration was two days away, hundreds of harried police officers patrolled the area. I nervously expected at any moment to be confronted by a zealous constable going about his duties.

Holmes slowly drifted away from me as I looked around. He turned to face another portion of the crowd and study their faces. Suddenly, I noticed a group of officers gathering near a man dressed in civilian clothes.

I tried to keep my discovery a secret, but I was too excited at this breakthrough. I couldn't keep quiet. "Holmes! It's Philadelphia! He's here!"

"Calm down, Higgins," he said sternly, while reminding me of my new role. "You're drawing attention to us."

"It's him. Philadelphia!" I pointed to a man who was speaking to another group of police. "That's Philadelphia! I'm sure of it."

A loader's dolly rolled by. The workman steering it parked it near us. Holmes yanked me so that we both crouched behind the handcart. We watched as the group of police officers snapped a smart salute at Philadelphia. Philadelphia spoke to them briefly, as if giving orders, and then seemed to dismiss them. The officers broke ranks and walked away from our target. Seeing that they were dispersing, Philadelphia sauntered off toward a large knot of people.

Holmes and I lingered in our spot behind the dolly. When a contingent of the men in blue uniforms walked by, we overheard one of them say, "It's not right, I tell ya."

Holmes stepped from behind the dolly and startled the group with his question, "What's going on?" Holmes looked totally at ease in his uniform, and the constables quickly accepted him as one of their own. "It's that bloody Chief Inspector," replied one of the police officers angrily, pointing to the receding figure of the man in civilian clothes.

"Who is he?" Holmes asked, although he and I both knew the man was our infamous quarry, Philadelphia.

"He's a commissioner of some sort, I would imagine, but I don't know him and don't much care to be his new mate, either. His bark nearly tore me head off. Since when's a detail like this called off? I mean, how we goin' to protect the Royals if they keep sendin' us on fool's errands? He wants us to clear this entire area. Not one civilian on the platform, he says." Dropping his voice in an entirely chummy way, the constable continued, "Listen, it's your own lookout if he sees ya dallyin'. You'd better fall in with us."

Holmes ignored the officer's suggestion. With a quick glance over his shoulder, Holmes said, "Look, I would advise you to find a man in authority whom you-"

"He *is* in authority," the constable said. "That's what I've been trying to tell you."

"I mean someone *else* in authority," Holmes said. "Tell him that this is all wrong. Surely he'll listen to you."

"Don't much matter to me," said the constable, piqued by Holmes' obvious slight. When Holmes didn't encourage him, the complaining constable shrugged and went back to his group of fellow officers.

"Where's that Chief Inspector?" Holmes turned his attention back to me.

I peered over his shoulder and watched Philadelphia continue moving the police away from us. I said, "He's behind you, halfway down the platform."

"Stay here and keep an eye on him. I'll return shortly." With that, Holmes walked away.

Hiding behind the dolly, I continued to spy on the mysterious Chief Inspector. I was so absorbed in my task that I waited too late to leave the area. With a jolt of surprise, I realized that I was one of only five constables left hanging around—and I was still doing my best to hide. Curiously, these few police officers all seemed casual in their efforts. They made no attempt to follow the other policemen as they dispersed. Occasionally, one of them would cast a nervous glance in my direction, but they didn't see me. In response, I pressed myself deeper into the shadows behind the dolly. From that spot, I continued to watch the officers in silence.

Philadelphia came back and walked over to the final five. He made some remark that I was too far away to hear, and they all burst into raucous laughter. Fearing that I might be spotted, I found another hiding spot behind a large crate.

As silently as a shadow, Holmes returned to my side. He whispered, "I have secured an excellent sanctuary for us to watch the activity. Come."

Crouched over, we shuffled our way through the maze of crates and parcels till we were well away from the dolly. Finally, we were able to stand upright, and we headed towards the buildings that faced the quay.

"In here," Holmes said, grabbing my arm. Leaning close to catch my ear, he said, "Follow my lead, and remember, you're Constable Higgins."

We entered a chemist's shop where a nervously twitching, wild-haired and bespectacled man wearing a white coat stood half-hidden behind a large display of coloured apothecary jars.

"Constable Higgins," Holmes said to me in a booming voice, "meet Mr. Terrance Brewer. This kind gentleman recently acquired this commercial establishment. I've informed Mr. Brewer of the Commissioner's desire for us to use the flat above as our observation post. He, being a law-abiding citizen, has been kind enough to accede to the Commissioner's wishes."

I nodded in as stern a manner as possible. The scrawny little man in the white jacket withered and shrank from my attention.

"And," Holmes continued as he lifted a pair of binoculars from a nail on the wall and handed them to me, "as luck would have it, Mr. Brewer is an avid ornithologist. He's allowing us the use of his best pairs of binoculars. Sir? Would you lead the way to our new quarters?"

The man scurried to lead us up the stairs. Staying in character, I still did my best to glower at the man.

"Thank you, Mr. Brewer," Holmes said. "If we require anything else, I will let you know. You've been more than accommodating." With that, Holmes escorted our host out of the flat and slammed shut the door behind him.

"What are we doing here?" I asked, as soon as we were alone. "Shouldn't we—"

"What of our man down there?" Holmes asked me, while ignoring my question. "What's he up to?"

"I'm sorry, Holmes, but I've lost sight of him," I said as I stared out the window.

"Hmmm, I thought as much." Holmes strode to the window and parted the curtains with his finger. "It was all too convenient."

Pointing outside, Holmes asked, "What about that man? Do you recognize him?"

I peered through the opening and saw the lone figure leaning against an iron post near the very end of the platform.

"No," I answered. "But he does look familiar. Who is he?"

"No one," Holmes said, pulling down the shade and leaving it an inch or two from the top of the sill. Next, he dragged a chair across the floor, placed it in front of the window, and straddled the seat backwards, while resting his chin on the chair and peeking through the crack of the shade. Holmes said, "Watson? Post yourself at the other window, if you please."

"All right." I did as he asked and then sat down. "Since we have time, Holmes, something has been bothering me. Back at Baker Street, you said that we were the targets?"

"Yes." He grimaced. "If you recall, as I flipped through the photographs of the assassination it seemed that we made no sudden moves to cause the assassins to react or panic. Yet, they fired anyway. If it had been the Prince they were after, then why didn't they wait till he had completely disembarked from the train?"

"Come to think of it, after the initial shock of seeing our murders, I wondered why all the shots appeared to be low. Except the one that —" I was unable to continue, recalling the final shot that had torn through Holmes' skull.

"I know," said my companion, softly. "The *coup de grace.* I saw it."

His face hardened as he mentally reviewed the killing shot that had been delivered to his person.

Speaking over his shoulder to me, he said, "So it is agreed, we were the targets. The Royals were a prop to put the police off the scent. The murderers wanted it to appear that we died in the act of saving the Prince."

"But who would do such a thing? I know Philadelphia is mixed up in this, but what has he to do with us? Is he perhaps an adversary from a previous case of yours? Someone seeking revenge?"

"Ah, perhaps it would be wiser to ask, *why?* Why would they risk exposure to the Royals' security forces? When it was plain that they could have killed us any time they wanted? I feel that when we ascertain the reasons *why*, we'll find out the *who*. What's the matter, Watson? Why so glum?"

❧ 22 ❧

I didn't answer, but I turned to gaze out the window. The Channel Squadron, including Her Majesty's newest and finest ships of the Royal Sovereign and Majestic classes (all built within the last six years) sat anchored the farthest from Portsmouth. Unrivaled in speed, armor, and cannon, they were undoubtedly England's most potent vessels in the first and second class battleship and cruiser classes.

The flag of the Commander-in-Chief of Portsmouth hung limply in the heavy air above the H.M.S. Renown. I was proud to note that without a single ship being withdrawn from the Mediterranean or any other foreign station or patrol, the Admiralty was able to call up a total of 165 warships to participate in the Queen's Diamond Jubilee. Other battleships, cruisers, and torpedo boats made up the bulk of England's presence for this glorious occasion.

Some of Her Majesty's most famous and infamous ships were present. Though much older than the Sovereign and Majestic classes, these gallant ships continued to cast deadly silhouettes against the skies.

There was the Alexandra, which was the historic ship of Admiral Sir Geoffrey Hornby and the Mediterranean Fleet's flagship. I could not help but recall the valiant episode of the Alexandra training her guns on the Russian army outside the city of Constantinople back in '77.

Near to her was the Inflexible, which was once the world's mightiest battleship. She'd laid waste to Alexandria. Now, she sat there regally with the muzzles of her four eighty-ton guns pointing to the heavens and menacing the encroaching black clouds.

There was the single-turreted Sans Pareil and her 110-ton guns. Sadly, I recalled her sister ship, Victoria, had been sunk by the Camperdown in '94 while on maneuvers. Outside the line of British battleships were the foreign ships of war. Of the twenty or so governments invited to participate, fourteen had responded, most sending the best their navies had to offer.

The most striking vessel to my mind was the U.S.S. Brooklyn from the United States. This heavily armored cruiser was the pride of the American Navy and painted entirely in white.

Not to be outdone, the Russians brought the Rossiya, a fast-running warship that was the largest one ever built in Russia. Norway was represented by the ominously black cruiser, the Fritjhof. Rounding out the foreign contingent was Italy's battleship, Lepanto, France's Pothuau, and the Japanese cruiser, Fuji.

I was so enthralled by the awesome display of warships that I had completely forgotten our purpose. Leaving the watchdogs of the world's powers to stand in silent vigil, I turned my eyes back to the station and quay. I was about to turn away from the window when I thought I saw Philadelphia's familiar figure hiding in the shadows.

"Holmes!" I shouted.

"I see him. He prowls the shadows like a man familiar with such places."

𝕾 23 𝕾

"Why are *we* hiding?" I asked, feeling my anger rise. "I say let's confront him here and now!"

"Watson, please be quiet. There's more to this case than meets the eye. Philadelphia is clever, but I sense someone else pulling his strings. Look at him down there." Holmes pointed at Philadelphia, "He appears to be waiting for someone."

"But Holmes, I—"

"Halloa! Halloa! What have we here?" Holmes was excited by the sudden appearance of two other men. Philadelphia spoke with them for some time, before nodding enthusiastically. "Do our two new friends down there look familiar to you, Watson?"

"There's something about them, but..." I shoved my hands in my pockets.

"Look at their clothes, man! Those two are supposed to be us. Look at the physical similarities. They are about the same height and weight."

"What are you saying?" And then the realization came crashing through. The man obviously portraying Holmes was wearing a top hat and carried a calabash in his hand. Although Holmes never smoked a calabash in our rooms, my illustrator had taken license with the images that he had created for my books. Thus, the public at large had grown accustomed to associating the curved pipe with the great detective. It was a fiction that Holmes tolerated, and one I regretted. The man acting on my behalf carried a medical bag. Both men were dressed in defiance of the threatening weather.

"Remarkable!" Holmes said. "But they have already made a most grievous error. Do you see it?"

Encouraged by my friend's words, but unable to glean the error, I turned to Holmes for an explanation.

"The pipe, man! Look at the pipe. Of course I would be carrying my favourite counsellor." Holmes reached inside his pocket and held up an old and oily slender clay pipe. "As I am now."

This was the small black pipe that I have often seen him "consult" with frequently when he is greatly troubled or in dire need of deep and quiet meditation.

Though my companion's words appeared to be mocking, he was in all actuality deadly earnest in his appraisal of their judgment. However, I thought the entire affair was absurd at best.

"Holmes, you can be..."

"Look, Watson!" said Holmes, pointing below. "More actors are coming onto the stage."

Five more men came into view and huddled with Philadelphia and our two counterparts. After some quiet conversation, Philadelphia nodded and the group separated.

"Where are they going, Holmes? Shouldn't we do something?" I asked.

Holmes whistled softly. "Watson, we are about to witness our assassination."

"What!?"

"Sh! Watch closely."

The two men playing our parts traveled down the length of the platform and stood there silently. Philadelphia, remaining down below us, watched as the other five men posted themselves at different locations throughout the area.

"Interesting," Holmes said. Philadelphia raised his hand, then let it drop to his side. The fake Holmes and equally phony Watson waved in acknowledgement. Then the two imposters slowly walked in our direction. In unison, the five other men moved from their different positions, making an elaborate pattern with their travels.

"A *danse macabre,*" said Holmes as the scene began to play out. "We are being stalked by Philadelphia's men, and we don't know it. Look how slowly they are encircling us from all points of the compass."

Once the ever-narrowing circle of men drew near their prey, they swooped in, seemingly without any outward signal. Our counterparts followed their captors' flow of direction. The exercise served to steer the fake copies of us towards the quay. As they neared the edge of the platform, the two men closest to the tracks stepped to the side. Our imposter counterparts were prodded forward. They glanced up the tracks as if waiting for a train to arrive.

"They're playing their parts admirably," Holmes observed.

The ensemble of actors pantomimed their reactions upon the arrival of an imaginary train. The man playing Holmes stepped forward as if greeting someone. In the blink of an eye, another the man lurched forward. Reaching behind his back, he suddenly swayed to the right, with his left hand clutching at his side. I turned my eyes on the man playing me and watched as he slowly slumped to the ground, clutching his throat. The man playing Holmes twisted round and then fell forward to his knees. As he attempted to rise, Philadelphia, who had been moving forward, and who had gone unnoticed by me, stepped into the circle of men. Raising his hand and his gun, he mimicked giving Holmes the fatal blow

The men stood round and studied their handiwork for a few seconds. Then they quickly broke from the circle by strolling calmly away. Philadelphia watched the men. Just before they were out of sight, he whistled and they came trotting back.

The two men who had been felled by this imaginary assassination jumped to their feet and brushed themselves free of dust and dirt. As the group reassembled, they laughed and patted one another on the back.

"Holmes!" I said, feeling infuriated by the jubilant manner in which these strangers had pantomimed our death. But when I turned round to plead my case with my friend, I was shocked to find him gone.

I turned my eyes back to the men and was startled to see my friend hiding in the shadows. Holmes was well within earshot of the group, and though from his concealment place he would remain unobserved, I was nonetheless furious with him and his careless disregard of my sensibilities. But at present I was helpless to do anything else but watch my friend Holmes spy on the enemy camp.

The circle of men slowly broke up and they went their separate ways. Even so, Holmes continued to fix his gaze on the receding figure of the man we had come to know as Philadelphia. Looking up at my window, Holmes frantically waved for me to join him, and I hurried out of the chemist's shop.

"Holmes!" I called after him, as I slid to a stop after catching up with my friend.

"The name is Bounder, Constable Higgins. Remember that. Come, we mustn't let him out of our sight. We have to find out who else is involved in this scheme." Holmes talked to me as we followed our quarry, taking care to stay thirty feet to his rear.

"But Bounder, won't he see us?" I asked. Calling Holmes "Bounder" was hard for me. For one thing, the name did not suit him at all.

"Perhaps, but look about you. Now that the rehearsal is over, this place is teeming with people again. Why, even the constabulary has returned to their duties. Just keep up a natural pace. Let our conversation remain as casual in appearance and demeanor as possible."

With Philadelphia leading the way, we initially remained anonymous because of the confusion of people jostling their way in and out of the station. As our journey continued, the task of remaining undetected became impossible. When the crowds thinned, it became obvious that should the man simply turn around, he would see us.

By crowding against me, Holmes steered us to the opposite side of the street. We followed Philadelphia in this manner for some time. Then this, too, became untenable because we three were the only individuals on the street.

"Higgins," Holmes whispered, as our predicament became desperate. "If he spots us we'll have to apprehend him."

"It's about time," said I, but the decision was taken out of our hands as Philadelphia suddenly veered left, climbed the stairs to one of the row houses on the quiet street and disappeared inside.

❧ 24 ❧

"Keep moving," Holmes ordered me. First, we came even with the building and then we walked past it. When we turned the corner, Holmes pressed himself flat against the building and stuck his head out so he could see round the side.

"An interesting turn of events," Holmes said.

"What do you think he is doing in there?" I asked.

"A meeting of the minds. Or so I would assume."

"What do you mean?"

"Most assuredly, Philadelphia does not reside here. As he walked along, he continually glanced down at a piece of paper. Seemingly, he was comparing it with the addresses on the buildings he passed. By the way, did you observe the windows along the street? They are boarded shut. Also, if you will look at your shoes, you will note white residue on them. We picked that up as we walked by the building's entrance. It is plaster dust. This building is undergoing extensive renovation. At present, this place is not suitable for habitation. So, what other purpose would he have for going in there?"

"I'm sure you have a theory," I said. I worried that our lurking about in this manner was sure to draw attention.

Holmes read my thoughts. "We do appear to be rather exposed, thanks to the sparse number of people on the street and our circuitous route. What do you suggest we do?"

"We should confront him here and now," I said. We would have to storm the building, but the weight of my pistol reminded me I was prepared for this eventuality.

"If you recall, you asked me whether our presence here could in some way fulfill the prophecy of our own assassinations. Then it follows that I must ask: What if he is not alone? Suppose we are walking into a trap?"

"Dash it all." I was frustrated by our dilemma. "You're saying we can't go in after him, and yet we cannot stay here. The time has come for us to either act or—"

"Halloa!" Holmes said, while pointing to a carriage as it turned onto our street and stopped at the kerb. "Our friend Philadelphia has visitors."

The first man to step down from the carriage was unknown to me, but by Holmes' startled reaction, he recognised the tall stoop-shouldered man. There was no mistaking the second gentleman now alighting from the carriage with some effort. That second man was none other than Mycroft Holmes!

"What on earth is my brother doing with that man?" Holmes said. He was dumbfounded.

"Who is that stranger, Holmes? The man who arrived with Mycroft? What is going on between Mycroft and Philadelphia?"

Sherlock Holmes removed his handkerchief from the pocket of his constable's uniform. He wiped his brow before leaning against the side of the building. I could see complete bewilderment in his eyes, and that worried me. I asked, "Who is the man who just arrived with Mycroft, Holmes?"

My friend whispered the stranger's name, "Giovanni Tuscano."

"Who?"

"Giovanni Tuscano. He is reputed to be the world's most prolific and successful assassin."

"What did you say?" I couldn't believe what I was hearing. "What has he to do with this? And what is he doing in the company of your brother?"

"I don't know," my friend said, "but whatever the connection is, we're witnessing a deadly consortium. My brother, of course, is the government. Tuscano represents the sordid world of murder for hire."

"Where does Philadelphia fit in?" As I said this, Philadelphia walked out of the building. The white dust was evident on his dark trousers. With a quick word to Mycroft and Tuscano, Philadelphia took his place at their side and waited.

The sounds of an arriving carriage explained what he was waiting for.

"Ah, Philadelphia is an unknown quantity. He is too calm to be an underling. There is more to him than meets the eye." Holmes pointed to the men as they climbed into a second carriage.

Curiously, Mycroft was exceedingly deferential to Philadelphia. Mycroft lingered to watch Philadelphia as he stepped up into the carriage. Tuscano climbed in second. Once he knew his guests were secure, Mycroft moved gravely to the other side of the conveyance. His limp was a reminder of the fall he'd taken getting out of his bathtub. With some effort, Mycroft climbed into this new carriage. As if sensing that his brother and I were hiding nearby, Mycroft glanced our way. Holmes and I hugged the wall, wondering whether he had seen us or not. If the elder Holmes brother had seen us, he'd kept quiet about our location. The carriage slowly pulled away from the kerb.

"What do we do?" I asked Holmes, as we watched the carriage turn the corner.

"It is obvious that we cannot follow them," he said, and I heard his disappointment. "I suggest that we enter the building and see what it has to offer. Wait here."

Before I could voice a protest, Holmes sauntered off in the direction of the building. Upon reaching the building, he paused and looked round before slowly and carefully climbing the stairs. I stepped out and away from my position down the block and watched as Holmes stooped to inspect the door's lock. In very short order, he had the mechanism open and waved for me to join him.

As I approached, he cautioned me to avoid stepping in the plaster dust on the steps. I navigated them by hugging the handrail. Upon reaching the top of the landing and coming to stand next to my friend,

Holmes gestured for me to bring out my revolver. He inched open the door and peered inside.

Satisfied that the place was empty, he grabbed my arm and pulled me inside. Once both of us were hidden away, he carefully and quietly shut the door behind us. He brought his finger to his lips and urged me to silence. We stood motionless for some time with Holmes cocking his head from one side to the other to listen for any sounds within the building.

There were none.

"Let's see what my brother has been up to," Holmes said. Brushing his hands together, he looked about, taking in the dilapidated and exposed skeletal remains of the walls. The building was obviously undergoing extensive renovation.

On the main level of the house, Holmes and I went from room to room in search of any clues as to what the men had been doing here. Not finding anything of note, we ascended the stairs to the second landing.

"Stop!" shouted Holmes, grabbing my arm. "Look." He pointed to a slender thread stretched taut across the second step.

"Interesting," the great detective said, stepping gingerly over the thread. "Mind your step, Watson. There's another one."

"All right," I said to Holmes. "I see them."

We carefully made our way to the top without any further incidents.

"It seems that up here they are much further along in their renovation." Holmes wiped a long, bony index finger along the mouldings. "Look, Watson. There's not a speck of dust."

We stood looking round at the newly plastered and wallpapered area. There were two doors on this landing, both of which were closed. Quietly, Holmes and I crept to the first door on the left. He stopped and examined the wood frame.

"Ah, here's one!" he exclaimed, pointing to a piece of thread that sat high up on the right hand corner of the door. "Make note of the thread's location, Watson. We must return it to its original position when we leave. And by no means wander away from my side from here on out. Understood?"

"Of course."

My friend plucked the thread from its perch, folded it into his clean handkerchief, and placed it in his pocket. He then opened the door a crack and peered in. Slowly poking his head inside, he finally said, "All clear." He swung the door fully open on its hinges. Inside the small room were seven cots and nothing more.

"Obviously their sleeping quarters," remarked Holmes, surveying the room. "There's nothing of import here."

He led me out of the room and then carefully replaced the thread in its original position.

"Next," he said, stopping in front of the second door. As before, he examined its frame and removed a hidden thread.

This time when the door swung open, we gazed at a barren room.

"Nothing!" Holmes said, pulling the door shut and replacing the thread. As he started walking to the next room, a thought popped into my mind.

"Holmes," I called, causing him to stop in mid-stride, "why would they go to such lengths for an empty room?"

"Why, indeed?" Holmes slowly turned round and surveyed his environment once more before heading back to the empty room we'd just left. Once again, Holmes removed the thread, tucked it carefully in his handkerchief, and entered the space. Holmes stood quietly and studied the barren surroundings without moving his head. He acted so much like a dog on point that any moment I expected a covey of quail to be flushed. He allowed his eyes to play over this seemingly empty curiosity. Then he slowly walked to the near wall. Pressing his cheek flat against the upright surface, he paced the entire outer perimeter of the room. He placed his hands on the flocked wallpaper and let them feel the rolling imperfections (or perhaps clues).

Disappointed by his meager results on this particular day, Holmes got down on all fours and crawled in an ever-widening circle. From this awkward position, he studied the deal boards of the carpetless area until he again found himself examining the outside edge of the room. Though he was keenly alert to its every nuance, his eyes were hollow. Rising from the floor, he impatiently brushed off the dust and shook his head.

He turned to me and said, "I'm at a loss here, Watson. I cannot detect anything singular about this room. Yet, there's the matter of the thread to contend with. As you stated, why would they set a trap for an empty room?"

"Perhaps the room hasn't been prepared yet." I offered, "Are they waiting for furniture?"

"I think not. There must be an answer." Holmes examined the door jamb, using his hands to explore the edge of the door. "I believe these walls are thicker than the ones in the other room. Look here, Watson. There is something curious about this door. See how it moves in the other direction?"

Holmes stepped into the doorway and stood sideways, facing the hinge. He studied the width of the wall by placing his hands first on the inside wall and then on the wall in the hallway. He held up his hands and stepped away, holding his hands at least twelve inches apart. Then he smiled broadly and placed his hand on the door. Holmes pushed it slightly towards the hinged jamb.

To our amazement, the hinges separated. The door glided across the threshold and disappeared into the wall.

"A pocket door," Holmes said.

"Why the two different constructions?" I examined the empty space the door had left behind.

"Wait." Holmes pressed his ear against the wall. "There's something else happening here."

The right side of the interior wall of the room suddenly sprang to life. It moved into the room.

"By Jove!" I leaped to one side. "You did it, Holmes!"

The wall continued to move silently into the room until it stopped to reveal a three-foot-wide, dimly lit passageway.

"Your pistol, Watson?" The detective prompted me.

"At the ready, Holmes."

With Holmes leading the way, we inched into the passageway.

"What if the wall should close in on us?" I asked. My fear of enclosed spaces made our exploration increasingly uncomfortable for me.

"There will be a similar release at the other end of this."

"Are you sure?"

"Of course. My brother would never leave his escape to mere chance. There will be another way out. Watch your step. There's a turn to the left, and a set of stairs."

Making our way down the stairs, we found ourselves standing below the surface of the street outside. We were in the cellar, or so I thought.

"Why not simply use the door beneath the stairs on the main floor?" I wondered.

"I believe we are below the level of the cellar." Holmes looked round and walked over to one of the walls. I joined him and was immediately sorry I had. Attached to the walls were a variety of gruesome photographs that depicted our assassinations and our final moments alive. A heavy silence weighed on both of us as we moved from one photograph to another.

"I have a sense of being in a museum," Holmes said, making an absurdly ironic observation. "It feels as if we are casually viewing and critiquing the efforts of a newly discovered artist."

"That's preposterous," I said. Holmes' fascination with his own death had begun to annoy me. Even so, I understood the perverse implication of his observation.

I abruptly turned away from the "wall of horrors" and nearly fell over a large tarpaulin-covered table in the center of the room. Steadying myself, I said, "Holmes, look at this."

Reluctantly, my friend abandoned his morbid inspection of gruesome images and came over next to me. We both stared down at the tarpaulin. Once Holmes nodded his head, we carefully rolled back the heavy canvas covering.

My mouth dropped open as I viewed a miniature rendering of the immediate environs. "What the devil?"

"Outstanding," my friend said. His eyes were bright with wonder. "A diorama!"

The three-dimensional tableau spread before us was a meticulously crafted effort, obviously depicting the surrounding area, the interior of the train station, and the Royal Quay to exacting specifications.

The representation was built on top of a thin veneer of wood. In fact, it must have been freshly cut because the familiar fragrance of sawdust filled the air. The base measured approximately eight feet wide and a little more than four feet deep. At the front of the scene were the train tracks. They ran the entire length of the piece of wood. The Royal train sat on the rails. Numerous and heavily detailed miniature castings of people had been placed about the scene. To my dismay, two of the miniature people were obviously us! On the left-hand side of the scene, a small squat row of commercial buildings had been painstakingly recreated. The artist had included the chemist's shop where Mr. Brewer had allowed us to set up our observation post.

The attention of the great detective was excitedly drawn first to one miniature casting and then another. To Mr. Sherlock Holmes' way of thinking, we had stumbled upon Christmas in June. But to me, the diorama was a grotesque and morbid blight on my sensibilities.

"What have we here?" Holmes' face flushed with discovery.

The item that had excited my companion was a hand wheel. I judged it to be very similar in size and shape to what one might find on a steam boiler. In that situation, the hand wheel would act as a pressure release or regulator. This particular wheel had a knob jutting from it. Holmes eagerly wrapped his fingers round it and gave it a slow turn.

To my horror and his great delight, the train and the miniature figures traveled around the board. As Holmes kept cranking, the Royal train chugged into the quay. More ominously, our figures were slowly and inevitably surrounded by figures conceived for the sole purpose of engineering our deaths. As Holmes had previously observed, their pattern of motion was indeed a *danse macabre*.

Our figures moved forward towards the edge of the train station platform as the locomotive came to a stop. Figures representing our assassins closed in on us. As if by magic, a figure came out of the train's coach and then suddenly moved back inside. Obviously, the doll represented Prince Edward. My figure fell to the ground, and then Holmes' figure followed suit. Meanwhile, our assassins quickly wheeled about. As Holmes kept cranking, they traveled the length of the diorama.

"Incredible!" exclaimed my friend, as he removed his hand from the hand wheel. I stood there stunned by the violent scene, but he ducked his head beneath the table to examine the mechanical workings of the diorama. "Watson, look here."

I dipped my head below the table's surface. There I saw the complex and myriad systems required to bring the diorama to life. The creator had used cables, pulleys, flywheels, counterweights, and magnets all acting in a balanced unison to perform their complicated tasks. As Holmes manipulated the hand wheel back and forth, the well-oiled and carefully crafted mechanical parts performed silently and flawlessly.

"Watson, have you ever seen such a marvelous device?" queried Holmes, coming out from under the table and straightening himself to a standing position.

I shook my head. "Unlike you, Holmes, I am not at all swayed by the ingenuity of this contrivance. In point of fact, I am appalled that such a contraption can be created by a brain that sits in the skull of a human being. This is nothing more than a blasphemy. What sort of perverted individual would find pleasure in viewing our deaths over and over again? This toy is an unconscionable crime of the highest order."

As my tirade rumbled to a stop, the fascinated expression on my friend's face turned dark. Once again, he crouched, this time to study the miniature row of buildings on the table's surface. "Watson, what do you make of this?"

I looked to where my friend indicated, but I saw nothing singular. My expression conveyed enough confusion that Holmes decided to physically tap a finger against the facade of the building I had noted as the chemist's shop.

"What of it, Holmes? I see nothing out of the ordinary. But look. There we are, painted right there in the window. I don't see anything."

"If those two figures in the window are supposed to be us, then who are the two men who were shot? The ones who are dead over there?"

I glanced at the two fallen figures on the platform. Again, my expression showed my befuddlement.

"I don't know," I said. "By all that's holy, what is the purpose of this... this... damnable toy?"

Holmes' bland face was his only reply. My friend clasped his hands behind his back as he walked back and forth, clearly lost in thought. I stood by in silence, because I was unable to fathom a clue as to the purpose of the diorama. Suddenly, Holmes stopped. He turned his questioning eyes to the photographs on the wall. Then he bent his lanky frame at the middle, placed his hands on his knees, and examined the photograph of our prostrate bodies. As he inched his face closer, I moved to his side and mimicked his stance. I also inspected the photograph.

"What is it, Holmes? What are you thinking?"

"Unbelievable," he said, slapping his hand against his thigh. "See if you can find a magnifying glass. Unfortunately, I left mine in my valise back at the chemist's."

I scurried about in search of the glass and tore into a chest of drawers standing against the far wall. Sitting on top of a miscellanea of papers was a large glass.

"Here's one." I held my prize aloft and trotted back to my friend.

Holmes never took his eyes off the subject of his attention. It was as if he worried that if he looked away, the image would disappear. Instead, he clenched and unclenched his hand for me to place the glass in it. He brought the glass up to his face and scanned the length of the photograph. His eyes stopped to study something in particular. As I watched, he moved the glass closer, then farther away from the photograph, bringing it into different focuses.

"Amazing," he said.

"What is it?" I asked when I was unable to withstand the mystery any longer.

"Look," he ordered me, as he passed along the glass and pointed to the photograph. "Next to my hand. On the ground. What do you see?"

I brought the glass into focus and stared at the picture. Surprisingly, I was able to ignore the carnage of his death as I peered objectively at the small item that showed up just outside of Holmes' dead fingers' reach.

"Your pipe?" I asked.

"Yes," he said. "Do you recall what I said back at Brewer's rooms, when we watched the rehearsal?"

"Of course," I bluffed, not understanding his meaning.

"If you recall, I made mention of the fact that I don't smoke a calabash. I recognize that illustrators have added that particular accessory in your books, Watson, but as you know, that's a matter of artistic license. Nothing more."

"Yes, I recall you saying as much. Well, what of it?"

"The pipe, man! Look at the pipe in this photo of our assassination!"

I did, and I was surprised to see that it was a calabash.

"Oh, my," I whispered.

"Yes. *Oh my,* indeed. Come, Watson, we must return to Brewer's as soon as possible. Put the glass back in its original location. We must make sure that any clue to our visit here is erased. Everything must be exactly as we found it."

Using the hand wheel, Holmes returned the diorama to its original position. We replaced the tarpaulin and surveyed the room.

"Good show," Holmes proclaimed with a nod, grabbing my elbow and leading us back up the stairs and through the passageway. He went to the door and slowly pulled the wooden barrier out of its pocket. The wall returned to its starting point. In a matter of minutes, the hidden room was in its initial state, giving no hint whatsoever that a secret waited behind the papered walls.

"Incredible." Holmes shook his head in wonder.

With the door closed tightly behind us, Holmes reached inside his pocket and withdrew the slender thread. Extending his hands to the top of the door, he placed it back in its original location.

"Come, Watson. The wheel has turned, and it is time for them to go." He clapped his hands gleefully.

"What do you mean by, 'The wheel has turned?'"

"Before I can answer, we must go back to Brewer's. It is there that I think we will find the solution to this puzzle."

We carefully retraced our steps. Once we were outside, we quickly headed away from the building and down the street. As we neared the corner, the loud neighing of a horse caused Holmes to stop. He craned his head back round the building because the sound was coming from behind the edifice.

"Interesting," he said. Holmes tugged at my sleeve and pointed. I took the cue and poked my head around the corner just as he had done.

"Philadelphia!" I cried hoarsely. "What's he doing back here?"

We watched the man take the steps two at a time and disappear into the house. A moment later, he came bounding out of the building. He stood at the kerb with his arms akimbo. His eyes darted up and down the street.

Holmes jerked his chin as a signal for us to leave the area. I followed him. The great detective spoke over his shoulder, "Sadly, we were not clever little mice. Our presence has been detected."

I did not ask him why he thought this. Instead, I held my tongue as we headed towards the chemist's shop.

25

Brewer stood outside his establishment, watching the tumult of the station's activity. When he spied our hurried advance, he stepped aside to allow us entrance. The poor man also made an attempt at conversation, but Holmes cut the chemist off in the midst of a pleasantry as we hurried past. I called over my shoulder, "Urgent business from headquarters." I hoped this would discourage any further attempt at conversation.

"Yes, of course," came Brewer's suspicious reply as we continued our way up the stairs.

As we burst into the flat, I warned my friend, "I think Brewer is having second thoughts as to our being here."

My words fell on deaf ears as my friend dropped to his knees and rummaged through his valise. I slumped down in one of the armchairs and watched Holmes until he shouted, "Eureka!" He held aloft the photographs and his magnifying glass.

After getting up off the floor, my friend ran to the table. Very carefully, he set the photographs on the surface. His hands shook with excitement as he brought his glass to bear on a particular photograph. Holmes studied the offensive item, lowering his head and moving the glass nearer to that horrible pictorial testimony. After a deep exhalation, Holmes straightened and stepped away from the table.

"Aha! Got them!" he said.

I jerked to attention. "What is it, Holmes?"

"The pipes. They're identical," he said. "See for yourself."

After my own scrutiny of the photograph, I was at a loss to understand my friend's joyous mood. "Tell me," I pleaded, collapsing back into the chair. "I see the pipe, but why are you so pleased? I don't understand."

"Ahh, Watson, Watson, Watson," groaned Holmes. "Sometimes your inability to reason with clarity astounds me."

"Holmes, you can ridicule my deficiencies at your leisure when we are back at Baker Street. Should we survive this ordeal, that is. However, given the gravity of our current situation—"

He rushed over next to me. "It was not my intention to cause ridicule. But you are the author of your own misery."

Angered by his words, I frowned at Holmes, but he only shook his head. "You misunderstand my meaning. Actually, I am praising you. If it hadn't been for your discovery of the hidden passage, I would never have had the opportunity to examine those photographs on the wall in the hidden room."

"I still don't understand," I said.

"Follow my thinking, because it's important that you understand. Please remember that I was able to compare those photographs with the photos of the rehearsal that we saw here. There was one singular clue..."

"The pipe?"

"Yes, the pipe. Now we have had the opportunity to compare the rehearsal of the event to the photographs that Wells gave us in 221B. I am pleased to report that the pictures all show the very same pipe, the calabash."

"Yes, but it is only a pipe, after all."

"Watson, open your mind to the obvious. You know that I do not smoke a calabash. That's a fiction perpetuated by your illustrator and by this actor! Furthermore, I have shown you the pipe that I prefer when away from home."

"Yes. Yes. That little black beggar. Why you continue to have that in your possession is a mystery to me. It is a filthy thing!"

"Watson, do not take offence, but lately, everything is a mystery to you. Don't you see? Let us suppose that these photographs, as well as the ones we examined at my brother's secret lair, are authentic. We can safely suppose that they most assuredly are. However, we both know that we're here, and we know that I do not smoke a calabash, even though the photos show me holding one. Therefore, the conclusion we had drawn from the photos that Wells gave us was incorrect. We did *not* witness our murders. Rather we fell upon a clever ruse of such epic proportions that my mind has yet to comprehend its extent or purpose."

It took a moment for his words to register.

"I knew it!" I shouted, hopping out of my chair and dancing the first steps of a jig. "I knew it. It's nothing but flapdoodle."

Holmes grabbed me and stopped my pirouette.

"Flap a what?" he asked.

"Flapdoodle!" I exclaimed again. "Nonsense! Pure twaddle and balderdash!" After a bout of uncontrollable laughter, I fell back in my chair. My friend's observation about his nonexistent calabash had greatly eased my mind. So we'd been tricked into thinking we would be assassinated! Hurrah! I've never felt so happy to be fooled! My relief, along with Holmes' ignorance of modern slang, left me feeling giddy. Finally gaining control of my emotions, I asked, "So it's over? We can go back to Baker Street now?"

My friend's quiet stare answered my query with an emphatic no.

Heaving a sigh, I resigned myself to continuing the case, though I was at a complete loss as to what it was about. More trickery? A missing time machine that our government wanted? A threat to the Royal Family? Were any or all of these possibilities realistic?

As I took a straight-backed chair near the table, I felt completely befuddled. Commandeering the chair opposite of mine, Holmes sat across from me with the keenest of expressions. His logical and methodical brain was already worrying over the inconsistencies of the case. While I had been celebrating, he had begun to deduce the meaning of what he'd only just learned. He was pondering the direction his inquiry would take next. Quickly making up his mind, Holmes jumped out of his chair and rummaged through his bag once more.

"Watson, it would seem that our disguises are no longer profitable or necessary. I suggest that we change back to our own clothes. We are in the courtyard of Mycroft's estate before the hunt. If he is the Master of Foxhounds in this particular chase, it will cost him dearly from his personal resources. Come, Watson! The drag has been marked. And we will run our prey to ground."

So remarkable and purposeful was our day's venture that I had completely forgotten that we were in disguise. With Holmes' mere mention of it, I became aware of how suffocatingly constricting were my makeup and habiliments. I tore open my constable's tunic and removed the wadding from round my waist. Breathing a sigh of immediate relief, I went to the washstand. There I set about the labourious task of removing my pancake and rubber appendages. Soon, the reflection in the mirror told me that I had, indeed, returned to my normal self. While I dressed, Holmes removed his disguise, and he, too, soon returned to his typical visage.

Our labours were not accomplished in silence. Rather, our thoughts and actions were often interrupted by pronouncements of theories and ruminations as to what this case was actually about. During this particularly high-spirited exchange, my friend displayed his remarkable ability to spot the obvious flaws of my postulations. Holmes managed to reject my reasoning without discouraging my continued participation in the exercise. This was a particular talent of his that often goes without mention. When trying to puzzle out a case, the man can show all the attributes of a career diplomat. Every idea, every proposal, is considered and accepted or rejected in such a way that more consideration is encouraged. In point of fact, with each realization of my flawed thinking, my mind became less clouded. I found myself approaching the problem in a more concise and orderly manner, and that delighted my friend.

As our efforts to deduce this case's direction continued, Holmes would on occasion, wander over to the window and peer outside. He would stand there for some moments in rapt silence before bringing forth another theory. Then he would immediately dismiss his own words as pure folly. After a while, our conversation ebbed. Holmes balanced himself on the windowsill and leaned his head against the glass dejectedly. His eyes were open, but they saw nothing.

I came over next to him, hoping my presence would offer a degree of comfort. From this new vantage point, I happened to glance down at the people in the area. To my great surprise, I noticed our temporary landlord, Mr. Brewer, speaking with a number of men. Something about his manner and his gestures told me that his words were desperate and angry.

"Holmes, look at Brewer down there. What do you think he's going on about? Something has him upset."

My friend was very dispirited because it had taken him so long to glean the truth of the case. His sense of disappointment had sent him into the doldrums. However, the great detective raised his hooded eyes and studied the scene below

Holmes watched Brewer for a minute or two. "Most probably Brewer is involved in a quarrelsome business dispute."

"I don't think so," I said, continuing to watch the growing dispute between Brewer and the other men. "Brewer looks to be in a spot of trouble. Look, Holmes, those men are closing in on him!"

Suddenly the dynamics changed. Using quick and much-practiced techniques, Brewer succeeded in bringing each one of the four men to their knees in stunned and abject confusion. A glimmer brightened Holmes' eyes. His interest was piqued by the remarkable swiftness and ease in which the chemist had brought his foes from pugilistic stances to complete helplessness.

We watched as Brewer, satisfied with his efforts, walked away from the group of defeated men. They crawled round in the dirt, attempting to gather their senses and pride. Holmes continued to watch as the chemist made his way to the building where we watched from the window.

"Remarkable!" I said, marveling at the man's capabilities.

"Jiu-jitsu," said Holmes quietly. He was clearly impressed by Brewer's mastery. To my unspoken question, Holmes added, "It is a method of defence that employs the actions of one's opponent against himself.

I have utilised the techniques on occasion, thanks to the teachings of a Japanese master."

"Our Mr. Brewer is quite an enigma," I observed. "I would not expect a man such as he to possess such a deadly arsenal. Would you, Holmes?" Attempting to brighten the mood of the room, I continued, "Remind me to pay Mr. Brewer for the shaving powder that I used. I wouldn't want to be on his bad side."

Holmes walked to his valise and removed the dossier with its witnessed accounts of our murders. It was the same dossier that he had held onto rather than returned to Wells. He studied the papers intently, while I watched.

Absentmindedly, he took out his black pipe, filled it with tobacco, and tossed me the pouch. With nothing else to do but await the completion of his study, I filled my own pipe with the coarse plugs. Soon the room blurred with our chimneying smoke.

❧ 26 ❧

"Aha!" Holmes shouted, slapping the report with the back of his hand and startling me. "Watson, read this and tell me what you find curious." He handed me a page.

Whilst Holmes continued to scrutinize the other statements, I hurriedly read the one in my hands. After doing my study, I gazed up at Holmes expectantly, but he was deeply involved in comparing his findings against the remaining accounts by witnesses. I again reviewed the paper I held. After reading it for a few minutes more, I focused on the name of the constable who'd taken the witness statements.

"Philadelphia!" I shouted, dropping both my pipe and the paper in my hands.

"Philadelphia?" Sherlock Holmes repeated.

"Yes!" I shouted. "The statements concerning our assassinations were all taken by one man, Detective Chief Inspector Philip A. Delphi. Philip A. Delphi or Philadelphia!"

After a gleeful dance step or two, I glanced out the window.

"And there he is!" I said to Holmes, while I pointed to Philadelphia. He was standing in the middle of the group of men who had caused the altercation with Mr. Brewer. Holmes let go of the witness statements he'd been holding. They fluttered to the floor as he hurried over to the window.

A second later, he yelled, "Stay here, Watson!" and he went racing down the stairs and out of the door.

"Holmes!" I yelled. "You're too late! Look, there's a carriage!"

But he was already out of the range of my voice. As I watched, Holmes skidded to a stop outside the chemist's shop. All of the men on the street, including Philadelphia, hurriedly climbed into a carriage. Holmes ran toward them, but he wasn't fast enough. He watched helplessly as the carriage driver snapped his whip, wheeled the carriage about, and raced dangerously out of the area.

Holmes' posture collapsed in response at having missed his prey. I braced myself because I knew a foul mood would follow. But my friend did not come upstairs immediately. So I approached the open door that he had hurried through earlier. From that vantage point, I could hear his breathless voice as he confronted Mr. Brewer. His words were too indistinct for me to make out until he bellowed for me.

"Watson! Your presence, if you will!"

I made my way down the stairs with some hesitation, knowing how disappointed Holmes must be after missing Philadelphia. But I was surprised to find Holmes and Brewer acting quite civil as they shared a pot of coffee.

"Ah, Watson. Good, you're here." Holmes smiled broadly at me. I stood on the threshold, feeling reticent to enter the main area of the shop. "Come here. Sit down and have a cup of Mr. Brewer's excellent coffee."

Brewer eyed me with keen interest as I took a seat next to my friend at a small counter. I nodded at the chemist, hoping to impress upon him my congeniality.

His reaction was unexpected. He blew out a long sigh of relief. "I say, your countenance while in disguise was rather cruel and intimidating. Now I can see that it was not a glimpse into your true nature. It is a pleasure to meet you, Dr. Watson. I am honoured."

I mumbled an embarrassed response. Holmes, sensing my discomfort, broke the awkward moment by complimenting the ease in which Brewer had brought his attackers down.

"Thank you, Mr. Holmes," the chemist said, and tried to look modest. "To be the recipient of a compliment from you is, indeed, the zenith of my dull existence."

Rather than respond in kind to the chemist's words, Holmes quietly gauged the measure of the man before saying, "All right, Mr. Brewer, suppose you tell us precisely what occurred outside your establishment. And I would appreciate it if you do not omit a single detail, no matter how insignificant you deem it."

"Of course, Mr. Holmes. It's all rather peculiar, I must say."

"Go on," coaxed my friend. His face was measured and calm.

"A little more than a fortnight ago, a man previously unknown to me came into my shop. He identified himself as a highly placed representative of our government. He informed me that for the next few weeks, agents acting on behalf of the Queen would be conducting a secret exercise. During the commencement of these exercises, the railway station would be closed to the public. Any and all commercial establishments within the nearby area were to be shut down as well. The proprietors of these businesses would be forbidden to view or discuss the matter with each other."

"Watson?" my friend interrupted the chemist and turned his attention to me. But I had anticipated his request to take notes. My notepad and pencil were both already in use.

"I'm sorry, Mr. Brewer," Holmes apologized. "You were saying, I believe, that you were restricted from conducting business?"

"Pray, do not misunderstand me. It's not as mercenary as you have made it out to be, Mr. Holmes. Of course, I was concerned over the loss of revenue, as would be any merchant. But my losses, as well as those of the other business owners were a necessary obligation, owed to the Queen herself. Even better, I was assured by this man that we would be fairly recompensed for doing our duty."

"This man," Holmes interjected, "does he have a name?"

"I'm sorry. I thought you knew. It was your brother, Mr. Mycroft Holmes."

"I see. Do continue," said Holmes, his voice crackling with energy.

"For the first few days, because of the deplorable weather, we suffered little inconvenience, as the citizens of this area sought shelter from the heat and were not of the mood to frequent merchants near the station. I must also admit to you, that at first the entire circumstance was splendidly exciting, and I was honoured to be a part of it, however small was my contribution. But one particular evening, I happened to witness a very troubling incident.

"As had become routine at the end of each day, the merchants were all assembled and escorted out of the area. I say this, understanding that it may sound rather unjust and cold, but you must remember that it had been impressed upon us that this was a matter of national security. So we went along willingly. However, there came a circumstance—completely unexpected by me—when I was forced to close my shop early. As you both have learned from the loan of my binoculars, I am truly an avid ornithologist. Recently I converted a space in my cellar for me to use in pursuit of my hobby.

"Unfortunately for my specimens, my carpentry skills are not as proficient, nor are they as conscientiously applied, as is my bird watching. The shelving that I had constructed to hold my chemicals came crashing down. Being a chemist of some capability, I was at a critical stage of partially oxidizing methyl alcohol and—"

"Formaldehyde?" Holmes queried.

"Yes. I use it to render my collection safe from deterioration."

"I see. Continue."

"Because of the accident, my shop became uninhabitable. The fumes, you see."

"Yes. Yes. It can be a deadly brew," Holmes agreed impatiently, while lighting his pipe. "Please go on."

"Of course, I had to vacate the premises early. I posted my notice that the shop would be closed for the remainder of the day, and I went home with the intention of returning later that evening to vent the building. In the aftermath of this chemical calamity, I had completely forgotten the restrictions on my being round the station and my shop during the government's exercise. Airing out the premises was foremost in my mind when I returned without thinking. Thankfully, I was not observed. It wasn't until I had entered the shop that night that I realised my error in judgment. However, it was still imperative that I vent the cellar.

"So, under purely innocent circumstances, I found myself to be acting contrarily to our Queen's wishes. Yet, as innocent as were my intentions, I nonetheless regarded my predicament as being unwise. Therefore, I made a conscious effort to go through my shop and down into the cellar without being unobserved.

"As I fished for a box of matches behind the counter, I heard voices outside my building. I peered over the top of the counter. I was startled to near panic when one of the men jiggled the handle on the door.

"Thankfully, Fortune was smiling on me. I had managed to relock the door behind me when I entered. You must remember the station area was completely deserted and as quiet and still as a tomb. Now, what I am about to tell you are the exact words one man said to the other, and pray remember that I could hear them clearly because there wasn't any other noise to obscure the conversation.

"'So,' said the man, 'whose turn is it to be murdered, tonight?'" The chemist paused to see the impact of his words. Holmes did not flinch, although I did. Seeing that the great detective was still listening expectantly, the chemist continued, "Mr. Holmes, I swear I nearly passed out then and there, but the other man laughed and said something even more peculiar."

Holmes had brought his pipe halfway to his mouth. Now he paused with it in midair as he waited for Brewer to continue.

"The second man said, 'I know it's Sherlock Holmes and that Watson fellow, but I sure wish it would be Whisper.'"

I shuddered. Holmes said nothing.

"Sirs, those were their exact words. I swear!" the chemist said. "As God is my witness, they went off laughing."

The chemist trembled noticeably. As a doctor, I found his physical distress worrisome. It would not do for the chemist to have a seizure. I got to my feet and went to Brewer's aid. "There, there, my good man," I said, as I planned to take his pulse.

"Watson? Please allow him to continue. I believe Mr. Brewer has more to add to this mystery. Am I correct, sir?" Holmes' question took on an accusing tone.

"Y-y-yes, I'm afraid I do."

"Go on," Holmes ordered, while tamping his pipe and nodding for me to return to my seat.

"As the men walked away, I found my courage. I crouched and scuttled to the window. Without exposing myself, I watched as a group of men seemed to be involved in a terribly morbid and deadly rehearsal of some sort. Alas, I was too far away to see clearly. Then I remembered my binoculars! As luck would have it, they were behind the counter, as I had the full intention of cleaning them before the trouble arose in the cellar. It's just that—"

"Kindly address the matter at hand," Holmes said. "I'm sure this is all very frightening, but I assure you that whatever you say will remain in the strictest of confidence. Your safety is—"

"I am not seeking nor do I require your protection!" shouted the chemist, jumping out of his seat. Spittle ran down the corner of his contorted mouth. "Has it already escaped your notice that I am more than capable of defending myself?"

Both Holmes and I were shocked by Brewer's outburst. My friend stared at the man who had erupted in a sudden and violent tirade. Holmes sat with tight-lipped patience, letting the man's temper to run its course.

Brewer realised he was out of order. "I-I'm sorry, Mr. Holmes. My anger is not directed to you or the good doctor. I am angry that I could have been so easily manipulated by our government. They preyed on my patriotism and used it against me."

"They will be dealt with, Mr. Brewer. On that you can count, but please describe to me what you witnessed that evening. It is imperative that you be as precise as possible."

"Of course, Mr. Holmes, but you must understand that I am not trained in the science of surveillance. I am merely—"

"Come, come, Mr. Brewer," interrupted Holmes. "Not trained in surveillance? You are an ornithologist. From your very own mouth, you've stated that you live and breathe to observe birds. It is in your blood to see that which others overlook. This is your chance to apply your very special skill and tell me what you saw."

Surprisingly, Brewer smiled good naturedly at my friend's enthusiasm. "Don't think your rationalisations hold sway with me, Mr.

Holmes. Nevertheless, I will endeavor to satisfy your exacting demands."

I must admit that my previous opinion of the man was as far off the mark as any estimate that I can ever recall. He was confident with what he knew of his world, and the rest of society could be damned! How had I misjudged him so thoroughly? It gave me a measure of relief as I sensed that Holmes' opinion of the man had also changed.

Brewer said, "I crawled behind my counter and retrieved my binoculars. There were five men positioned at twenty-foot intervals. Three of average-to-medium height. All were dressed in greatcoats. One of the remaining two was much taller than the others, whilst the last man was short and rather broad-shouldered. He seemed to be the leader of the group. I was too far away to hear what they were saying, so I risked opening my door a little bit to see whether or not I could listen in on them.

"As I'm sure you know, Mr. Holmes, sound travels exceedingly well in the station when there are no people milling about. Therefore, I could easily hear what they were saying. Unfortunately, I had cracked open the door too late to hear most of what was said, but I am positive one of them said something about Philadelphia. Isn't that a city in America?"

Seeing that his question was ignored, Brewer continued with his observations, "The tallest one spoke to the leader, and he nodded. With a wave of his hand, the men stood motionless as they all looked towards the far end of the platform. From out of the shadows walked two more men. Of course, you know who they were."

"Us," Holmes whispered. "You saw us."

"Yes. You and Dr. Watson. Can you tell me what it's all about, Mr. Holmes? I mean, why would you practice—"

Holmes cut him off. "Please go on with your narrative. You are doing excellently."

"Thank you, but you already know the rest. You and Dr. Watson moved towards this end of the station. The others quickly stepped forward and escorted the two of you to where the special trains enter the quay. For a moment or two, everyone waited. First, it appeared that Dr. Watson was shot. Then you, Mr. Holmes, were shot. In a matter of minutes, it was all over. After some discussion, you stood up. Everyone went back to the starting points and did it all again. That's it, Mr. Holmes. Did I leave anything out?"

Mr. Brewer looked to Holmes expectantly, but my friend was too preoccupied and deep into his thinking to respond to the chemist. Having roomed with the world's first consulting detective all these years, I knew that when he was this deep in thought, nothing (short of a fire) would penetrate his whirling brain.

Sensing that our silence would extend into an embarrassed discomfort, I decided to query Brewer regarding the altercation he'd had with the men. I tentatively asked, "If you would, can you tell me about the confrontation you had earlier? What was the cause of it?"

The chemist smiled at my attempt to ward off the growing silence. He was more than happy to provide me with details.

"Of course, Doctor. There's nothing much to it, I'm afraid. Save for the ignominious end of my career as a spy. You see, once I had discovered that I could safely watch the rehearsals, I continued my efforts night after night. I learned that the men were on a strict schedule, and I was duly prepared for the performance. Each evening I chose a different man in the group and watched his every move. I became familiar with their mannerisms and affectations, made copious notes and detailed drawings of my observations, and—"

Holmes' head shot up in reaction to Brewer's last remarks. "You have drawings and notes!?"

"Why yes, of course," affirmed Brewer, startled by Holmes' agitations. "They are an invaluable and requisite commodity in my birdwatching. My modesty prevents me from espousing my capabilities, but I have become quite—"

"Where are they, man?" Holmes demanded, hopping to his feet and pacing the floor in excitement.

"Why, they're down the cellar. I keep all of my notes and drawings down there."

"Quick! I must have them! Would you be so kind as to go and fetch them for me? Hurry!"

"Of course," replied the chemist, rising from the table.

As we waited for his return, Holmes studied me in silence. Finally, he said, "Thank you, Watson."

"For what, Holmes?"

"For being a terrier. Because of your tenacious curiosity, we may gain some valuable clues."

"You are welcome, Holmes," I said.

Flushed with his efforts, Brewer returned. He handed a stack of sketches and small notepads to my friend. "That's all of them. Do you think they will help you?"

"Outstanding!" said Holmes, perusing the artistic renderings of the chemist. "Mr. Brewer, you have acquitted yourself admirably."

The man positively glowed crimson, buoyed by Holmes' praise.

My friend added, "Mr. Brewer, while I review your efforts, please go on with your dissertation of your, uh, spying, I think that is how you described it. You were explaining to Watson the cause for the altercation, I believe."

❧ 27 ☙

As my friend studied the drawings and notes, Brewer continued, "I came to know their routine. When the exercise concluded, I foolishly decided to follow the man whom I believed to be the leader. Knowing in advance where he would exit the station, I posted myself outside and waited for him. Right on schedule, he appeared on the street. I fell in behind him. I must admit that I was excited by the game as I shadowed him along the streets. He walked as if he hadn't a care in the world and I grew more confident with every step. But then he suddenly veered down an alley and simply vanished! I'll tell you, Doctor, it was the most unsettling experience that I have ever had. One minute he was there, and then he was gone!"

"No one simply vanishes," I said, choosing to ignore the numerous times when Holmes would suddenly appear out of nowhere when I believed I was alone.

"Perhaps he simply went into one of the side doors," I offered.

"That's just it, Doctor. There weren't any."

"Over a fence, perhaps?"

"Nothing of the sort. Just sheer walls," Brewer said.

"Impossible! A window?" I kept trying.

"None."

"A coal chute or cellar?" I asked.

"Nothing."

Holmes' eyes wandered from the drawings. His brow arched in amusement, as he watched me struggle for a solution. He asked, "Mr. Brewer, can you tell us where this mysterious alley is?"

"I can do better than that, Mr. Holmes. I'll draw you a map, but you won't find anything there. That much I can tell you."

"Yes, of course," Holmes sounded congenial. "Please indulge me this one last favour, will you? Show us where he disappeared, according to your maps. But before you do that, pray continue with your adventure."

"Yes, of course, I'll provide you with the map, but nothing will come of it," the chemist said, like a petulant child. "Now, as I was saying, having lost sight of the leader in the alley, I returned to my shop, feeling much the fool for having failed in my surveillance. A period of time elapsed. I was busy tending to a customer when I noticed a man peering in my window. I recognized him immediately. He was the tallest of the men whom I had observed. When my customer left, the man came into my shop and threatened me. He said I should mind my own business and not meddle in something that could have dire consequences against my person."

Holmes asked, "Was there anything about this man that struck you as being singular in nature?"

"Why, yes. Now that you've brought it forward, there was something."

Holmes stared at Mr. Brewer and waited.

Brewer said, "I could barely understand the man when he spoke. In fact, I had to ask him to repeat what he had said."

"An accent?" I offered.

"No. His voice never rose above a whisper. That's what I found curious. Here was this big strapping individual, and his voice was *sotto voce,* if you know what I mean."

"Go on," Holmes encouraged Brewer.

"We argued, or I should say that I argued whilst he merely smiled and shrugged. I'm not afraid to admit that I was unsettled by his calm reaction. Nonetheless, I spoke of my intentions to inform the authorities of the strange goings on if he didn't leave my shop immediately."

"To which he responded?" asked Holmes.

"He laughed. He said that he *was* the authorities."

"What else, Mr. Brewer?"

"He told me that there would be no further warnings. Then he left the shop. My anger was at full boil, and I'm afraid that I acted rather crudely. I swore an unholy oath at him. Then today, the rest of his men came to the shop and threatened me with bodily harm. That is the altercation that you observed. I took it upon myself to explain to them that they cannot go about threatening England's citizens, especially if they are in fact, the authorities. One thing led to another, and I just decided to tangle with them."

"Amazing!" Holmes said. "Sir, your bravery is commendable, if somewhat foolhardy. I am surprised that you are alive today to tell us of your experiences."

"Thank you, Mr. Holmes," said Brewer, as he used a pencil to mark the map. "Ah, here you are. That's where the man disappeared. Just follow my markings and you will find the alley." Brewer handed the map back to Holmes.

"Thank you." Holmes glanced at the diagram and smiled knowingly. "Mr. Brewer, would it be too terribly inconvenient for us to continue using the flat upstairs? Watson and I need a safe haven. More importantly, I need to observe these mysterious rehearsals."

"Would you require a key?"

"No, I think not," Holmes said.

I have written before about Holmes' ability to circumvent all the usual methods of securing a room. His prowess at picking locks is legendary. Brewer caught my friend's meaning and understood that Holmes could gain entrance without the assistance of a key.

Brewer continued, "Of course, you may use the flat, but be sure to stay well hidden. And do not in any way give them cause to look in here. Mr. Holmes and Dr. Watson, these are dangerous men. But you already knew that, didn't you?"

"Yes, but the question is, 'On what side are they playing?'"

"Does it matter?" Brewer asked. "Danger is danger, after all."

Holmes studied the man standing before him. Brewer was loose-limbed and relaxed, even as he spoke of the violence that could take his life.

Holmes must have agreed with my silent assessment. He said, "Mr. Brewer, you intrigue me. When this affair is over, I would very much like to talk with you again in a more relaxed environ."

"It would be a great honour, Mr. Holmes. But, please, can you tell me what this is all about?"

"Perhaps later," Holmes said, wheeling about and walking toward the door. "Come, Watson! We need to hurry. I want to be back here before Mr. Brewer closes his shop for the day."

One glance back at our host told me that Brewer was obviously surprised that we'd taken our leave so suddenly. By way of explanation, I offered, "I'm sorry, it's just that... well... he is Sherlock Holmes."

Brewer stared at the profile of Holmes, as he strode past the shop window. "He is at that," the chemist said. "He is at that."

❧ 28 ❧

I raced out of the shop and quickly caught up to Holmes. "Aren't you going to look at the map?" I asked.

"There's no need. I know where we're going. I've been a fool, Watson. As I said earlier, we are in my brother's yard."

"What do you mean?"

"All along we have been playing in Mycroft's world, and I should have deduced his lair from the beginning."

"Of course! We were there earlier. The cellar! The photographs! But Holmes, this is not the way back to that house."

"That is not our destination. We're heading for another one of my brother's sanctuaries."

Not having paid attention to the direction of our travel or considered our destination, I was caught unawares by Holmes' sudden stop. With a sweep of his arm, my friend impeded my moving forward by pushing me behind him.

"The area where Brewer had lost sight of Philadelphia is midway down the street. On the left," Holmes whispered out of the corner of his mouth.

I moved from my spot behind my friend and looked where he indicated. I said, "There's nothing remarkable about it. Are you sure this it?"

"Quite. Several months ago, I needed to keep this place under watch. I discovered that it's another of Mycroft's dens of deceit."

"You were spying on your own brother!?" I asked. I was shocked.

"No, but the individual I was hunting led me here. It was then that I discovered my brother's involvement and this evil place." Holmes spat out the words in disgust.

"Now what?"

"Come. It is time to face evil head on."

My friend headed for the narrow alley as I followed. Our pace was quick, bold, and purposeful when we crossed the street on the diagonal. We walked directly towards the alley. With each step, I had the uneasy sensation that we were being watched. I glanced up at the windows, but I saw nothing. Nevertheless, the feeling of eyes watching my every move felt familiar. Accordingly, I reached for the comfortable heft of my revolver.

Before we arrived at the entrance of the alley, my senses were assaulted by the putrid smell of boiled meat and cabbage. There were also other repugnant odors from unknown sources. I half-expected to find, at the very least, a rotting corpse. The stench was that all-consuming. But as we drew closer, I was surprised to find the area absent of any sign of foul play. In fact, there was nothing amiss at all. The alley was precisely as Brewer had described it. No doors, windows, fences, or any way for Philadelphia to have hidden.

I turned round, expecting to find Holmes scowling in disappointment. But his eyes played on the brick structures that comprised the narrow corridor. Eventually, his gaze wandered to a lone rusting hook embedded in the mortar. His eyes sparkled with delight and discovery. Holmes asked me, "What do you make of that?"

"It is nothing but a fossil from past lives," I said, wondering why my friend found this curious. "It long ago surrendered its purpose of supporting a line to hang clothes."

"I see. And where is the other one? Its partner?"

"I don't know, Holmes," I said, growing impatient and wondering why my friend would not admit to the obvious. "Perhaps its mate was taken down or broken off when the line was no longer required."

"But look at the height of this one," Holmes continued. "It is well above my head. I have to reach to touch it and I am taller than most."

Feeling that he was countering my words with desperate logic, I was surprised to see how nonchalantly he leaned against the wall, directly beneath the hook.

"All right," I said. "I give up. Tell me what you believe."

"Believe!?" Holmes' said, raising his voice. "Watson, you of all people should know that I believe in nothing! Nothing, that is, but logic reasoned by sound and judicious applications of the senses. Do you not find it curious that this lone hook exists at all?"

"No, Holmes. As I said, it is the remainder of a wash line and nothing more."

"I see. And where, pray tell, are the windows from which these imaginary people hung their clothes?"

I gazed up at the walls. For the first time, I realised that they were windowless. Not a single one existed on any of the buildings.

"Yes," Holmes said. "Now you've got it. If these buildings are what they pretend to be, imagine how dark and airless these flats would be."

"But why?" I wondered. "Why no windows at all?"

"There are no windows so that the legitimate inhabitants of these hovels, if there are any, do not see what they are not supposed to see."

"And that would be?"

In answer to my question, my friend reached up and pulled on the hook. At first, nothing happened. Then there was a click. The drainage cover in the middle of the alley popped open.

"My God!" I whispered, following my friend to the lip of the hole.

❧ 29 ❧

With the courage of a miner who goes daily into the unknown darkness, Holmes lowered himself into the abyss. He ignored the dank smell, the fug of air too long sequestered from the sunlight. "Mind your step, Watson, the rungs are slick," he said, as his head disappeared beneath the surface. Taking one last look round, I followed him down.

Moving carefully one rung at a time, eventually we arrived in a dark and moist underworld. Water dripped from above us and the scrabble of claws around our feet suggested we shared this subterranean spot with rodents of all sizes. Holmes crept forward steadily, and I followed him through the narrow, dimly lit tunnel to its end. My nostrils flared with the pungent odor of decay. Our passageway stopped abruptly when we found ourselves standing in front of a large iron door. Holmes' fingertips danced round the edge of the doorframe until he pushed a recessed lever. With a groan, the door sprang open.

My friend gestured for me to take out my revolver. As I did as he asked, a voice on the other side of the door spoke to us: "There's no need for a weapon, Mr. Holmes and Dr. Watson. You are among friends. Come join me, won't you? I so hate talking to someone without being able to see their eyes. Come, come. I promise that this is not a trap. If we wanted, we could have taken you any time."

Holmes inhaled deeply, shrugged his shoulders, and went through the door. I did not want to fall prey to deception, notwithstanding what the stranger's voice promised as truth. Therefore, I took out my revolver and checked its load as I walked through the doorway.

"It's a pleasure and an honour to meet you both," said a man who sat casually on a corner of an ornate mahogany desk. The carved trim suggested the piece was both old and valuable. The scent of beeswax assured me the piece was well cared for.

As Holmes took in our surroundings, the man said, "My name is—"

But my friend interrupted the stranger. With confidence born of scrutiny, the great detective said, "We know who you are, Mr. Delphi."

The man chuckled. "Very good, Mr. Holmes."

"Relocating, are we, Mr. Delphi?" Holmes asked, while smiling and nodding at the crates stacked in the center of the room. "Or would you prefer to be called Philadelphia?"

"Yes, by all means. Call me Philadelphia, please. I have grown to like the name. It has panache. And you, Doctor," the shadowy figure continued in a threatening voice, "kindly put away your pistol or I will have it removed from you."

Philadelphia snapped his fingers, and two men stepped out of the shadows. They appeared as if they had walked through the wall itself. Their sudden arrival seemed to have little effect on Holmes. In all actuality, he seemed rather smug despite their presence. His next words offered irrefutable testimony as to why he is considered the keenest of observers.

"I was curious to learn how long your men could remain motion-less," Holmes said, his voice laced with mocking cruelty. "If they dare to attempt the taking of my associate's revolver, they will deal with me. And I assure you, I will not be as generous or merciful as was Mr. Brewer." Holmes clenched his fists for emphasis.

Philadelphia raised his hand, and the men stopped their advance.

"That will be all, gentlemen. Your presence is not required," said Philadelphia, watching them retreat into the darkness. He continued to sit there on the corner of the desk, swinging his legs as if he didn't have a care in the world. I studied the shadows that swallowed them up and attempted to lift the veil of darkness. I hoped to determine exactly where the men had disappeared. Only after some effort was I able to spot their clever deceit.

The walls appeared innocent at first glance, but to our right, I saw that the shelving was out of alignment. Each shelf stuck out nearly two feet. A clever use of lighting allowed an illusion of sameness in their horizontal line, and that trick disguised a hidden passage. Mycroft's men had hidden themselves behind the shelves.

So absorbed was I in ferreting out the ruse that I suddenly realized I hadn't heard a single word of the conversation that Holmes and Philadelphia were having. I returned to the discussion in mid-argument.

"That's preposterous, Mr. Holmes, and you know it," Philadelphia continued. "Your reasoning and suppositions are all wrong."

"How so?" Holmes said calmly.

"Consider the person you believe is conspiring and plotting against you. Your own brother! That in and of itself should cause you to doubt your assumptions."

"Sir, I never assume."

"If I may quote Shakespeare 'Aye, there's the rub.' Are you sure you have all of the evidence? An obscure writer once suggested that you yourself have said, 'It is a capital mistake to theorize before you have all the evidence. It biases the judgment.'"

I grit my teeth in response to Philadelphia's obvious attempt to poke fun at me. He was, of course, referring to a quotation made by Holmes and chronicled in my first published effort, *A Study in Scarlet*.

"Go on," said Holmes, relaxing his threatening stance. "If you have other evidence to the contrary, I would forever be in your debt if you would provide it."

"Patience, Mr. Holmes." The man smiled as he sensed that he now had the upper hand. His manner was supercilious as he said, "You will be provided with what you call evidence—" and then he added with a snarl "—when it suits me!"

Holmes reacted with the speed of a pouncing cat. The great detective closed the distance separating himself from Philadelphia in the blink of an eye. With a lightning-fast motion, Holmes knocked Philadelphia flat against the desktop. Wrapping his hands around his adversary's neck, Holmes made as if to throttle Philadelphia. The man sputtered in shock. His eyes bulged with surprise. Clearly our host was terrified.

Seeing that he had succeeded in overwhelming his opponent, Holmes released his viselike grip around Philadelphia's neck. But Holmes didn't back down. Instead, he swiftly grabbed Philadelphia by the lapels and pulled him into a seated position. With his own face mere inches from Philadelphia's, Sherlock Holmes smiled into the terrified man's eyes. Holmes said, "I shall beat you within an inch of your life, Mr. Delphi, should you ever choose to use that tone with me or my associate again."

Philadelphia nodded meekly.

"Good. I am glad we have come to an understanding," Holmes said. He let go of Philadelphia in such a way that the man nearly toppled off the desk. Without taking his eyes off of his adversary, Holmes took two steps away from the man. Philadelphia massaged his neck and watched my friend with new respect. I could not help but wonder if Mycroft Holmes' unwieldy bulk and sloth-like behavior had caused Philadelphia to underestimate Mycroft's younger brother. If so, that was a mistake that Philadelphia would never make again.

Holmes continued, "Now that we have the unpleasantries out of the way, suppose you tell me what this is all about."

Philadelphia spoke in a raspy voice. "Believe me when I say this, Mr. Holmes, I wish I could, but I cannot."

Holmes balled his fists and took a step forward once again. This time the man jumped off his desk and raced around to cower behind the piece of furniture. As he scurried, Philadelphia raised his hands to his head as if to ward off an expected blow.

Holmes' face was totally blank as he watched Philadelphia's frantic maneuvering. When Philadelphia had assumed a crouch behind the desk, Holmes rocked forward on his toes.

He leaned over the desk to speak to Philadelphia in a confidential tone, "Now look here. You can give up your little charade. I know that you are not as cowed as you make yourself out to be. If you truly felt that I was any sort of threat to your person, your two friends would have come running. Out with it! What is your game, and how is my brother involved in all this? Surely it does not include our murders!"

Philadelphia rose to his full height and smiled wickedly. Once again, he came out from behind his desk. Now he took his time coming round to sit on the corner again. Once there, he resumed his casual posture with his legs crossed.

"Bravo, Mr. Holmes!" Philadelphia exclaimed, his voice sure. "I was wondering how long you could maintain that little farce of yours. I knew you would never believe in your brother's duplicity in such a crime. Before you deign to throttle me again, I will tell you this much: Everything that you have heard or seen is being done, in fact, to save the lives of the Royal Family, not to mention the life of your brother. That is all that I am prepared to say."

"Just who are you? Who do you work for?" I asked, moving next to Holmes.

"Ah, we now hear from the good doctor," Philadelphia laughed, mockingly. "If you must know, Dr. Watson, I am from Special Branch of Scotland Yard." He waited for my response with a lopsided grin upon his face, but Holmes had a question of his own.

"And Giovanni Tuscano and Whisper? They are with your Special Branch?"

At the mention of the two men's names, the smile disappeared from Philadelphia's face. He continued, "Alas, Mr. Holmes, I am not at liberty to divulge whether they even exist. I'm sure you understand."

My friend was disappointed by his inability to glean any useful information. The tone of his voice conveyed his growing impatience with being thwarted at every turn in this strange, sad affair. "Mr. Delphi, it is obvious that your purpose here is to block my investigation, but I assure you that I'll continue on. If you or any of your cohorts should interfere with my progress, there will be heavy dues extracted."

"Sir! I do not take kindly to boastful and idle threats. And I say *idle* because should I wish it so, you and your bumbling fool of a doctor would be out of it. In an instant! Do you hear? In an instant! I never should have involved you—"

Surprisingly, my friend backed away from the growing confrontation, and instead tried a different tack. Holmes said, "I am sorry, Mr. Delphi, but you must consider our position. We are brought into this case because of a warning that we are both to be murdered. How would you have reacted if you had been provided visual evidence that upon first examination, depicted your death? And then you discovered that what you had seen was actually just a record? A photographic representation of a curious rehearsal connoting your death? What would you do, if you found yourself in similar circumstances?"

"Ah, Mr. Holmes," crowed Philadelphia, smugly. "So it is a clue that you want. Perhaps I can assist in that regard without sacrificing my integrity."

"You preening little popinjay!" I said, suffering the fool no more. "You speak of integrity as if it were an infirmity! You are nothing but—"

"Watson, please," said Holmes, softly. "Mr. Delphi was about to offer a suggestion as to how we should proceed."

Philadelphia's glowering expression brought me a sense of satisfaction. I drew comfort with the knowledge that I could get the man's goat so easily.

"Hmm, yes, of course," Philadelphia said, but he was wary as he turned his eyes away from me. "I was about to suggest that you both return to Mr. Brewer's chemist shop and watch tonight's rehearsal. It may provide you with the evidence you need. I must caution you, however, that what appears obvious is not as important as changing one's perspective. And perhaps, in some small way your reputation of being a keen observer may assist us in finding the true assassin. Now, sirs, I have said all that I am prepared to say. If you will kindly show yourselves out."

He rose and came to stand directly in front of Holmes. "I will add this one other item, Mr. Holmes, and I say this in all sincerity. I am a great admirer of yours, and I assure you that we are working on the same side. The world would be a much more desolate place if you were not around to tilt at windmills."

And then, Philadelphia extended his hand for a shake.

"Thank you," Holmes said, curtly ignoring the peace offering. "Come, Watson."

Holmes spun on his heels, and I followed. We left Philadelphia standing with mouth agape and outstretched hand hanging in the air. The man's discomfort gave me a modicum of joy. As we made our way to the street, I asked, "Holmes, was that a compliment or a threat that Philadelphia made at the end?"

Holmes responded, "I think to Philadelphia they are one and the same."

❧ 30 ❧

O nce more above ground, the depressing heat quickly sapped my strength. Holmes could see that I was wilting under the blazing sun. He spoke to me over his shoulder, "Let's hurry and get out of this oppressive heat."

Mr. Brewer was standing outside his shop when we arrived. He looked genuinely pleased to see our return. Stepping aside to allow us entry into the shop, he greeted us by saying, "Good, you're here. I was afraid that something might have happened to you. Well, was it just as I said? Was I correct that there was no place for that man to hide?"

"Yes, there was no place to hide," answered Holmes, smiling thinly. "Mr. Brewer, isn't it about time for you to close your shop?"

"What? Oh, no, sir. It is much too early to—" Seeing my friend's face and catching the implied command, Brewer interrupted his own words, "Oh, I suppose if I must close shop, I must." He looked to Holmes quizzically.

"You must," Holmes echoed.

"I see," the chemist responded, morosely. "Well, I'll leave it to you two gentlemen to secure the place—if you leave."

"Of course, sir." Holmes was happy that our new friend required no further coaxing or explanation. "And Mr. Brewer, thank you," Holmes continued, as we watched the man slip out of his white coat.

Brewer smiled. "One of these days you will have to explain it all to me."

"Certainly," Holmes assured him.

Brewer bid us goodbye and made to leave, but before he could reach the door, Holmes stopped him.

"Sir, at the appropriate time, I will personally be sure to include you in the solving of this case. Again, I am sincerely appreciative of your cooperation."

"Thank you, Mr. Holmes. Good evening, gentlemen." Brewer smiled again and nodded. The bell jingled above the door, and he was gone with a wave over his shoulder.

I watched him go. "An extraordinary man, wouldn't you agree, Holmes?"

"Yes. He is extraordinary," confirmed my friend, his eyes narrow.

After locking the door and lowering the gas, we trudged our way up the stairs to the flat and waited for the rehearsal to commence. As the time wore on, I noticed that my companion was worrying over something.

"What is it, Holmes? What gears are whirring inside that brain of yours?"

"What?" Holmes blinked back my intrusion, and his mood became pensive. "Oh, it is something that Philadelphia had mentioned. He said that what appears obvious is not as important as changing one's perspective."

"Yes, I recall his saying that. What of it?"

"I'm not sure, but I can sense that he's trying to tell me something."

My prejudices against the man came to the fore. "What he is trying to say is that he knows the answers and we don't. He's a miserable excuse for a man, Holmes."

"He is that, but his words have meaning. He chooses them carefully, Watson. I'm sure he was providing us with an avenue we have yet to explore. 'Change your perspective,' he said."

Again, my friend fell into silence. I closed my eyes and tried to nap as I sat in one of the stuffed chairs. I had almost nodded off when a shout from Holmes jolted me wide awake.

"That's it! We have been concentrating our efforts on the choreography of the *danse*—and not on the man who is pulling the strings. Watson, when the time comes, you keep an eye on the activity below. I'll return after it is all over."

"And just where are you going, Holmes?" I asked. I was tired of being in the dark. "If the rehearsal is unimportant, then I surely will not sit here and watch something that will serve no purpose. I'll going with you."

My friend said, "Fine. The answer we are seeking is not to be found in the puppets below, but on the perimeter of the stage. Just who will we find when we look behind the curtain? Who will be just offstage, outside the view of the audience and directing this little play of ours?"

"I haven't the foggiest," I admitted.

"Sadly, neither do I, and that is why I must position myself to better see the entire area. There is someone in the shadows who does not want to be found out, but I vow to you that I will find the one responsible."

"Then what?"

"I don't know," responded Holmes, his mood turning inward.

As he ruminated on this, I stared through the windowpane and looked at the majestic ships once more. When I tired of that view, I slowly brought my eyes back to the scene directly beneath us. The station platform was nearly deserted, and all of the shops had been closed.

"Holmes," I said, interrupting his silence. "Why would your brother not make his intentions known? At least to you? It seems that at every turn he has done everything possible to dissuade you from pursuing the matter."

"I had been wondering that very same thing, Watson, and I have yet to reach a satisfactory conclusion. But if I may, I would like to start from the beginning. Let me recite to you the chronology of the case. Perhaps reviewing it aloud will assist us in placing the matter on the square."

"A splendid idea," I said.

"Excellent. Of course, there was our meeting with the Queen and..."

"Your appointment to be the Protector of the Realm."

"Yes. There was the curious reaction on my brother's part to my appointment."

"You mean his disapproval of it?"

"So, you noticed that also? Not only did he have to stifle his dismay when I was given the task, it also seemed that he did not want us— both you and me—to participate in the celebration." Holmes' eyes narrowed as he recalled the incident.

"Any idea why?" I asked.

"I'm not sure, but something is beginning to stir." Again he closed his eyes and let his mind drift. This was his way of willing the solution to come forward. "Where were we? Oh yes. After our meeting with Queen Victoria, we received a communication from Wells."

"Yes, I recall it said, 'Mr. Holmes, you have been followed...tomorrow.'"

"Right. Then there was my chase of the robber viscount. I read of my adventure in the contents of the envelope that I had received a day previously. My near-death adventure had been published in the next day's newspapers."

"Then our meeting of Einstein and Wells and those horrible photographs," I reminded him.

"And let's not forget our meeting with my brother at the Diogenes Club and our being followed to and from that place."

"All right, Holmes. We're here now and what have we to show for it? I still cannot determine the purpose of these rehearsals. Why would they reenact our murders?"

"We've already discounted them on that score, Watson. Those pictures were not images of our murder. Although the actors looked like us, they were not you and I."

Throwing up my hands in disgust, I said, "I give up, Holmes. I say we pack our things and head straight back to Baker Street. I—" and I paused mid-sentence. "Holmes! A thought has just occurred to me. Do you recall your bringing up the point that it had to be Philadelphia who used the time machine without Wells' knowledge, and he did so for the purpose of—?"

"Reconnaissance," Holmes interrupted me. "Well?"

"Why that date?"

"What do you mean?" Holmes asked. My question had piqued his interest and his face was coming alive.

"I mean, why not the 30th or the 16th, or any other date? Why did he travel to that specific date? Remember, Wells did not travel to the 27th until he had noticed the disparity of the date indicator."

"Why, indeed!" he shouted, snapping his fingers. "Of course! Philadelphia already knew of the assassinations."

"How?" I asked, pleased with my contribution.

"There can only be two ways. Either he was informed of it by someone else or—"

"Or that is the date on which *he* had already planned to have us murdered."

"Yes. Suppose we continue on with that hypothesis first. Philadelphia, deciding to murder us during the Queen's Jubilee, had the good fortune of hearing about Wells' invention. He saw an opportunity to use the time machine for his own purpose. After gaining Wells' confidence, Philadelphia traveled forward in time to the 27th of June so he could observe the security measures we had taken to protect the Royal Family. He saw—"

"Wait a minute, Holmes. Aren't you forgetting that Wells saw our murders? If Philadelphia went on a scouting mission, that must have been before the murders were planned. They wouldn't have occurred yet. How do you explain that?"

Holmes thought for a moment before responding.

"Obviously, if we go along with this theory, then it is safe to assume that Philadelphia had traveled to the 27th on more than one occasion. I would wager that he has used the machine many times without Wells' knowledge. It was pure happenstance that Wells caught on to it at all."

"All right. But there are still our murders to contend with. When did Wells see them? Or should I ask, when did Philadelphia commit them?"

"Wells didn't. What he saw was another rehearsal. Remember the photographs he provided as testimony have me carrying the wrong pipe."

"I'm sorry, Holmes, but again there is a flaw in your reasoning. Don't forget the Prince. The photographs also showed him in them. Are you saying that Prince Edward and the entire entourage were in on the rehearsals?"

Holmes went to his valise and once again removed the photographs he had gotten from Wells. Examining them one by one with his glass, his eyes suddenly narrowed after the painstaking scrutiny of one in particular.

"What do you make of this?" he asked, handing me the photograph.

I studied the rotund face of Prince Edward. The nattily dressed young Royal was as impeccable as always, but there was something unusual about his expression. Normally Queen Victoria's young son looks exceedingly pleased with himself. Not this time.

"He's frightened, Holmes."

"Yes, but of what? Look closely. Look at his eyes. When I first saw the photographs, in their whole—I mean in the collected and assembled form to allow the viewing as if they were moving pictures—I noticed the fright in his eyes and took this reaction to be in response to some movement that he had noticed. But again, look at his eyes. They are looking directly at me. Or the man acting on my behalf, anyway. Don't you see? Prince Edward understood that it wasn't me who stepped forward to greet him. He knew right away that the man was an imposter."

"My God, Holmes, you're right."

"So, now armed with this additional knowledge, what do we do with it, and what are we to surmise?"

"Prince Edward expected to see you. Not the other man. So, he wasn't in on the plan?"

"Correct. But what do we take away from this?"

"I'm not sure I understand what you're looking for."

"If Prince Edward wasn't in on the plan, as you put it, then what else was different from his expectations? Think, man!"

"I don't know."

"Watson, since we both know that we aren't murdered on the 27th, then why are there reports of war in the future? Remember Wells said that England went to war over the matter."

"But Prince Edward, as well as your brother, knows that we were not murdered," I replied, seeing where Holmes was leading. "Then what would cause them to conceal the fact that we were not the ones murdered?"

"Ah, that is the question. I propose that they kept silent for one reason and one reason alone. They did not want it known that they themselves rehearsed the assassination."

"But why?"

"Because too many people would enquire as to how the authorities had come upon the advance knowledge of our murders."

"The time machine!"

"Precisely."

"Do you mean to say that England would rather we go to war? Kill all those men and willingly sacrifice our own boys, just to keep the time machine a secret?"

A cloud descended on my friend's face. Slowly, he spoke a sad conclusion, "Wars have been waged for far less reasons."

"That's horrible. I will not believe us capable of such madness," I said, growing more and more furious.

"Then what are the alternatives?" Holmes asked.

After some thought, I offered a glimmer of an idea. "It's a hoax! The entire affair is a fraud!"

"The murders? The photographs? The newspaper accounts?"

"Yes to all three," I answered him.

"Go on," Holmes encouraged me. He seemed surprisingly relaxed.

"Wells traveled to a time destination that he was meant to discover. Someone wanted him to find what he did. He was led by the nose, all the way."

"Bravo!" said Holmes. "But why?"

Again, I tried to tease out the solution, but at long last, I surrendered without attaining one. I felt melancholy as I admitted, "I don't know, Holmes. I just don't know."

"Was it an experiment, perhaps?"

"How do you mean?"

"I mean, that by continuing to follow with your second hypothesis, it soon becomes clear that Philadelphia is not planning to have us murdered. There are just too many variables to contend with should we continue this line of reasoning. At each instance, we come to the realisation that in order for our theory to hold up, we must contend with either my brother's culpability or ignorance. And I refuse to believe his complicity or that he is to be regarded as incapable of discovering the plan. Don't forget, he now has the time machine. And we have already agreed that both Prince Edward and my brother know that we weren't the ones lying dead on the ground."

"I suppose you're right," I agreed, feeling unsure as to what I should believe.

"I know I am right. But what are we left with?"

The room grew silent as we pondered the twists of this vexing case.

"Still no action down there," I remarked to Holmes while I pointed out the window.

"The night is young. It is still too early for the show to start." Holmes glanced at his watch.

Before the silence grew insufferable, I focused on my friend's use of the word, *experiment*. "Holmes, you made mention of an experiment?"

"Yes. In order for us to discuss this intelligently, I suggest that we revisit our first hypothesis."

"Which is?"

"The hypothesis is that quite innocently, Philadelphia or someone else on his team, discovered the plot on our lives. And I say 'innocently' meaning without the intervention of the time machine. Their knowledge must have come from some other means."

"All right, I'll accept that, but if that's the case, why didn't he warn us? Surely we could have prepared. And, more importantly, we would not have allowed the Prince and the Royals to be exposed to the dangers."

"But suppose Philadelphia did warn us?"

"What do you mean? He did no such thing!"

"Ah, but he did. He told Mycroft."

"What?"

"That is the only logical conclusion."

"Then why didn't Mycroft warn us? And I do not want to hear that hogwash he tried to peddle us back at his club!"

"To answer that we must once again establish the relevant time period that he became involved."

"Oh, and when would that be?"

"He was told about the danger to us well after he knew of the existence of the time machine. It's the only answer."

"Why?"

"Because my brother has always had the uncanny ability to seize upon any opportunity that arises and shape it for his own purpose. Follow my thinking: Philadelphia tells Mycroft of the plot, and my brother, knowing of the existence of the time machine, sees the warning as an excellent opportunity to test the time machine's capabilities. He learns all that he can about Wells and his experiment. Mycroft places Philadelphia on Wells' doorstep. Wells badly needed an assistant, if you'll recall, so Philadelphia soon becomes an indispensable cog in the wheel. Wells became more and more dependent upon the man's talents and his seemingly unwavering adoration of the author."

"I'm with you so far, Holmes, but what about our murders?"

"Think, Watson. Philadelphia informs my brother of the plot, and my brother with the cunning that would shock Machiavelli, decides that rather than tell us of the dangers, chooses instead to use the time machine to observe the event. And then, having obtained the information from the gathered reports, he arrests the culprits before they can do their dirty deed. To Mycroft, the time machine is a tool which he, being the sole arbiter, can use as a weapon against injustice..." Holmes paused, an amused smile slipping across his face.

"All right, Holmes," I said, knowing that look. "Out with it. What do you find so ironic?"

"Oh, I was just wondering what my brother finds more valuable," said Holmes. "The information he would possess by using the time machine—or the satisfaction he would enjoy by keeping me out of the case."

"I see." I couldn't help but feel angry that Holmes could be so easily distracted by his and his brother's ever-expanding game of one-upmanship. Especially when our lives might be at risk.

"Oh, Watson, allow me my little amusements," said Holmes, seeing my face. "I have not given up the investigation. We are still very much involved."

"Have it your way, but while you indulge in your amusements, you have missed a very important point."

"And that would be?" Holmes raised an eyebrow.

"That we are still here, trying to make sense of it all. If your brother had used the time machine so wisely, then why have we, and in this I include your brother as well, why have we yet to determine the purpose, or for that matter, the man behind the assassins?"

Feeling the weighted scrutiny of my friend as he pondered my words, I turned back to the station and platform.

After a strained silence, Holmes said, "Your question has merit, Watson. We've obviously missed something. Do you see anything?"

"No, Holmes. There's nothing at all happening," I replied, knowing the meaning of his query. Again, an uncomfortable silence loomed.

"Holmes, there is another man in all this who has me concerned, and you seemed as bothered by his presence when we first laid eyes on him—Giovanni Tuscano," and so saying, I turned round to observe my friend's reaction.

There was none, save for his stony silence. "Yes," Holmes finally muttered, under his breath. "Tuscano."

Upon the speaking of the man's name, I noticed a slight variance in Holmes' voice.

"I have followed his exploits with some interest," Holmes said, with admiration building in his tone. "He's a remarkable study, Watson. The man is as ruthless as they come—yet he has never been appre-hended. He applies his deadly trade with great imagination and style. He..."

"Before you anoint him, Holmes, what is he doing with your brother?"

"I don't know."

"Is it common for Mycroft or our government to associate with such men?"

"When it suits their purpose, I suppose it is."

"All right, Holmes. I am not so naïve as to find that horrible reality unacceptable, but again, why would Mycroft have this man in his employ? Is Tuscano here to assassinate us?"

The automaton took over for Holmes, the man. "Mere speculation on my part would set a most dangerous precedent. Without a well-reasoned foundation, my thoughts on the matter would surely prejudice our course of action. We could be acting contrary to the realities."

"Holmes," I scoffed, exasperated by his unreasonable caution. "I, for one, would rely more heavily on your mere speculations, than any other man's reasoned conclusions."

"Thank you." Holmes smiled, pleased with my faith in him, "But if we act on my speculations, and they prove to be wrong, our lives may be forfeit. Are you willing to risk everything?"

"Yes," I responded without hesitation.

"Very well. Let us suppose that Tuscano is here to murder us. Then what of the other men? Why do all of the shots appear to be coming from those who are standing directly behind us?"

"Could he be here to insure that the assassinations are successful? I mean, perhaps he is present just to inflict the killing shots, should they be required?"

"I think not. In fact, I'm not at all sure whether our deaths were a necessity. They were only the result of the action. A bonus, if you will."

"What do you mean?"

"From the beginning, I believed that we were the targets. Yes?"

"Why, yes, of course, but..."

"But suppose we're wrong. Is it not possible that the intended target all along was Prince Edward and the other Royals?"

"I suppose it is possible."

"Watson, though you served as a surgeon in Afghanistan, you have told me that you also were involved in some singular skirmishes as a soldier," Holmes interrupted, joining me at the window. "Imagine this area as a battlefield, and your objective is to kill the opposing general. You have information that he will be at this precise location for a conference on a specific day. But he is suspicious of having strangers meet him when he arrives. As his enemy, what would you do?"

That was an easy question. "I would do everything possible to put him at ease, of course."

"And that would be?"

"Sending us!" I cried, understanding his drift. "Of course! I would have my opponent met by men whom he trusted implicitly to guard his safety."

"Would it be required that they be conspirators?"

"No, but it would be preferred."

"Excellent." My friend was pleased with my reasoning. "Now, let the events unfurl. What do you see?"

"The train pulls into the station," I said, picturing the event in my mind. "Upon seeing what he expects to see, his friends and his protectors, the Prince begins to descend the steps. Suddenly, he realises that the men who came to greet him are impostors. Sensing a trap, he clambers up the stairs and back inside the train."

"Very good, Watson. If I may continue? The men surrounding the impostors are under orders to kill the two men who stepped forward to greet the Prince and--"

"Yes! I see it! What was supposed to happen was that when the Prince stepped down, another assassin situated far away was to kill him with a rifle shot. Our murders were a mere diversion. Tuscano!"

"Excellent! But this is all supposition. Again, I cannot believe my brother's complicity in all this."

"Which brings us back to my original question: Why is Tuscano here?"

"An adviser?" Holmes offered. "Let us continue with the problem. We'll return to Tuscano later. Watson, put yourself in the position of being this other unknown assassin. Where would you station yourself to accomplish your mission?"

"I don't know, Holmes. It depends," I responded, not sure what my friend expected. "For a strategic advantage, I suppose that I would take to the high ground in order to observe the entire field of battle."

"Yes, but look about you. There is no high ground. What do you do now?"

"Why I would...I would...I don't know, Holmes. Wait a second!" I shouted, with an astounding realisation of clarity, "But there is a high ground."

"Watson, we have been all through this station and there is no high ground," Sherlock Holmes argued, deflated by my obtuseness.

"Oh? And just where do you think we are?" I asked.

Holmes responded, "In the diorama, do you also recall noticing Brewer's shop? Especially the rooms above?"

"Of course."

"And there were two men painted in the windows?"

"Of course. They represent us. What are you driving at, Holmes?"

"What fools we have been," said my friend. "I'm afraid it is all my fault."

"Holmes, for the last time, why the mystery? We saw our figures painted in the windows of that terrible toy. And are we not, in fact, actually here in Brewer's shop?"

"You are correct in the second part of your observation, but you are-or shall I say *we are*-wrong in the first presumption of your statement."

"What do you mean? We both saw our figures painted in the window, did we not?"

"No. We assumed that those figures were us, but if you recall the diorama-" Holmes shouted, running to the window and gazing down. "Watson! We must in all haste abandon this place! Hurry!"

"What of our things?"

"Take everything!" he shouted, while excitedly stuffing his bag.

We hurried about the rooms of the flat and gathered our meager belongings.

Holmes tossed me the police uniforms. "Take our disguises. We'll hide them downstairs. They're too much to carry. Hurry!"

As Holmes bounded down the stairs, I laboured with the mountainous pile of clothing and padding, and carried the mess down to the cellar. Once there, I hid everything behind a stack of crates. On my way back through the shop, I heard the door handle being jiggled. I had no choice but to quickly hide behind the counter. I felt my heart pounding in my chest as I nervously peered over the counter and saw the two men trying to look into the shop. They alternated cupping their hands around their eyes and shaking the door handle. Finally, they moved on.

I took the steps two at a time in my haste to join my friend. "Holmes, there were two men—"

"I know. I saw them." My companion walked to the window. "The curtain rises." Holmes pointed to Philadelphia and the group of men standing idly by. "Watson, your revolver."

I looked at my friend in silence, worrying that he was about to commit an act of violence.

"Just a precaution," he assured me.

I reached into my pocket to grab my weapon. At the same time, I glanced down at the group and noticed that Philadelphia had formed his men with their backs towards us. I said, "I don't trust that man, Holmes."

As I joined my friend at the door, he said, "Neither do I, but it is an opportunity, nevertheless. Hurry, will you? We must be gone before he arrives."

"Who?" I asked, following Holmes down the stairs. "The advisor?"

"Yes."

Holmes led us to the rear of the shop. Behind a curtain, he found a window and quietly raised the sash while making as little noise as possible. We climbed out, being sure to shut the window behind us.

32

We stood listening for what seemed like a long time. When Holmes was satisfied that nothing was amiss, he grabbed my arm and led me along the rear outside walls of the shops. Upon reaching the end, Holmes studied the area. Then he headed at a diagonal, away from the buildings.

At first, we hugged the walls and remained hidden in the shadows, but when there was no cover remaining, Holmes calmly stepped out beneath the faint glow of the streetlamp. The gaslight provided the only illumination for the street.

"Come, Watson. We are far enough away that we can be relaxed."

"Where are we going?"

"To the other side of the platform. I want to watch Brewer's shop from a different perspective."

"That's what you said earlier." I didn't understand how we could watch anything, given the darkness that surrounded us. I prayed my eyes would adjust and the gaslight would lend us a semblance of visibility.

At the far end of the platform, we stepped across the rails and found refuge behind what I took to be an abandoned utility shack.

"Here," said my companion, handing me a pair of binoculars.

Holmes must have borrowed them from Brewer again and stashed them in his valise. "We'll move farther up on this side. I suggest we go midway between Brewer's shop and the end of the platform. We need to get nearer the signal indicator. By positioning us in that manner, we should be able to see both ends of the station equally."

Holmes did not wait for my response, as he immediately set off for the signal box, the armoured, elevated structure from which the signals were displayed. I followed in a half-crouch and then squatted next to my friend. The signal box offered us magnificent cover from prying eyes if the person carried a lantern.

As my eyes adjusted to the lack of light, I could see the great detective's face. He was staring suspiciously at a round melon (obviously forgotten by one of the railway workers) that was precariously resting upon a crate, approximately twenty feet from our position. At the base of the crate sat detritus from other melons that must have rolled off the crate and burst when they hit the ground. Small flies enjoying the fruity feast buzzed loudly as they swarmed their fallen treasures.

"You are enjoying this, aren't you, Holmes?" I asked as I scanned the area with the binoculars.

He shrugged his shoulders, gestured for the binoculars, and turned his attention back to the platform. "Watson, my dear fellow, this is what makes life worth living. To face a challenge head-on. To fight the good fight. No matter what the risk. If you have an ounce of blood and a heart that beats, you must in all good conscience feel similarly disposed."

"You're impossible," I said. "But yes, I understand the exhilaration you feel."

"Good old Watson." My friend, sitting cross-legged on the damp ground, brought the glasses to his eyes. Shaking my head, I settled down on my haunches and used my hand to request the binoculars for another turn at looking.

Raising the glasses, I let them play along the flat landscape of the deserted railway station. The moon came and went under a cover of clouds. When its light shone down, I could see the silhouette of the train and its engine, as well as the building. I prepared myself for a long wait. But to my surprise, the area became suddenly alive with a burst of activity.

"Here we go," Holmes whispered excitedly. I handed over the binoculars. He took them and swung them to the right. Again, I was thankful for the bulk of the signal box as it gave us an excellent spot for spying on the others. Added to the dark of the night, our position was in the shadows cast by various stacks of crates.

At the far end of the platform stood the two actors who were playing our parts. One of the men carried a lantern to help the group find their positions. It was remarkable and somewhat unsettling to see how meticulously they aped us. Their mannerisms, affectations, and style of dress all suggested their desire to be as accurate as possible when portraying us.

"Remarkable," observed my friend in a voice tainted with anxiety.

A shrill whistle signaled the actors to begin their stroll. The man with the lantern climbed a ladder and held his light aloft. With that small amount of illumination, the play began.

I studied the men as they casually walked by. They were on their way to the other end of the platform. I glanced at Holmes to see his reaction. To my surprise, his glasses were trained on the area where the two men had first appeared and not on the men themselves.

I returned my gaze to the spot where my friend was concentrating his scrutiny. At first, I saw nothing of note. But suddenly, there appeared a familiar figure emerging from the shadows and walking directly behind the troupe of actors.

"Got you!" Holmes exclaimed, breathlessly.

There, in all of his bureaucratic and bulky glory, was Mycroft Holmes. Sherlock's brother followed the two actors at a discreet distance. Mycroft lumbered from side to side. His limp was even more pronounced than it had been earlier. Despite the pain, Mycroft ambled near the fronts of the commercial establishments that lined the way. Even walking slowly, he overtook the actors. Passing them on their right, he moved along without as much as a sideways glance in their direction.

To my great consternation, Mycroft stopped at the doorway of Brewer's shop. With an impatient removal of his watch from his vest pocket, he noted the time. He turned his eyes back to the two men who were portraying us. Then he watched as first one, then another, then another, and another of his men came forward from behind the columns. These new players fell in behind the two actors. The man with the lantern continued to shine his light on the ever-changing scene. The glow did not extend far, but it provided enough illumination so the men could take their positions.

Mycroft turned away from the gathering knot of men. Again, he glanced at his pocket watch. Raising and swiveling his head to the right, he watched as a man who was carrying something wrapped in canvas came from round the corner of Brewer's shop. Mycroft and the newcomer nodded at each other and disappeared inside the chemist's store.

The actors portraying us were now surrounded by a crowd. The fake Holmes and Watson stood near the edge of the platform where the train carrying the Royals was expected to arrive.

"Watson, look at Brewer's flat," Holmes instructed me. Shifting my weight on my haunches, I gazed in the direction he was pointing. To see around the signal box, I had to lean out just a little. As I did, I was shocked to see the silhouettes of two men standing in the window. The bulky shape of one instantly gave away his identity.

"My God! It's Mycroft up there in the flat," I said.

"Yes, and our friend, Tuscano," Holmes added.

"Where's Philadelphia?" I asked, searching for the man.

"Look in the doorway of Brewer's," Holmes said.

I did, and I noticed Philadelphia leaning against the building's façade while watching the rehearsal.

Holmes directed me. "Keep your eyes on the window of the flat upstairs. The play is of no importance, as we already know its outcome. Our efforts should be directed to the movements of those two up there. What on earth can they be up to?"

The second floor room we'd recently inhabited was awash in the glow from a lamp. Though I could only see shadows cast against the curtains, there was no mistaking the rotund shape of Mycroft and the tall, stoop-shouldered form of Tuscano. The window sash slowly lifted. The snout of a black-throated rifle sniffed the air as the curtains were moved to the side. The room over the chemist's shop suddenly went black as the lamp was extinguished. But I could still see the shape of the rifle's barrel as it inched farther out into the night air. The rifle traced an arc, as the man who was preparing to fire found his target. The barrel was now pointing in the direction of the men who'd been tasked with reenacting our murders.

The sickening realisation that Mycroft Holmes was involved in the attempted assassination of Prince Edward caused me to look away. The duplicity of the man, the disloyalty, and the treachery caused my stomach to roil. I turned to speak with Sherlock Holmes, but he was no longer by my side. He had managed to slip away without making a sound. I glanced left and right, feverishly trying to locate him, and then I heard my name.

"Watson!" he whispered. Sherlock Holmes had crawled over to the crate that had the melon sitting on top of it. Staying low and out of sight, I crab-walked to his side.

"Look around us. See the ground?" he commanded as he pointed to the half-moon mounds of broken overripe melons. Their shattered rinds were covered with rippling blisters as thousands of ants and flying insects feasted on their remains.

Holmes was squatted close to the decaying flesh of the melons. Paying little attention to the festering swill, he plunged his fingers into the meat of the slimy fruit. The overripe smell was sickeningly sweet. Again and again Holmes stuck his hand into the gooey flesh. At times, his fingers violently clawed through the melon's guts until he finally found what he was looking for. His dripping, nectar-slicked hands clutched a number of small, blunted objects that he held out in his palms for me to examine.

"What are those?" I moved closer. I could not make out what my friend had found, but I could tell they were metal by their glint.

"A clue," he said, stuffing his prizes into his pocket, "and if we desire to not be pelted by pieces of exploding melon, I suggest that we return to our position over by the signal box."

Running low, we came to kneel behind the signal box. Bringing up his binoculars, my friend studied Brewer's window. Even without glasses, I could see that the rifle was still directed at the men on the platform.

"Watson, we are about to witness a stunning feat of marksmanship."

"What are you talking about?" I said. "Why even I, using my revolver, would be able to hit the Prince from there."

"Perhaps, but the target is not the Prince. Continue to keep your eyes on the rifle. I believe that in very short order, the assassin will select his primary target and—"

My friend's words were cut short by the sudden swing of the assassin's rifle, as it turned in our direction. I noticed an eerie green glow emanating from the black of the room above Brewer's shop. A small puff of smoke silently leaked out from the rifle's barrel, and the green glow disappeared.

Thuck!—Thuck!—Thuck!

The melon exploded with a sickening, fleshy sound.

33

Holmes whistled softly. "Come, Watson. We must leave this place."

My friend and I hurriedly ran, first towards the abandoned utility shack, then we made our way across the rails, and finally we ran back behind the buildings. Gasping for breath from the exertion, I leaned against a brick wall.

"Well?" Holmes queried, obviously pleased with the excitement.

"Well, what?" I retorted angrily, dropping my hands to my knees as I attempted to catch my breath. "We were nearly killed, and you stand there grinning from ear to ear like the proverbial Cheshire cat."

"Nonsense," returned my friend. "We were safely away from danger."

"Do you call this safely away from danger?" I asked, plucking a piece of melon from my hair.

Holmes ignored me and went to his pocket, taking out the items he had removed from the melons. After tossing and then catching them in the palm of his hand, he picked out one and handed it to me. I raised it to my eyes and examined it closely.

"It's a spent bullet—but it's like none that I've ever seen before." I handed the projectile back to my friend.

"Nor have I. Watson, did you hear anything?"

"You mean a report?"

"Yes. Did you hear the sound of the rifle being fired?"

"Come to think of it, no, I didn't. Surely you're not suggesting that the man fired from the flat above Brewer's? The distance and the light would make that impossible."

"What else would cause a melon to explode like that?"

"There had to be a charge in it. Some sort of explosive set to go off at a predetermined time."

"For what purpose?"

"A diversion?"

"No. That melon was the target. So were the others that littered the ground. Tuscano fired the shots at the melon from Brewer's window."

"Holmes, that's preposterous!"

"Watson, your inability to reach the most obvious of conclusions will always baffle me. The melon was the approximate size of a man's head. Of course Tuscano could not use a live person to practice his deadly skills. The melon was-"

"Holmes, you know very well I understand the purpose of the melon. I was referring to the impossibility that Tuscano could hit his target from that great of a distance. It can't be done! The melon sat there in dim light. From that distance, Tuscano would have been unable to see the target—no less hit it."

Sherlock Holmes persisted. "Did you by any chance observe a curious green glow?"

"Yes," I said. "There was a pulsating green light. Just before the smoke came out of the rifle, I noticed a green glow. What was it? I thought it was just a trick of the light behind the shooter."

"I don't know, but you're certain that you heard no sound?"

"Of course, I'm certain," I said. "Except for the sound of the melons exploding, this place was as quiet as a church."

Holmes nodded his agreement. "We'll remain here for now. When the area is clear we'll return to Brewer's and take some much-needed rest."

My friend and I took turns watching the group from our hiding place. It was risky staying out in the open, but necessary nonetheless. Some time had passed before Holmes felt it safe for us to move. All of the actors had gone, and so had the supporting cast members.

"What of Mycroft and Tuscano?" I asked my friend. "I believe that they did not pass us. Might they still be at the flat?"

"No. When I was taking my turn on watch, I saw them exit the shop and leave by the entrance at the other end. Come, Watson, we need our sleep."

We walked back to the front of Brewer's. Holmes expected to have to fiddle with the lock. We were both surprised when the door swung easily open.

"That was careless," observed my friend, slipping inside and locking the door behind us.

"Could it be a trap?"

"Perhaps, but I think not. Take out your revolver. Let's err on the side of our safety."

"I am ahead of you," I said. Holmes smiled when he saw that I already had my pistol in my hand.

Alerted to the light leaking from beneath the door, we quietly made our way there and stood outside the entrance to the flat. Holmes stared at the fan of light bleaching the floor, waiting for any sign of movement from within, and after a number of disquieting minutes had elapsed, he inched open the door then pushed it fully open.

Nothing.

Holmes smiled, but his flaring nostrils and shallow breathing spoke of the tension and uncertainty of the moment. But having found nothing of note in the three rooms, our caution ebbed.

On the small table in the center of the room was a cardboard carton that wasn't there when we left. Holmes eyed it suspiciously, including the folded note that sat on top of the box. With the wariness of a feral cat, he reached for the paper and read its contents.

❧ 34 ❧

Holmes visibly relaxed and smiled. "We shall dine in tonight," he said, handing me the note and opening the carton. The box held an assortment of sliced meats, cheeses, bread, a clutch of fine cigars, and a flask of brandy.

The note read: *Sherlock — Eat, drink and be merry, for tomorrow... Mycroft*

I was surprised to discover that I was famished, and by my friend's quick devouring of his portion of the fare, it was obvious that he, too, suffered from lack of food. Sitting at the table and feeling relaxed after availing ourselves of Mycroft's gifts, we again discussed what we had seen earlier that evening.

"Watson, old friend," Holmes began, "since we must await my brother's pleasure till the morning, I would like to present to you a theory that has suddenly revealed itself to me."

"Gladly."

My friend rose from the table, lit his cigar, walked to the window, and gestured for me to join him.

"What do you see?" he asked, gazing through the glass.

"A deserted railway platform."

"Ah, but place yourself into the future. I meant to say that I want you to picture, if you will, that it is now daylight and it is the day of the Queen's Jubilee. The throngs of England's citizenry are below us and you and I are standing at the edge of the platform waiting for the train to arrive."

"I'm with you so far, Holmes."

"Good. Now we see the train entering the quay. It comes to a stop in front of us. Look! There's the Prince beginning to exit his coach. Wait, suddenly there's fear in his eyes and he scrambles back inside. You and I fall to the ground, mortally wounded."

"Yes. Yes. I see it." I didn't like this ghoulish revisitation, but for the sake of solving this mystery, I reluctantly played along.

"Excellent. Now, with everyone's attention being centered on the commotion of our murders, I want you to place yourself here, in this very room. Can you do it?"

"Yes. I'm here." My mind whirled as I grasped what he wanted.

"Fine. Now let's say you are Tuscano, and you have a mission. What is it?"

"I'm to kill someone."

"Yes, but who?"

My enthusiasm suddenly evaporated, as I was at a loss to glean the identity of my target. I said, "I'm sorry, Holmes. I don't know."

"It's all right, Watson. I'm frozen at this spot also, but I want you to follow my thinking. Our stand-ins below are dead. The crowd reacts to our murders by adding confusion to the jubilation, and unseen by anyone, because of this distraction, someone else gets off the train farther down the track. Someone who *must* be killed."

"Yes, but again, who is it?"

"I think we'll be told of his identity tomorrow. But another question is why? Why is it necessary to kill someone with such a dramatic flourish?"

Putting a match to my cigar, I allowed the smoky haze to conceal my face and hoped it would be sufficient camouflage to mask my growing concern. I turned the scenario over and over in my mind while gazing far down the platform to the spot where Holmes and I had earlier hid.

"Impossible," I remarked.

"What is?" queried my friend.

"The distance. Look at the distance! I tell you, Holmes, I was a fair shot while in the army. No...better than fair...and no one can hit a target this far away."

Holmes moved me to the side and leaned far out the window. A moment later, he brought himself back in. A curious expression was on his face.

"What is it?" I asked.

"I thought I saw something."

"What?" I again asked, leaning my head out the window.

"That strange green glow we had seen coming from here earlier. I believe that I—" Holmes shouted, "Watson! Get down now!"

Satiated with the food and fine brandy, I did not react as quickly as I should have. As I hesitated, Holmes grabbed me with both of his hands and yanked me hard toward the floor. I didn't have time to duck as he pulled me out of the window and so I conked my head on the bottom of the raised sash. When the back of my head hit the floor, Holmes threw himself on top of me, using his body to cover my face. The window exploded in a shower of jagged glass and wood.

Thuck—Thuck—Thuck!

Holmes and I stayed motionless. Shards of flying glass and splintered wood had rained down all over us. If Holmes had not landed on top of me, a piece could easily have pierced my eyes and blinded me.

"Are you all right?" he asked, speaking to the top of my head. "I don't think I should move. Not yet, at least."

"I concur," I told him.

After some time had passed, Holmes scooted off of me. Moving carefully, he rolled to his haunches. Gingerly, he brushed the broken glass and chips of wood from his arms. Wrapping his handkerchief around one hand, he swept much of the litter away. "There," he said. "I've cleared a patch for you."

"Thank you." I slowly rolled to my knees. Concentrating on staying inside that small area of the floor that Holmes had cleared, I got into a crouching posture.

Holmes crawled to the window and raised his head just enough to see over the sill. He stared out into the darkness.

"Watson, the lamp! Put out the lamp. Then come over here and bring the binoculars. Quick!"

While staying low, I scrambled awkwardly past the jagged expanse of glass shards. When I reached the table, I lowered the wick of the oil amp. The flame sputtered, then died. I grabbed the binoculars as they hung over a chair. Only then did I stand up and hurry to Holmes' side. The room was now as dark as pitch, but my friend's laboured breathing provided a beacon for me to follow.

"Here they are, the binoculars," I whispered, giving them to Holmes.

He rested the glasses on the sill, turning them diagonally to the left. Being sure to keep his head low, he brought his eyes to the lenses. He reached up with his right hand and slowly turned the focus knob until he was satisfied. He peered through the lenses for some time, before smiling.

"Got you, Tuscano. Take a look, Watson."

I did as I was told. In the dim light of the streetlamp, I could barely make out a tall, stoop-shouldered man calmly sitting on the crate. A twinkling ember suggested he was smoking a cigarette. From the outline of his body, I could tell he was cradling a rifle in his lap.

"As you were saying?" asked Holmes, interrupting my incredulity.

"What was I saying?"

"I believe your exact word was, 'impossible.'"

Holmes squatted on his heels and leaned his back against the wall to stay low. He ran his fingers through his hair. Bits of glass fell to the floor. "I think your choice of words should have been *incredible* instead of *impossible*. Not another man alive could accomplish such an extraordinary feat of marksmanship. Tuscano has put to rest any doubts we may have had as to his capabilities."

I, too, balanced on my heels with my back against the wall. Holmes' obvious admiration for a deadly assassin bothered me. After what I considered a reasonable length of time, I twisted, straightened slightly, and brought the binoculars back to Tuscano. He was gone!

"I know," my friend said, without my having uttered a word. "He's gone. He remained long enough for us to see that it was his handiwork that sent us into this confusion."

"I would be dead right now, Holmes, if you hadn't warned me. Thank you."

The great detective shook his head. "With all due respect, I should point out to you that Tuscano is such a master of his trade that should he have wished us dead, we would in fact be so. He was merely providing us with a demonstration of his prowess with the rifle."

"Oh, I see," I replied, feeling my colour rise.

My friend raised himself from his squat and extended his hand to assist me from mine. Sherlock Holmes went to the window and studied the damage the bullets had inflicted on the window sash.

"Remarkable," he said. "Watson, observe the grouping of the bullets. Did you ever see a more profound example of marksmanship?" Holmes fished in his pocket and took out a half-crown. Holding it between thumb and forefinger, he placed it over the area where the bullets had penetrated the wood. The coin covered their point of entry entirely.

Pleased with this finding, Holmes flipped the coin in the air and palmed it back into his pocket. We stood in awe of Tuscano's deadly precision. Holmes folded his arms against his body and turned to face me directly. Meanwhile, I walked over and turned on the gas, adding light to the room.

"Of course, you heard nothing? No report?" asked my friend.

"No, Holmes, nothing. No report at all."

"Curious. And what do you estimate the elapsed time to be between the first and last shots?" He came over to stand next to me at the table.

"It's impossible to say. Since I have no sound reference of when the first shot was fired, how can I determine the time it took to reach the last?" I was being reasonable and cautious.

"Right. Let's ignore our inability to hear the rifle's report. Will you not agree that the time elapsed between hearing the first bullet and the last hit the window frame was a remarkably short span of time?"

"Yes. Impossible as it may be, I would estimate that it required less than a second between the first and the last." As I said these words, a cold finger of dread skated around my collar.

"I would agree," Holmes said, understanding the import and implications of our observation. "I know of no such rifle capable of firing at such a rate, much less one with the capacity of remaining totally silent."

"Nor do I." I added, "Nor do I know of a weapon with the power to pierce the darkness as this one obviously has."

"It would be a safe conclusion then that the rifle we are talking about does not exist."

"But..."

"Relax, Watson. My remarks are not meant to confuse you. I merely stated what we, in our collective knowledge of weaponry, know to be the truth. A rifle having such capabilities does not exist at this present time."

"And yet here it is."

"Yes. And yet here it is. And you would attribute its presence to what?" Holmes raised an eyebrow.

"The time machine?"

"Yes. The time machine," he said with a tinge of exhaustion in his voice.

"They are bringing back weapons of incredible destruction from the future!" The realization unnerved me. As a soldier, this was too terrible to contemplate. The thought of our government's willing participation in such a horrifying activity caused bile to rise in my throat.

"That would appear to be the case."

As we mulled over the extraordinary repercussions of our latest reasoning, another thought occurred to me. "Holmes, we have not dealt with the two men that are portraying us."

"What about them?"

"Were they actually murdered?"

Holmes went to his valise and carried the photographs to the table. After positioning them to take advantage of the lamp's light, he brought his glass to them and studied them for some time before smiling.

"No," he said, as I came to stand behind him. "Look." He flipped through one and then another and another. "See their hands? If they are dead, how do you explain the hands being in different positions as we go further and further into the scene? No, they are most definitely still alive."

"What's going on here?" I asked. "First we're dead, then we're not. Then we determine that it is not us, but others playing our parts. Then they're dead, and now they're not. Is anyone dead? I ask you. Or is this entire affair just someone's cruel hoax?"

"I don't know, but come the morrow, we shall have some answers. I suggest that we try to get some sleep."

"Sleep?" I said, as I kicked at a stray bit of broken glass. "Who can sleep with this hanging over our heads?"

"At least we can try to get some rest," said Holmes as he grabbed a broom from a nearby closet and put his back into sweeping up the mess. With a grunt of annoyance, I ran downstairs, found a dustpan, returned to the flat, and set about scooping up the broken glass and bits of wood. Not long after, we drank more of Mycroft's excellent brandy and fell into our cots.

❧ 35 ❧

Despite my complaining, I awoke the next morning feeling somewhat rested, even though I was bleary-eyed and grumpy. Glancing over at Holmes' cot, he was nowhere to be seen. Rising from my bed, I was about to call out when I heard Holmes' voice drifting up from downstairs.

I splashed water on my face and attempted to control my unruly hair by wetting it and brushing it flat. Somewhat refreshed and feeling slightly more comfortable with the prospect of participating in the human race, I went downstairs.

"Ah, Watson," sang out my friend upon seeing me. "Mr. Brewer here has just informed me that he will not seek a solicitor or bill us for the damage inflicted upon his premises. It would seem that he has as much patience and compassion as our dear landlady, Mrs. Hudson."

Feeling groggy from my fitful sleep, I could only muster a half-hearted smile in the direction of the chemist. When Brewer offered me a steaming cup of coffee, I accepted it thankfully.

"Watson? While you were languishing under the influence of Morpheus, I was continuing a previous discussion I had yesterday with Mr. Brewer. In fact, I was telling him that last week in St. James Park, I sighted a Bohemian Waxwing. You may recall my mention of it being from the family of Bombycillidae? To my great surprise and pleasure, Mr. Brewer remarked of a similar sighting the very same week!"

"I am thrilled beyond words to hear that, Holmes," I growled, sarcastically.

"My, but you are a bear today, aren't you?" the great detective said.

"Surely we have more important matters to discuss other than a scrawny little bird," I said. Before my inexcusably rude behavior could go any further, Mr. Brewer coughed politely.

"Your visitors have arrived, Mr. Holmes," he said, nodding at the door. "Of course, you gentlemen may use the flat upstairs for your meeting. I will insure your privacy."

I was startled and alarmed to see a large contingent of men entering the shop. And I was equally troubled to see Giovanni Tuscano bringing up the rear of the group.

"Good morning, Sherlock," Mycroft said with a sniff, acknowledging his brother's presence, but ignoring mine. The corpulent civil servant pushed his way between Sherlock and me as he headed for the stairs. Pausing before making the arduous climb, Mycroft said, "These men are with me, of course. I believe you have already met Mr. Delphi. And Mr. James French, known to his friends and associates as Whisper, was observed by you outside my club. The next two gentleman are, under the present circumstances, to remain nameless. For obvious reasons, they are as much a part of this scheme as you and the good Dr. Watson are. And though you are not familiar with that dour-looking gentleman carrying the water for us, you are undoubtedly familiar with his work. His name is—"

"Good morning, Mr. Tuscano," interrupted my friend, trumping Mycroft's self-importance. "My name is Sherlock Holmes, and this is my friend and associate Dr. Watson. I am, of course, a great admirer of yours. Although I must caveat my admiration that it is your expertise that I find singular. I strongly disapprove of your deadly and mercenary profession."

Tuscano smiled in a relaxed manner, but said nothing.

"Yes, I see," Mycroft Holmes responded to his brother's familiarity with the assassin. "We have no time to dawdle, Sherlock. If you are to be of any value to this investigation whatsoever, I suggest that we hold in abeyance this useless prattle and get on with the meeting."

"Whatever you say, Mycroft," Sherlock Holmes said, as his brother struggled up the stairs. The older brother huffed and puffed his way up the stairs, with his retinue dutifully following him. Holmes sidled up next to me and whispered, "It would seem that my brother is rather thin-skinned this morning."

When at last we gathered in the flat, Tuscano went to the window and examined his work from the previous evening. Holmes, noticing the man's keen study, followed and stood next to the assassin.

"A remarkable accomplishment," observed Holmes, as I drifted towards the two men.

"I beg your pardon?" Tuscano responded, with a surprisingly British accent. He was genuinely startled by the nearness of my friend.

"Your grouping." Sherlock Holmes pointed to the splintered wood.

"Oh. And how many bullets do you count in this...this grouping?"

"Three."

"Yes—three," he clucked disappointedly.

"I don't understand," said Holmes, sensing the man's dissatisfaction.

"Of course, you don't," came the sarcastic reply. "If I were up to my exacting standards, you would only see one point of entry, but I had to wait for your foolish Dr. Watson get clear of the window. I'm afraid his rather unusual and unpredictable behavior resulted in a distraction."

My hands balled into fists, but I bit my tongue rather than lash out at the overly proud assassin.

"Gentlemen?" Mycroft Holmes called out. "If we are through marking our territories, can we begin our meeting?"

I looked to the assembled men and nodded gruffly. Then I turned back to the shooter. "We are not finished, Tuscano," I hissed, walking away from the man.

"I await your pleasure, Doctor."

"That will be enough, Mr. Tuscano," Sherlock Holmes said with menace. "If you so desire, I will..."

"Sherlock!" barked Mycroft, "Please take your seat."

My companion's face twitched tightly.

"Come, Watson," he said, pulling me away, "we will deal with them all appropriately. All right, Mycroft, what confounded mayhem have you wreaked upon the citizens of England? I will not accept your excuse about the nation's security forbidding you to tell me what's going on here. You and your kind play these evil games with such cold and calculating abandon that the people of the land are treated as nothing more than chattel. I, for one, will not stand by and allow your thuggery to continue. Do you understand?"

My friend's words were so stunningly violent that the murmurings of the room evaporated as the group waited to see what Mycroft's reaction would be. To my astonishment, Mycroft Holmes nodded meekly.

"It's your way from here on out, brother," answered a solemn Mycroft. "There will be no further impediments. I have advised these men to answer any and all of your questions without reservation, but there are a number of facts that are privileged and not meant for their consumption. Towards that end, I suggest that you and I talk in a more private setting."

The manner and tone in which Mycroft was now comporting himself gave his brother little satisfaction. In fact, the realisation that Mycroft Holmes has been incapacitated to this alarming extent caused his brother obvious consternation. Sherlock Holmes altered his approach.

"Very well, but whatever you have to say will be told in the company of Dr. Watson. He holds a marker in this game as well. Brewer's cellar should suit our purpose nicely. Besides, I have a small desire to see his specimens."

Again, Mycroft Holmes nodded. He spoke most agreeably. "Very well. You men are to remain here." Mycroft studied the group. His eyes came to rest on Tuscano. "There will be no reason to leave the premises under any circumstance. Do I make myself clear?"

The assassin glowered at his employer but nodded his compliance.

As Holmes opened the door to exit the flat, he was startled to see Mr. Brewer standing on the landing with a tray of coffee and rolls.

"Ah, Mr. Brewer, your timing is impeccable," said Sherlock Holmes, recovering from his surprise. The great detective lifted a roll from the tray. "I was about to search you out, but here you stand. We require the use of your cellar for some private discussions. In addition, I'm interested in seeing your chemical laboratory. I'm sure you don't mind. Thank you. Come on, men!"

Of course by "men," Sherlock meant Mycroft and me. My good friend brushed by the nonplussed chemist without a sideways glance. However, when Mycroft and I passed Brewer, I thought there was a look of strain on his face. But I assigned it to his task of holding the tray upright and level as we maneuvered our way by him and headed down the stairs.

Arriving on the main floor of the shop, I saw that Sherlock Holmes was on the verge of biting down into the roll he had taken. Curiously, he paused and lifted the roll to his nose instead. A satisfied smile crossed his face.

"If you have taken any rolls, I suggest that you wait before eating them," he said to me and his brother. Without turning round, Sherlock tossed the roll in the air over his shoulder. It bounced in and out of Mycroft's hand, then in again, as he struggled to catch it. Following his brother's lead, Mycroft brought the roll up to his own nose and nodded. As we continued our way down to the cellar, Mycroft passed that same roll to me.

"Smell it, Doctor."

I did, and was surprised to find a subtle chemical odor blended in with the fragrance of sweet dough.

"All right, brother," Sherlock Holmes sneered, whirling round when we had arrived in the chemist's experimental area. "Out with it!"

Mycroft's massive physical stature visibly deflated as he gingerly tested a stool to see if it would hold his weight. When he was satisfied it would, he sat upon it and mopped his brow with a starched white handkerchief.

"Chloral hydrate?" Mycroft Holmes asked.

"Yes. The rolls are laced with it," Sherlock Holmes said. "Judging by the strength of the odor, I believe it has been introduced to merely render the victims unconscious. When we return to the flat upstairs, I imagine that we'll find your men rather quiet."

"I agree."

"And, Watson, before your blood boils, Brewer is already gone. I heard his panicked steps as he vacated the premises just a minute ago."

"Let's go after him," I shouted, bewildered by the brothers' complacency.

"He is where I want him," Holmes replied, cryptically.

"But what of the men upstairs? Are we to allow them to remain in their stupor without medical attention?"

"I was up and about very early this morning, Watson. Well before the arrival of Brewer to his shop. I have made the necessary arrangements for their recovery. Unless I miss my guess, they have just now arrived."

The sound of hurried footfalls raced through the shop and headed up the stairs to the flat. One step of footsteps came back down the stairs and stopped at the entrance to the cellar. "Everything is well in hand, Mr. Holmes!" shouted a voice from above.

"Very good!" Holmes returned loudly, glancing up at the ceiling. "And what of our friend, Mr. Brewer?"

"He is on the line, Mr. Holmes. My men are trailing him, as we speak," the voice responded.

"Excellent! Be sure that we are not disturbed!"

"You've got it, Mr. Holmes."

A smug smile of satisfaction lit my friend's face.

"Holmes?" I shook my head at him.

"Yes, Watson? As I told you, I had risen early. In fact, I have yet to go to sleep. While you were off dreaming, I came down here and explored Brewer's laboratory. I found it curious that most of the chemicals here are made to render someone unconscious, or they're poisonous and-"

"He explained that," I interrupted. "He uses them for his specimens."

"Look about you, Watson. Do you see any specimens? Any evidence of taxidermy? Any jars with wee creatures floating in formaldehyde?"

Of course, Holmes was correct. There were none of those to be found. I turned in a slow circle and sputtered, "I don't understand.

With such a trivial observation, you harbored suspicion toward Brewer?"

"That, and my remark about the Bohemian Waxwing."

"What do you mean?"

"The Bohemian Waxwing. It's a bird, and..."

"I'm aware of that, Holmes. You said that you yourself saw one just last week and—"

"That's just it, Watson. If I were fortunate enough to observe one, I wouldn't be here talking to you."

"What do you mean?"

"The Bohemian Waxwing's habitat is North America. Brewer's confirmation of his own sighting here in Britain told me that he was an imposter. Any reputable ornithologist would have seen through my fraud."

Taking my silence as a signal to continue, Holmes went on, "My suspicions were aroused early on. In fact, when I first met Brewer he seemed to be expecting me. Maybe not Constable Bounder, but someone demanding the use of his flat. I found that somewhat curious. Also, being a casual observer of human behavior, I found that contrary to his meek countenance, he belied a man of resolute capabilities and temper. Admittedly, these are small observations, but taken as a whole, to me they bespoke of a man that struggled mightily to maintain an aura of innocence and harmlessness. Based on these judgments, I found it necessary to err on the side of caution.

"I made contact with a number of specialised individuals with whom I hold acquaintance. They are the ones who are at this very moment judiciously following my orders. Soon our friend Brewer will be apprehended. And now, Mycroft, suppose you tell me what this is all about."

36

"This is about..." Mycroft hesitated, shifting his weight restlessly. Clearly this confession was costing him a great deal of discomfort. "This is about a serious lapse in judgment on my part, I'm afraid." The older Holmes brother sighed and a slow crimson stain crept up the fleshy rolls under his chin. "Someone came to me with certain information of an assassination attempt—"

"Philadelphia?" asked his brother.

"Yes, Mr. Delphi. He is what we call a 'floater.' He works outside the constraints of our governmental boundaries and travels in circles that you cannot begin to imagine. He came upon the plot of your murders through an associate of his—"

"Whisper?"

Mycroft nodded in the affirmative.

Sherlock Holmes continued, "It was then that you decided, having already acquired information of the existence of the time machine, to use it as a source to gather evidence and experimentation?"

Mycroft noticeably paled in reaction to his brother's astute observations and deductions. After several attempts to clear his throat, the corpulent man finally said, "Yes."

Sherlock pelted his brother with questions. "How long have you known of the existence of the time machine? More importantly, how long have you known about the attempts on our lives?"

"Regarding the time machine, I'm not prepared to respond. As to the assassinations, nearly four months. Sherlock? Watson? I want you both to understand that I in no way believed the matter would reach such a confusing state of affairs. I believed that we could use the time machine as a tool for observing the event and capturing the assassins on our return to the present."

"And why haven't you?" I asked angrily. "You have had all of the information required to apprehend the culprits, and yet we are here now, as much in the dark as before. Not to mention, we've been shot at several times."

"I'm sorry, Doctor. I understand your misgivings, but I assure you that we have gone as far into this as possible and have yet to realise a conclusion."

"You should be very proud of yourselves," I said. "Your selfish incompetence has led us nowhere."

My stinging words of rebuke surprisingly caused Mycroft to laugh nervously. "I am not accustomed to being spoken to in such a manner, Doctor, but alas, I can find no fault in your criticism."

"How did it come to be that Philadelphia was planted in Wells' home?" my friend asked his brother.

"I knew of Wells' experimentation for some time. When Mr. Delphi came to me with information about it, I had already groomed him to be Wells' assistant and he had been working with the author for a while. It was upon receiving his warning that I decided to put the time machine to use. Knowing the date of the attempted assassinations, I had Mr. Delphi visit the future and witness the murders."

"But they are not, in fact, the murders depicted in the photographs that have so conveniently been placed in our laps, are they? And they are not the ones we have run in circles trying to understand?" Holmes asked.

My friend's question caught Mycroft by surprise. His puffy face flushed with anger. "How did you ever deduce that?"

"Tuscano. His presence is an anomaly. His purpose is obvious. He's here to kill the true assassin. Judging by his performance last evening, his target will be in front of the train's locomotive. If he were here to assassinate the stand-ins, what would be the purpose of his practicing on a melon so far away from the event? Who is this other assassin?"

"I don't know."

"Who is this mysterious assassin's true target?"

"I am." Mycroft removed a silk handkerchief from his vest and mopped his face.

"What's that you say?" Holmes asked.

"You heard me correctly, Sherlock. It is me."

"Who is the assassin, then?"

"His identity cannot be determined. I am to be killed by an unknown person in an unknown location."

"I don't understand," I said. "Meaning no disrespect, but if what you say is true, then why are we involved at all? Why the charade of our own murders?"

"Because we are a distraction," Holmes replied, turning to face his brother.

"Proceed, Sherlock, you have the floor," Mycroft said.

"From the beginning, your reluctance to have me as a security consultant regarding the Royals' safety was because my participation would force you to alter your plans. You knew about the attempt on your life, but because of the manner in which you have discovered the plot and certain details surrounding it, you understood that I would have questions. Furthermore, you would not be able to sustain in any logical and meaningful way the answers that I would have accepted. But this again, brings us back to Watson's question, 'Why us?'"

Holmes continued, "I would surmise that our two unconscious actors up there have been told that there has been a breach of security, and that it's vital for them to portray us in such a manner as to distract the true purpose of the exercise."

"Go on, Sherlock. You're doing fine," Mycroft prodded, proud of his brother's summation.

"Did they ever think to question why the true Sherlock Holmes and Dr. Watson were not involved in this playacting of yours?" I wondered.

Mycroft merely smiled.

"God save us from unquestioning soldiers," my friend lamented. "Before I go any further, exactly where were we to be held for our safe-keeping?"

"You were there the other day."

"Yes, of course. Your latest lair." Sherlock Holmes studied his brother for some time before shaking off a thought. "We'll return to that later. Tell me, if you will, why did Philadelphia leave the time-date destination on the time machine?"

❧ 37 ❧

"He what?" bellowed Mycroft, then was suddenly quiet. For what seemed like an interminable span of time, he fumed. The huge mound of flesh practically seethed with fury, and then slowly he calmed himself. "Oh, now I understand it all. So *that* is how you came into this."

"You didn't know? Hmm, that is curious. But to continue, Philadelphia left the tampered machine for Wells to discover. To what purpose? We have yet to determine. But Wells, in his bumbling way, visited upon the date and discovered what he assumed to be a plot on our lives. In actuality, what he had observed were the results of your rehearsals. The diversion of attention away from your murder and..."

Again, Sherlock Holmes paused to study his brother. This time he asked, "Why was it so important to distract the public in such a manner? What would be the imperative to keep everyone's attention directed to the back end of the train? Why would..." Sherlock Holmes' eyes widened with sudden realisation.

"You fool!" he said, glaring at Mycroft. "The time machine!"

"What?" I asked, confused.

"Don't you see it, Watson?" Holmes shouted, coming to stand inches away from his brother. "Mycroft was transferring the time machine. It was being off-loaded from the front of the train. Isn't that so, brother of mine?

"Where was it headed?" he continued. "Who was there to facilitate the transfer? Why was this foolhardy scheme of yours attempted at such a momentous occasion? Why wasn't it done in the dark of night, as you do most of your dastardly deeds?"

Holmes asked these rhetorical questions (for he truly did not expect answers) because he had trained himself to do so. His own words were more of a declarative statement, as Holmes sought to identify a possible course of events, rather than the actual solicitation of a response. It has often been my friend's wont to put forth a series of questions for the purpose of clarifying, and in his own unique way creating an inventory of direction that his thought processes must further explore or discard.

To Holmes, there was nothing more egregious and notorious than a cluttered and disorderly mind. I have often heard him say that in order to facilitate a logical investigation, one must first dispose of any useless data that may prejudice a rational pattern of thought. Upon accomplishing this monumental task, one could proceed with surety that whatever the naked result that becomes the conclusion, it has been reached without fear of contradiction.

As Sherlock Holmes continued his postulations, he was not sedentary. In both mind and physicality. Rather, he methodically explored every nook and cranny of the cellar.

"Halloa!" he exclaimed, moving to the side an assortment of foul-smelling chemical vials and beakers sitting on a shelf.

To my great surprise, behind the chemicals lay hidden a leather valise very similar to a medical bag. Holmes brought it down and placed it on top of the benchtop. Working the clasps, he spread open the mouth of the bag.

"Why, Mr. Brewer, you clever little devil!" Holmes said, spilling the contents out onto the bench. "Look, what we have here: an exceptional assortment of make-up and devices."

Holmes opened the lids to the jars and tins. Judging from the discoloured smudges of pancake and creams on the outside and the small amount remaining inside these containers, one could see that Brewer had been practicing the art of disguise for many years.

"I knew there was something about him," I protested, much to the amused grin of my friend.

"All right, brother," Mycroft said, impatiently. "Is there anything else?"

Holmes ignored his brother and continued his exploration of the cellar. When he was out of sight in a dark corner, Sherlock Holmes asked, "Watson! Where did you hide our constable uniforms?"

"I hid them behind a crate right where you are standing."

A humourless laugh broke the silence of the room. "They're gone," my friend said, coming out of the shadows.

Sherlock Holmes gave a sideways glance to his brother. "All right, Mycroft, as a matter of fact, I do have more questions. Why do you have Tuscano practicing his profession from such a distance? You said that the assassin is unknown to you, so you are working blind, so to speak. And yet you chose to position Tuscano here in the rooms upstairs, where he is targeting a subject. Why did you do that?"

"Because of where I fall. Tuscano has determined, thanks to his expertise in this sort of business, that the assassin would take this precise location upstairs in order to facilitate a successful assassination attempt. Thanks to our many rehearsals, we have been able to elimi-nate any other possible area from which the assassin would be able to both succeed and retreat."

"I see. Yet you still cannot determine the identity of the assassin?"

"No."

"And the time machine? Was it to be transported through your secure corridor at the quay?"

"No. We had planned to have it already transferred, prior to allowing the dignitaries to process through the corridor."

"Transferred to where?"

"I will not respond to that."

Holmes continued, although he was obviously annoyed by his brother's obstinance.

"Mycroft, if I am to be of... how did you put it? Ah, yes. If I am to be of any value to this investigation, I must have all the facts! To where was the time machine being transferred?"

"I'm sorry, Sherlock, but that is not a matter I can divulge."

"I see. Then tell me this: I take it that you expect to be shot?"

"Yes," said Mycroft.

"If it is not too troubling, how many times?" Sherlock Holmes asked.

"Once. Right between my eyes." The older man sighed.

"And witnesses—did they hear anything?"

Mycroft looked surprised. "What?"

"Fascinating," Sherlock Holmes remarked.

"Fascinating?" I echoed, startling the two brothers. "How can you sit there calmly and dissect, as if it were a student exam, this murder? It's an abomination of reason, I tell you."

Before they could respond to my outburst, a voice shouted down from the main floor.

"We're leaving now, Mr. Holmes!" came the shout. "The others are awake, and they have been instructed to remain where they are until you give them permission to leave."

"Very good, Davidson," Mycroft Holmes shouted in response, "Have Mortimer post himself outside the shop. Tell the others they can return to their normal lives. I will contact you by the usual means should I require your services again."

The door slammed shut without further utterances from this unknown stranger. The three of us—Mycroft, Sherlock, and I—followed the direction of the footfalls as they traversed the ceiling. Hearing them troop down the stairs, we knew that the men had vacated the premises.

"Who are they, Holmes?" I asked, aroused by the drama and efficiency of it all.

"Mycroft's men," was his reply.

"Can we return to the flat?" Mycroft asked. "These foul-smelling chemicals are proving deleterious upon my olfactory senses." (Though he is my friend's brother, I couldn't help but be amused by the pomposity of the man. Why couldn't he just say that the room smells?)

"Not yet, Mycroft," Holmes answered his brother. "Just a few more questions. First, do your men upstairs know of the time machine?"

"Just Mr. Delphi." Mycroft sniffed in annoyance. He was not accustomed to having his desires thwarted for any reason, and his brother's questions obviously irked him.

"Second, the rifle that Tuscano is using? What is it?"

"He believes that it is an invention of the government." Mycroft looked bored.

"Third, with the number of times that Philadelphia has visited the future to observe the, uh, event, how do you explain that he reports an inability to deduce the assassin?"

38

This question demanded Mycroft's attention. He hesitated before saying, "In truth, I couldn't believe it possible. I have my doubts as to his veracity and allegiance."

"I take it that is when you yourself decided to travel through time?"

Mycroft's shrewd eyes blinked in rapid cadence in reaction to his brother's observation. "I never told you that."

Sherlock Holmes pursed his lips and stared at Mycroft. "Come now, brother. Forgoing the seriousness of the matter, you and I know that your all-consuming drive to possess all that there is to know would have mandated that you could not have done otherwise. You had to see the time machine's capabilities for yourself. You would never rely solely on the discretion of an underling. Your lack of humility would have prevented you from being a mere spectator."

Sounding like an aggrieved child, Mycroft said, "Ignoring your rather unkind opinion of my character, you are, of course, correct. I have witnessed the murder. And though I am loath to admit it, I have been unable to determine the identity of the assassin. One minute I am alive, and the next, I am not. I have changed my position to observe the assassination, but no matter where I place myself, I fail in every attempt."

When his brother finishing talking, Mycroft added, "As I told you earlier, these noxious odors are sickening. I want to quit this space!"

But Sherlock Holmes ignored his brother's complaints. Instead, he explored Brewer's cellar and discovered a number of cut-metal tubes of different diameters. These were stashed beneath a pile of oily rags. He brought one of the black tubes up to his eyes and looked down its throat as one would do when looking through a telescope.

"Interesting," the younger Holmes brother said. He set it down, rubbed his fingers together, and sniffed the residue left on his skin. "Paraffin jelly. That is rather puzzling." His eyes narrowed as he surveyed the piping, then he slipped one inside another, then another —until they were at a collective length of approximately two feet.

His step quickened as he walked back to the wall. His hand reached behind the back of the shelving and withdrew a small box that had been hidden. With care, Sherlock Holmes placed the rectangular container on the bench and lifted the lid.

"Splendid!" he said, jubilantly while turning out its contents. A plethora of coiled springs, small metal parts, and screws rolled along the surface of the bench.

"Why the excitement?" I asked. "That looks like nothing to celebrate."

"On the contrary, these are everything. Mycroft, I require some information from the extensive records at your disposal."

"What do you need?" Mycroft asked. His voice quickened with excitement. Obviously his brother had deduced a clue of some importance.

Sherlock Holmes said, "Find out how long Brewer has owned this establishment and how he came to possess it. I would guess that it is just a matter of a few months, and the previous proprietor will not be located. I believe that the unfortunate previous owner—the one before Brewer—has been murdered."

"What do you have, Sherlock? I must know," Mycroft said, as he struggled to his feet.

"Obviously, I think I have the murderer."

"I have already assumed it to be this Brewer fellow. That is nothing useful."

"Ah, but it is. I know how he accomplished it." Sherlock sounded smug.

"What? How?" His brother pressed for answers.

"All in good time, Mycroft. Please get your men moving on my request. And I would suggest that you take possession of Tuscano's rifle. It wouldn't do to have him roaming the land with such an evil device. I believe that once you release him from this assignment and – that should be immediately after our meeting here – he will attempt to disappear with it."

"I suppose you're right. But what of the other men?"

"Send them all packing," Sherlock responded quickly, and just as fast, reconsidered. "No, wait! Keep the actors portraying us and let the rest of them return to where you have kept them hidden away until you need them again. Leave that man—Mortimer?—to keep watch over this shop."

"Very well. Anything else?" Mycroft sounded resigned that his brother held the upper hand.

"Yes, I suggest that you do not attempt to transfer the time machine tomorrow."

"But I have already made other plans!" Mycroft said.

"Of course you have," Sherlock said. "But I want you to create the illusion that you are still doing what you had set out to do."

"Meaning?" Suspicion clouded Mycroft's voice.

"Meaning I want you to manufacture a duplicate crate. It must replicate in every way the exact structure and markings of the real crate, but of course, it will be absent the time machine. Pay particular attention to the apparent weight. Fill it with rocks for all I care, but everything must be as close to the original as possible. You are to follow your exact plans regarding the transfer. Do you understand?"

"Done." Mycroft sounded defeated, but also a great deal relieved. He struggled to his feet. Sherlock offered no assistance, and I took my cues from my friend.

"Fine," said Sherlock Holmes as his brother walked wearily towards the stairs. "I believe that we have nothing more to discuss, Mycroft. I will contact you later. If you would kindly take your men with you as you leave. Oh, and just a personal observation on my part, it would be wise for you to speak the truth when I question you. If you recall when we were at your club, I queried you as to the identity of two men and you assured me you knew nothing of them except for the name of one, Whisper. Yet, as we now know, both of them are in your employ."

Even though his back was towards me, I could tell that Mycroft seethed at such treatment. However, he held his own counsel and laboured his way up the stairs. Each step presented a challenge to him as he moved one foot up and the other to meet it before repeating the process. About midway, we heard Mycroft bellowing for his men, and they came bounding down the stairs. From the ensuing commotion and the slamming of doors, Holmes and I chuckled as they struggled to help Mycroft upstairs.

When silence filled the cellar, Holmes seemed to diminish in size. Though there were times that he took obvious delight in jousting with his brother, it was plain that these latest exertions had caused him discomfort.

"Remind me to tell you about the time when my brother's intervention saved me from being hung at the gallows," he remarked, calmly. He then busied himself gathering up the black tubes and box of springs.

"What?" I asked with surprise. I assisted Sherlock Holmes in picking up the various pieces. But my friend took his time and didn't respond to my probe for more information. I followed the great detective back upstairs to the flat.

❧ 39 ❧

Entering the rooms we'd once occupied, Holmes placed his finds on the table. I did the same. Then he collapsed on his cot, shielding his eyes with his arm.

"Watson, I'm aware you have thousands of questions, but please allow me to think in peace. I must fashion a plan to capture Brewer whilst maintaining my brother's reputation. I do not want to be disturbed. Should I nap, please wake me in one hour. I dearly need to shut my eyes." He let out a heavy sigh before his breathing became steady and rhythmic.

Though my friend was correct that I had "thousands of questions," I was nonetheless surprised to feel a sense of relief at not having to discuss the matter further. Instead, I sat at the window in silence, mulling the confrontation that had just occurred between these two intellectual giants.

I rested my head against the glass and let my thoughts drift. But I became alarmed when I spied a man leaning against a column, staring up at our window. I was about to bring my discovery to Holmes' attention. Then I recalled his earlier instructions to Mycroft to leave one man behind, and I relaxed.

"How do we know if that particular man is on our side?" asked

Sherlock Holmes, who had magically appeared behind me. He hadn't made a sound. "He could be one of Brewer's men."

"What are you doing awake? I thought you needed to rest."

"There will be time for that when this is over. How did you know?"

Understanding that he was curious about my lack of response at seeing the man outside, I knew that I had no logical answer. Instead, I sheepishly revealed the revolver in my hand. "I didn't. But if he made a suspicious move, even I could have hit him from here."

"That is precisely what we need at this very minute." Holmes chuckled softly. "The banner would read *Dr. Watson Fells Man for Acting Suspiciously.*"

Again he shook his head, continuing his fiction, and pretended to read from a newspaper, "The doctor, when questioned, told the Scotland Yard inspector that the man's perceived actions would have disturbed the well-deserved rest of one Mr. Sherlock Holmes. When questioned further, Dr. Watson remarked that he didn't think the noise from the pistol would have disturbed his friend."

"Go on, Holmes, have your sport with me. I was only thinking of you."

"I know you were, old friend." Holmes waved to the man, gesturing for him to come up to the flat.

Shortly, we heard heavy footsteps as Mortimer, the man assigned to guard us, arrived upstairs. He introduced himself, reconfirming that he was the man Mycroft had ordered to stay behind.

"What do you need, Mr. Holmes?" he asked, but he eyed me curiously.

"Please, Mr. Belster. Sit yourself down while I compose a few notes. Oh, and I would like to introduce you to my friend and associate, Dr. Watson. Watson, meet the very capable Mr. Mortimer Belster. He and I have a rather unique history."

I wondered if this was the same Belster Holmes had spoken of when we met Mycroft at the Diogenes Club, and asked as much.

"That's right, Doctor." The man smiled broadly, taking on the conversation. "Mr. Holmes was clever enough to deduce that a man was bleeding me to near financial ruin. All because of a youthful folly. I have nothing but the highest regard for his capabilities and

the discreet manner in which he dispatched my case. Had the information come into the public domain, I most assuredly would have
been reduced to an untenable state of affairs. I will forever be in his
debt."

"I am happy to hear that the matter has been settled to your satisfaction," I said sincerely, noticing that Holmes had retired to a side
table and was busy writing.

Belster was a man of great physical stature. Standing a shade under
six-and-a-half feet and approximately twelve stone, his long frame
seemed at odds with his fluid movements as he draped himself over
the back of a chair. A lock from his magnificent mane of hair dipped
just above his right brow, giving him an air of rakish charm. His smile
and confidence were contagious and I instantly liked the man. His
hands, in constant motion, tapped vigorously on the back of his chair,
keeping time to an imaginary musical arrangement.

Waiting for Holmes to conclude his writing, Belster went over to
the window and examined the bullet grouping that marred the window
frame. He turned to face me and winked. With a smile, Belster said,
"Quite a deadly package, wouldn't you say Doctor?"

To the untrained eye, the scarred wood was a confusion of splinters
and gashes. Having never before heard a grouping described in such a
manner, I was unnerved by the ease in which Belster reached his
conclusion. I quickly realised that the man's affable manner was a
formidable tool to deceive the deceivers.

"It's all right, Doctor," Belster responded upon seeing my study of
him. "I know I have that effect on people."

I was embarrassed by my rudeness. Thankfully, Holmes' stirring
saved me from having to offer an apology.

Sherlock Holmes said, "Mortimer, here are five envelopes and a
piece of paper. The first envelope is for Davidson. The others have all
been marked with the appropriate names. I want you to personally give
this one to Davidson and await his instructions. Have one of your boys
deliver the other four to this one address. This telegram that I've put
on the piece of paper must be sent immediately. Have the boy wait for
an answer."

"As you wish, Mr. Holmes. Is there anything else?" Belster asked, glancing down at the name of the person to receive the telegram. His head shot up in surprise.

Sherlock Holmes gave the man a pat on the shoulder. "Just be prepared for any eventuality. There's many a way for this to go all wrong."

"Don't worry, Mr. Holmes. I'll take care of everything."

"Excellent." My friend smiled and grasped Belster's hand in gratitude. "I have lately come to depend very heavily on you and the men. Please be sure to extend my appreciation to them."

"I will. Doctor? Mr. Holmes?" And the big man gave a surprisingly graceful demi-bow before leaving us.

With the departure of Mortimer Belster, Holmes' relaxed nonchalance disappeared. As he perched on the window sill he said, "Tomorrow is the day, Watson. We are going to change history that hasn't occurred yet."

"What do we do now, Holmes?"

"We wait."

"What were in those envelopes and the telegram?"

"Plans for tomorrow. Each envelope holds specific instructions as to where I want a particular man positioned when the train arrives. Of course, the mock assassination has been discarded, but the actors will still greet the Prince as planned."

"Why aren't we assuming that responsibility? I fully understand your allegiance to your brother, but are we not putting the recovery of Mycroft's reputation before the safety and reputation of Prince Edward and the rest of the Royals? After all, Her Majesty—"

"Reputation, be damned," said Holmes, setting his jaw. "I accepted this obligation with all humility, Watson, but with great purpose of mind. I assure you that my primary directive remains the safety of the Royals. By continuing to have the actors portray us, we are free to capture Mycroft's assassin. It is not his reputation that I am concerned with. It is his life! And in protecting him, I believe that we are protecting the Throne. Say what you will of my brother's methods, but even you cannot question his value to England and the Crown."

"Of course, I understand. I concur with your brother's worthiness.

But, Holmes, if we are so engaged at the other end of the Royal train, what if something goes wrong? Must we divide our loyalties?"

"No," my friend responded. "The Prince must always be our priority. I believe, however, that I have taken the necessary precautions in the event it should be necessary—"

He hesitated and finished his thought. "Well, let us just say that no harm will come to the Royals."

"All right, Holmes. I trust your judgment, but I do have a question about Brewer. It is obvious that he is Mycroft's assassin, but how do you explain the failure on your brother's part to discover his own murderer? Mycroft had all the advantages of witnessing the event. How is it that you were able to look at lengths of pipes and springs and easily deduce the manner in which the murder is to be committed?"

Once more, Sherlock Holmes ignored my question. "Your mentioning of Brewer has suddenly alerted me. We haven't heard from the man who was tailing him. That is curious and troublesome."

Worry furrowed his brow, as Sherlock Holmes mechanically tapped his pipe empty into the palm of his hand. He let the black ash tumble into a china saucer. Absentmindedly, his fingers sifted through the previous day's remains of tarred plugs and dottles. These had all been saved in the saucer. Without looking my way, Holmes asked for his tobacco pouch and I tossed it. His hand flew up to catch it. Peeling the bag open, he pinched a tight shag and tamped it down in his Black Mamba clay pipe. Soon the room was filled with a billowing cloud of smoke and the acrid smell of his coarse blend of tobacco.

I knew from my years with him that he would remain in this stupor for some time, and though he appeared to be in the clutches of a paralyzing trance, his mind was in fact at its most active.

"Has it been impressed upon you, Watson, that Brewer took both of our disguises?" he remarked, breaking his own silence.

"No. What do you make of it?"

My friend had already returned to the safety of his protracted thinking. That left me to ponder the meaning of this latest observation.

"What of the black tubing? Do you not find its shape familiar?" Sherlock Holmes asked.

"Holmes, I cannot deduce whether or not you wish my participation. Believing that any words spoken by me would distract you, I wish you would provide me with a signal of some kind. Should I speak or stay silent? I cannot sit here and constantly worry."

With his eyes aglow and his elbows planted firmly on the tabletop, my friend laced his fingers together and rested his chin on the supporting bridge. The embers within his pipe cooled. His amused smile flickered in and out through the gauzy haze of the smoke he produced.

"With our long history, Watson, you still claim that I am unreadable? I am an easy read. I am a book whose pages are open for everyone to study."

"Ha! A book! A book perhaps, with pages that have been submerged in water. Every time I attempt to read one of your pages, it becomes a pasty mass of confusion. A book, indeed."

"What I mean to say, Watson, is that whether I am in quiet repose or rambling incessantly, I value your counsel too much to desire your silence. When you have something to contribute, I want it all. I must have data to form an educated opinion. There is no man wiser than you who can separate the wheat from the chaff."

I appreciated my friend's faith in me, but his next words dashed them all in an instant.

"Besides," he said, "your appreciation of my desire for silence was substantially compromised when you asked whether or not I wanted you to remain quiet."

"Holmes!"

"I apologise, Watson. It is not often that I bow to such boorish behavior—but the pressures of this case have been mounting. I pray that you'll understand and forgive.

"To the business at hand," he said, raising his long finger in the air, "Watson, I asked whether the black tubing reminded you of anything. Have these pieces made any impression?"

With that, he assembled the tubing on the table's surface.

"My word, Holmes! It looks like a policeman's baton!"

"Precisely, and don't overlook the symmetry of the make-up kit and Brewer's lifting of our disguises."

"Incredible! Why he's—"

"Yes. Unfortunately, though, there will be hundreds of constables here tomorrow. And since we do not know exactly what he will look like, they will all be under suspicion and will require our scrutiny."

Holmes got up and made himself busy looking out the window. "Ah, I believe we are about to receive some word about Brewer," he said, strolling towards the door. "Watson, while I confer with our visitor, see if you can make sense of the items in the box. I'll be back shortly."

While my friend was gone, I emptied the springs and other parts on the table, and disassembled the tubing. Having acquired an appreciation of puzzles, I studied the different items with an eye as to what piece fit where. I immediately realized that some of the pieces could only be assigned in a particular order. Having deduced their placement, my fingers toyed with the diverse elements until I had my solution completely assembled. Sitting back in stunned silence, I stared at the most diabolical weapon I had ever seen. A baton that could fire a projectile silently. Then I realised that the most important part of this puzzle was missing—the bullet.

Holmes entered the flat. Disappointment was clearly etched upon his face.

"They've lost Brewer," he said. "He gave them the slip in a warren of hovels down at Market Square. The men are remaining at their stations, just in case he resurfaces, but I believe that nothing will come of it. He is clever enough to change his appearance again. That means he will most probably walk right by them without attracting their notice. We will have to be ever-vigilant tomorrow."

"Why don't we just call the whole thing off, Holmes? It is far too dangerous for all concerned to allow this man anywhere near the Royal train. No matter what we surmised was his intent, it's fraught with the potential for violence. I wouldn't be at all surprised if he abandoned his plans and decided to target the Prince out of sheer spite. I tell you, Holmes, this man is clever and dangerous beyond my comprehension."

"What brings you so close to the precipice of surrender?" Holmes asked, eyeing me with concern. "It is not normally in your personality to succumb before the battle has begun."

"I'm sorry, Holmes, but look at what this man plans to unleash tomorrow," said I, pointing to the device on the table.

Holmes turned a chair around and came to sit at the table. He lifted the weapon and raised it to his eyes, holding it at different angles to study it more closely, a tight grimace on his face. Deducing its application, he pulled the forward tube towards him. It slid, collapsing over the second tube. A loud and forceful whoosh of air escaped from the far end of the tube. My friend's eyes were filled with wonder as he lifted his head to stare at me.

"The only item missing, I think, is the bullet."

I suddenly felt my confidence wane. I had wanted to believe that my piecing together of the various parts was all wrong. But I saw in my friend's eyes that he, too, understood the deadly nature of the weapon assembled on the table in front of us.

"Outstanding, Watson! You have deduced the manner in which Brewer will attempt to murder my brother. Give me one of the bullets from your revolver. Let us see whether your model will hold up under a test-firing."

I took one out and handed it to my friend. He pinched it between his fingers and examined it closely. Then he placed it on the slide that Brewer had somehow fabricated, Holmes drove the slide home with a quick pumping of the black tube. The bullet disappeared inside the device.

"Are you ready, Watson?" asked Holmes, scanning the room for a suitable target.

"I suppose."

First, he moved a chair against the wall. Then Holmes walked to the tiny cupboard and removed a tin tea canister. He balanced the metal container on the back of a chair. With a thin smile, Sherlock Holmes pumped the device once more. We could hear the bullet click as it settled into the breech. Sherlock Holmes paced off about ten feet and turned to face his target.

Lowering the tube to a nearly horizontal position, Sherlock Holmes grasped the front of the weapon with his left hand about three inches from the forward end and turned inward. He slowly pulled back on the rear tube and held it in this position for a moment or two. Raising his eyes towards me, he nodded once.

I brought my fingers to my ears to deaden the noise.

Holmes' right hand suddenly and violently moved forward. The bullet escaped the weapon's nose, and the tea canister flew off the back of the chair and came crashing to the floor.

"What happened?" I asked Holmes. "Was there a misfire? I didn't hear a thing."

My friend smiled as he stooped to pick up the canister. He held it up for me to see.

"No," was Holmes' one word response to a possible misfire. "Look."

He poked his finger inside the small hole at the very center of the canister. With only his long finger supporting it, he turned the punctured piece of tin round so I could see the back of the canister. A much larger rosette flowered from the back side of the torn tin. The hole testified to the massive extent of damage the bullet would inflict once it had penetrated its victim.

✣ 40 ✣

"**G**ood heavens, Holmes," I gasped, thinking as a doctor about the carnage such a weapon could inflict.

"Indeed."

"But I heard nothing!"

"That's the genius of this invention, Watson. It makes no sound. The assassin fires this weapon without fear of any attention being drawn to him. In the confusion, he slips away. By the time anyone realises there has been a shooting, he is long gone. Or at the very least, because of his disguise, he blends in with all the other gawkers. He might even assist others in holding back the crowd."

"It's diabolical," I said.

"The infernal brilliance," Holmes remarked, awed by our opponent's evil device.

"What are we to do, Holmes? Every man on the beat carries a baton. How are we to find him?"

My friend was already involved in solving the problem as he went to the window and waved. Seconds later, another man came into the room.

"What can I do for you, Mr. Holmes?"

"Deliver this to my brother, straightaway," said Holmes, scribbling and sketching on a piece of paper. "Make sure that he understands that this must all be accomplished before daybreak, and that no one outside the force is to have this information. Tell him that not one of these men must get by his inspection. Lives depend on it. And tell Mycroft I need the other items as soon as possible."

"You've got it, Mr. Holmes. Someone will replace me while I attend to this errand."

"Thank you." The man left as quickly as he had come.

"What's on your mind, Holmes?" I asked, filling the silence. "Have you a plan?"

"Of course," he said. His back was to me as his hands worked for the extraction of the brass from the weapon. "Watson, would you be so kind as to go to the cellar? I noticed a small can of white paint on the top shelf. Please bring it to me."

"Whatever for Holmes?" I asked, already heading out of the flat.

"To create singularity, of course!" came his confusing reply. "Now, be a good fellow and fetch it, will you?"

A short while later I returned with a tin of white paint and a brush. Holmes was standing and gazing out the window again.

"Here they are, Holmes," I called, upon entering. "I have the items you requested."

"Look, Watson," he said, pointing to the throng outside. Men, women and children were already sitting or lying on the deck of the station's platform. "They're already claiming their parcels of real estate for tomorrow's festivities. The police force will have their hands full, I think."

"We will never spot Brewer in that mess," I said.

"Be of good cheer," said Holmes, relieving me of the paint and sitting at the table.

"What's your game, Holmes? What do you plan to do with the paint?"

My friend popped the lid off the paint. He then daubed the thin brush in the colour and applied it to the weapon. With two quick strokes, he was finished.

"What do you think?" he asked, admiring his artistry. He had added a white X to the baton.

"Very nice, Holmes, but will you tell me what you are doing?"

"Creating singularity."

"I didn't understand your meaning earlier, Holmes, and I most certainly do not understand it now. Speak plainly, for once."

"Think, Watson," responded my friend. "We cannot strip the force of their batons, can we?"

"Of course not! Why would you even consider such a drastic proposal?"

Before Holmes could respond to my obtuseness, a sudden clarity came into my brain. "By God, Holmes. It's brilliant!"

"Not quite, but I do appreciate the simplicity."

❧ 41 ❧

The remaining hours were spent in quiet reflection, interrupted by an occasional bout of flurried activity, as Holmes reacted to the comings and goings of the messengers he had loosed upon the authorities.

In his attempt to anticipate every eventuality, Holmes correctly pointed out that we must once again go in disguise. A runner came in carrying our wardrobe for tomorrow. The man set the bundles down on a chair and gave his report. "The men are setting up the stands, Mr. Holmes. They'll keep them under guard until you and the doctor arrive. I was told to tell you that one man has been assigned to each of you. Your bodyguards will be by your side at the stand for the entire day."

"Thank you," said Holmes.

"Stand? What stand?" I asked, taking advantage of a lull in the activity.

"Tomorrow, Watson. Everything will become clear as glass tomorrow. I suggest that we send our friends packing and try to get some sleep. We'll be up very early tomorrow."

With everyone gone, and feeling secure with the men whom Holmes had posted downstairs, I was finally able to let down my guard.

Obviously, my friend was of a similar disposition, though much further along in the process, for he was already snoring away, lying face-down on his cot.

Feeling my head beginning to dip to my chest, I surrendered to my tiredness and lay down on my cot. Soon I was fast asleep.

I recall waking numerous times during the night in response to voices in the flat. Without rising, I turned my head and through bleary eyes saw my friend in various postures of wakefulness as he spoke in whispered tones with the different men. But my exhaustion was so compelling that I soon returned to sleep.

I awoke the next morning feeling dwarfed by the expectations of the day's events, and I rose from my cot with some trepidation. Holmes, to my great surprise, was already up and deeply immersed in the morning papers.

"Ah, good, you're awake," he remarked upon hearing my stirrings. "I've made you some coffee. It will bring you round to the human side."

Feeling that any words coming from my cotton-dry mouth would betray my reservations as to my humanity, I mumbled an unintelligible response and shuffled my way to the washstand.

Holmes' chuckling forewarned me that today would be a trying day. Nevertheless, I joined him at the table.

"If you are up to it, Watson," he said as he poured my coffee, "I suggest that you go to the window and see what has transpired whilst you slept."

Grudgingly, I took the proffered cup of steaming coffee and walked to the window.

"Where did they come from? There are thousands upon thousands!" I cried out in alarm. I was referring, of course, to the mass of humanity that had filled every inch of space on the platform below.

"They began coming in the middle of the night. Many of them camped out right on the platform. It's remarkable how the human pines for an encounter with celebrity, no matter how brief or far removed."

"Well," I said, "not everyone can claim the Queen as a friend."

I paced about the rooms, going from window to window and

SHERLOCK HOLMES AND THE TIME MACHINE

becoming more and more alarmed at the sight of the tumult and confusion down below.

"Watson, you're like a cat contemplating a moth. Kindly find a spot and settle."

"Holmes, look at them down there! How are we to operate with any sense of organisation? We'll be trampled by the mob. What we are contemplating doing is unreasonable, and we cannot guarantee the safety of the Royals—no less ourselves. I suggest that we warn them and call the entire matter off."

"Now who's being unreasonable? Can you imagine the uproar a cancellation will cause? Do you have any idea how-?"

"Perhaps not, but can you imagine the uproar when the Prince is assassinated? What will you tell England's citizens then?" I asked.

"I will simply tell them that it was because of my failure to do my assigned duty that the Prince was murdered."

I stopped my frantic pacing in mid-stride and turned to face my friend. Expecting to see a playful smile on his face, I was startled to see that he was in deadly earnest.

"Listen to me closely, Watson," he began tightly, looking at me seriously. "I truly believe that my grasp of the facts regarding this case is correct. The Prince is not the target. It is my brother, and my brother only, who will be felled. If my preparations are not sufficient enough to anticipate and deduce the assassin's plan, then I, as well as the citizenry of this great land with all of their righteous anger, will hold me accountable. It is the right of the people to expect nothing less than a complete and honest effort from those who are sworn to protect them. My fealty is to the very principle that makes England's heart so vibrant and essential."

"I hope you are right in your assumptions," I said, somberly. "If all goes well, then the people will owe you a debt of gratitude the likes of which—"

"In doing what we ought, we deserve no praise, because it is our duty," Holmes interrupted. "But there is one curiosity that perhaps you might help me understand. It has suddenly come to my mind."

"Anything that I can do to help, Holmes."

"Why did he take both of them?"

"What do you mean? Take both of what?"

"Our uniforms. The disguises we wore. Brewer took them both. Why? With the speed of his flight, surely carrying them both would slow him down."

"Perhaps he didn't know which one would fit and decided it was wiser to..."

"A blind man would be able to see the disparities. Remember, he took the cotton batting and the batons. He—"

"There's two of them! Two assassins!" I said.

"It would seem so."

"Then I was correct. The Prince's life is in danger!" The magnitude of our problem hit me squarely.

My companion's silence was profoundly disturbing.

"Well, there is nothing we can do but be vigilant in our purpose. If Mycroft has followed my instructions, the man will be easy to spot. Let us get into our disguises and report to the staging area."

42

After Holmes had completed his own disguise, and as he had done before, Holmes patiently applied actor's putty and pancake to my face and blended it all together. As I stared at my reflection in the mirror, I must admit that I was always surprised by the ease in which my friend could erase my previous existence.

"Those are yours," he remarked, pointing to the stained and tattered clothing separated on the table.

I dressed in the trousers first. I was relieved that Holmes hadn't required that I wear padding under my clothing. But I grew concerned when I noticed that the right sleeve on the long frock coat had been pinned up. Believing this to be a mistake, I worked to remove the pin.

"Leave it," Holmes ordered, seeing my effort. "It is a necessary part of the disguise."

"But, Holmes, how am I to operate my gun with only one hand?"

"You'll see. Put on the coat." He took my revolver and tucked it in the waistband of my trousers. Placing my left arm through the sleeve and letting my right hang loosely at my side beneath the coat, I reluctantly did as instructed. Holmes came over and buttoned my coat fully.

"This is ridiculous." I asked, "How am I to get to my pistol if it is needed?"

"Stand erect, will you?" he commanded, seeing my petulant slouch.

Again, I did as instructed and glared at my friend through angry eyes.

"Excellent. Now very slowly with your right hand reach up for your weapon and remove it from your waist. Then let your hand hang down at your side."

Holmes watched, as I followed his commands.

"Now, like this, I want you to bend your arm forward. Stopping midway at your waist." My companion mimed the movements he wanted me to follow. Mimicking his motion, I was surprised to see the barrel of my revolver jutting out from a cleverly disguised rip in my coat.

"Incredible." I laughed. "Holmes, you've thought of everything."

"We'll see. Just remember that you are now a one-armed cripple. It's imperative that you remain in character."

"I understand." I went to the mirror and practiced until I felt satisfied that my weapon could be drawn without anyone having noticed. Staring at my reflection, I became what my friend had envisioned, a helpless cripple who had been wounded during the war and was now a hawker of garish souvenirs.

"Remarkable," I said, enthralled by the reflection in the mirror.

I turned to admire my friend's disguise, but his back was to me. So I waited for him to turn round. Though his head drooped when he did face me, I saw the balding pate of a man far along in his losing battle with some unknown disease. Festering boils and blisters dotted the grey cancerous landscape of his head. As he slowly raised himself to full erectness, I jumped back in fright. His pallor was greyish-green, and the flesh round one of his eyes was swollen and bruised. The eye itself was a milky white colour. Tilting his head at an odd angle on a filthy neck, my friend smiled to reveal a set of barely attended to greenish and uneven teeth.

"Holmes! Your skin! Your eye! What happened?"

"Whoa, calm down, Watson!" he laughed, seeing my great agitation and worry. "As far as the eye is concerned, it is a glass lens that I have been working on. I am able to see through it quite clearly. As to my skin colour, I merely placed a daub of sulphur and gunpowder under my tongue. It requires a few minutes to take effect, and I must undergo a period of queasiness, but it has already passed. The mixture is quite harmless. I'm surprised that you haven't heard of it. After all, you were a surgeon in the war. It is a well-known scheme cooked up by soldiers at the front. This concoction is much used by malingerers when they can stand no more. If your reaction is to be believed, I have succeeded in conveying an image of a pitiable soul."

"In the future, Holmes, please warn me when you are about to frighten me to near death."

My friend only smiled. "Ready?"

"Whenever you are, Holmes."

🏵 43 🏵

We left the flat and Brewer's shop and were met by a broadly smiling Belster.

"Good show, gentlemen!" He laughed, looking us over with great admiration. "The stand has been set up and your orders have been followed to the letter. Follow me and I will take you to your new place of employment."

The platform was teeming with people, and it was with some effort that we made our way to a small table that had been set up for us. A man I had never seen before nodded at Sherlock Holmes, and stepped from behind the table.

"It's all yours," he said, acting relieved that we'd joined him. "These people are crazed! Watch them close or they'll steal you blind. The prices are marked on the items, and there's coin in the box. Good luck."

Mortimer Belster burst out laughing as he watched the man race away. The big policeman crowed, "There goes a man who takes life much too seriously. All right, Mr. Holmes, I'll be round to check up on you from time to time. Good hunting."

"Thank you. Where is my brother?"

"Posted exactly where you want him to be. He'll pass by here on his way to the far end of the platform at the precise moment the train noses into the quay. Anything else?"

"No. Oh, by the way, post someone to keep an eye on the window of the flat. The person you assign to the job must be a crack shot. He is under my orders to shoot anyone who appears in the window. Dr. Watson believes that there may well be an attempt on the Prince. And though I do not agree, it would ease both our minds if that particular venue is shut down tightly."

"I'll see to it personally, Mr. Holmes," Belster replied, his face never showing any annoyance at this unexpected turn of events. "No one will come out of that flat alive.

"Gentlemen." With a nod goodbye, Belster walked away and was immediately swallowed up in the crowd.

"Does anything faze that man?" I asked, drawing surprising comfort from Belster's confidence.

"If there is such a thing, I have yet to see it," Sherlock Holmes said with approval.

Looking round, I noticed that our position was directly across from where Tuscano's melon had been set up. My revolver was still concealed beneath my coat. I was about to slip it into the waist of my trousers, but a change in Holmes' posture caused me to become instantly alert.

Just then, a cackling woman enquired as to the cost of a small card with Queen Victoria's portrait on it. While she went on and on, Sherlock Holmes stiffened as he studied a police constable who kept coming nearer to our table.

As the woman's hands roamed our merchandise, I ignored her questions. Instead, my eyes flicked from Holmes to the constable and back to Holmes. My hand slowly tightened on the grip of my pistol. I brought it up to peek through the slit in the front of my coat. By then the constable had drawn even with our table. He glanced over our wares and nodded politely. His hand was resting on the butt of his baton. My eyes traveled the length of his weapon as I began to apply pressure on the trigger of my revolver.

"Wait," Holmes whispered out of the corner of his mouth, sensing my growing apprehension.

The anticipation became almost unbearable. Our tension was heightened by the incessant cackling of the old woman. Finally, when I was unable to contain myself any longer, I shouted, "Here! Take this!"

I tossed the card at the woman and continued, "Now will you kindly remove yourself from this table? Your voice is grating on my nerves!"

"There it is," observed Holmes. As the constable chuckled to himself and walked on by, I caught sight of the small white X painted on his baton.

Seeing my friend's prearranged sign of recognition so clearly, I relaxed my stance. But now I felt the withering glare of the woman that I had so rudely treated, boring into the back of my head.

As I turned round to apologise to the crone, I was greeted with a streaming current of invectives coursing out of her contorted mouth. She "harrumphed" haughtily and turned on her heel, but not before throwing the card in my face.

"I've said it a thousand times, Watson, you must keep up with your people skills." Holmes laughed, uproariously. His disfigured and grotesque face seeming to make my humiliation more complete.

If I hadn't put my pistol away, I think I would have shot him then and there.

44

As the morning wore on and neared the noon hour, I discovered that I had the capacity to barter with the best of them. Our money box soon overflowed its capacity. I was so deeply involved in the selling of our wares that ofttimes I didn't see Holmes' suspicious eyes follow the movements of the passing constabulary, only to relax when he saw the X on a baton.

From time to time, a runner would arrive at our table and whisper in my friend's ear. And he in turn, would convey his orders in a like manner.

"Are you enjoying yourself?" queried Holmes, watching my last customer disappear in the crowd.

"I'm sorry, Holmes. It's just that..."

Watching me stuff the money in my pockets, Holmes asked, "Do you feel it?"

"What?"

"The current. There's a sense of electricity in the air. The change is quite subtle, but it is here nonetheless." In response to his words, my heartbeat quickened.

"Stay alert," said Holmes, taking out his watch. "The time is fast approaching."

With our minds suddenly keen, we eyed each passerby with suspicion. A commotion stirred farther down the platform.

A terror-stricken man came running in our direction with a constable chasing close on his heels. "Stop, I say!" the policeman shouted, raising his baton over his head.

The man was running in a near crouch in an attempt to avoid the officer's swinging baton. He suddenly veered towards our table. Lowering his shoulder, he was about to plow into us, but Holmes neatly stuck out his arm, hitting the man in the chest, sending him sprawling to the ground. The constable, out of breath, caught up to the man and pinned him by lying across his chest.

I realised that my revolver was once again protruding from my coat. I quickly stuffed it back in my waist. Without further incident, the man was carted away with the assistance of three more strapping officers. Holmes tossed a canvas tarpaulin over our merchandise and sat down on a wooden crate.

"I propose that we make the rounds and check up on our preparations," he said, rising from the crate. "Stretching our legs will help keep us limber."

As he began walking away, I asked, "What about the merchandise?"

My friend frowned at me from over his shoulder. His look of chastisement made me wish that I hadn't been so distracted from our purpose.

"I'm sorry, Holmes," I said.

"It's a defencive quality that is unique to your person," said Holmes.

"What is?" I asked, confused by his words.

"The manner in which you deal with the unknown. You become so easily distracted when you are tense, but I know within you beats the heart of a lion. I myself, apply a number of mental exercises to relieve the stress of the moment. It helps me to think more clearly. I wonder which of us sets the better example: you or me?"

I could not tell if Holmes was offering a polite criticism or a simple observation. I resolved to think over his comment when I had a moment to give it proper consideration.

Meanwhile, the crowd had become unyielding in its purpose to discover and claim the perfect vantage point to observe the festivities. The mass of exuberant citizens was quickly becoming a wild mob.

"Holmes, this is a disaster in waiting!" I said. "The crowd is growing more unruly by the moment, and the constables are moving around so quickly that I cannot see the Xs. What are we to do?"

As we pondered our next move, Belster was making his way towards us. His worried face glistened with perspiration.

"Mr. Holmes! Come quickly!" he exclaimed, reaching our position, "Your brother has requested that you and Dr. Watson make your way to the storage facility immediately. He realises this is contrary to your preparations, but he feels that if things go much further, any corrective response would be..."

Belster's eyes went suddenly wide as he stumbled forward. His face crumpled in a mask of pain and confusion. He looked to Holmes questioningly as a tiny blotch of red appeared in the center of his chest. Belster looked down at the red dot quizzically. He seemed fascinated by its ever-widening pattern as it began to fill the front of his blouse.

"Lordy! I think I've been shot," he whispered hoarsely, as he slowly tottered to the ground. Holmes' eyes darted round in search of the shooter. I moved forward and grabbed Belster under his arms. Working together, Sherlock Holmes and I half-dragged and half-carried the man to a nearby column. Once there, we let him slip to the ground with his back being supported by the post. I knelt to examine him, but even as I got to my knees, Belster's eyes fluttered closed. With one final exhalation of his breath, he died.

Holmes locked onto the receding back of a constable who was backing away from us quickly. "Watson, stay here with Belster!" my friend ordered, as he trotted after the policeman who was quickly melting into the crowd. As soon as Holmes disappeared, I ran to our table and tore off the tarpaulin. Carrying it back to Belster's corpse, I draped it over him. It seemed the least I could do. I have seen good men die before, and I shall never become accustomed to it.

"What did he ever do?" I shouted at the heavens.

"His duty," remarked Sherlock Holmes, suddenly appearing at my elbow. "We have to leave him, Watson, and get down to my brother."

"What of the constable you were chasing?" I asked, looking into my friend's eyes.

His silence told me that the man had gotten away.

"There's nothing we can do here," Sherlock Holmes said, nodding to Belster's corpse. "We must see this through to the end. Come, we must hurry."

Taking one last look at Belster, I moved away and fell in behind Holmes. A flying squad of three constables happened by, and Holmes planted his hand in the center of one of their chests.

"Hey! Watch out there!" the officer protested.

Ignoring their anger, Holmes roughly grabbed the batons and looked for the white Xs. Seeing them, he identified himself and ordered the officers to stand guard over Belster's body. "No one is to touch anything. Am I clear?"

"Yes, sir," they said in unison.

"If you see other officers passing by, grab them and check for the X. If you don't see any such markings on their batons, you are to subdue them and hold them in custody."

"You have it, Mr. Holmes," said the most senior of the group.

"Right. Come, Watson!"

Abandoning any pretext of anonymity, my friend barreled through the crowds. As we drew even with Brewer's establishment, Holmes cast a sideways glance up at the window of the flat, and hurried on by. Spying his brother standing outside, my friend headed straight towards him.

"Ah, Sherlock." Mycroft beamed with joy. "I see that Belster has conveyed my—"

"Belster is dead!" Holmes interrupted, grabbing Mycroft by the lapels and backing him against the wall of the shed. "Your devious behavior has cost a very good man his life!"

"What!?" Mycroft bellowed, prying his brother's hands off his chest. "How? When?"

"It doesn't matter," said Holmes. "He is dead, and there is nothing we can do about it. Now, what is so important that you have caused me to abandon my position? And it best better be—"

The hollow wail of a train whistle contributed to the confusion and urgency of the moment, as the brothers stood glowering at each other.

Responding to the whistle, Sherlock raised his head and cocked it toward the noise. "Is that-?"

"Yes. The train is fifteen minutes out," Mycroft said, anticipating his brother's query.

"Look at this madhouse!" an exasperated Sherlock Holmes gestured at the teeming crowds. "How are we to accomplish anything? Mycroft, you must not proceed with our plan. The assassin who murdered Belster has gotten behind us. There's no way to determine where he has posted himself. The Xs are too small for us to see clearly. The murderer could be upon you in an instant, and we'd have no time to respond with any certainty of success. This is all wrong! Watson and I cannot be wandering round aimlessly, hoping to spot the murderers."

"Murderers?" Mycroft repeated, his eyes widening. "You said murderers, Sherlock? There is more than one?"

"Yes, I believe so. Brewer took both of our disguises. He has an accomplice."

❧ 45 ❧

"**P**hiladelphia," Mycroft said. He was sweating profusely.

"What about him?"

"He's gone missing. He was assigned the task of making the duplicate crate that contained the time machine, as per your instructions. This, as you can plainly see," Mycroft tapped the large crate sitting on two dollies, "is the result. But when we looked for Philadelphia, he was nowhere to be found. The crate was sitting here, just as you see it."

Sherlock Holmes eyed the crate curiously. He asked, "What did you use to add the sufficient weight that I requested?" To punctuate his request, he placed his hands on the wood case and rocked it back and forth.

"I'm sure I don't know," Mycroft replied, watching his brother.

My friend ran his hands along the crate's slatted frame and down along its side to the bottom. He suddenly crouched low and placed his long finger inside a slight separation of the wood. Still in his crouched position, Sherlock gazed up at Mycroft with a troubled expression on his face. Slowly rising, he brought his finger up for us to see. It was covered in blood. Sherlock turned to me. "Watson, ready your revolver, please. And someone bring me a prybar."

I stood with my pistol pointing at the crate as a man hurriedly handed my friend the tool he requested.

Cleaving the wood with a violent thrust of the prybar, Holmes separated the crate's side from the rest of the container and out fell the crumpled body of Philadelphia. He had been shot neatly between the eyes.

"Good heavens!" shouted Mycroft, deftly avoiding the corpse that tumbled at his feet.

"Look, Holmes, the pistol was in his lap," I said, pointing to the small calibre revolver on the ground. "Why would a man take his own life like that?"

"Oh? And did he nail himself in the crate before or after he had shot himself?" snapped Holmes impatiently. "Where's Tuscano?" He abruptly changed the subject and scanned the area for the man.

"Why, he is where you wanted him," replied his brother, looking down at the body of the mysterious Mr. Delphi.

"What are you talking about?"

"Belster."

"What of him?"

"Tuscano said that Belster, under orders from you, wanted Tuscano posted back up at the window of Brewer's flat. He—"

"Does he still have the rifle?" Sherlock Holmes asked, as he turned his head in the direction of the flat.

"Yes. I'm afraid he does."

Before Mycroft could further explain, the Queen's Band struck up their instruments in a final rehearsal before the arrival of the Royals.

"Blast!" shouted my companion, throwing his hands in the air with frustration. He grabbed hold of Mycroft's arm and led him round to the back of the shed.

When our group assembled, Holmes was already involved in a heated discussion with his brother.

"But that is why I summoned you here, Sherlock!" I heard Mycroft say loudly, as I neared them.

"I don't understand," said Holmes, scuffing the ground with the toe of his boot. "What horse!?"

Mycroft smiled and whispered in his brother's ear. As his brother continued to speak, Holmes' face, full of righteous indignation, melted into a tableau of acceptance and intrigue.

"An excellent suggestion!" Holmes beamed at Mycroft. "A Trojan horse it is. But first, we must deal with Tuscano. If he is at the window, we are far enough removed from his field of vision that he won't know we have discovered Philadelphia's body."

"How are we to approach him?" I wondered. "He will surely see us as we near the shop."

"With the confusion of the multitudes, if he spots us at all, he will see what I expect him to see, two disfigured old men of limited competence. He will not give us a second's thought."

"It sounds risky, Holmes," I remarked, shaking my head. "If he is at the window, perhaps we can aim up at him and kill him from a safe distance."

"Tuscano is a professional assassin, Watson. He has situated himself perfectly. Right now, he is scanning the area with his scope. He will easily spot any stationary target that is trying to intercede. Besides, there are two items that must be taken into account. First, who will attempt the task of shooting Tuscano? I am perhaps the best suited, but even I have my limitations. If I were to accept the mission, I would first be required to draw even with him. Look down the platform: do you see any area of concealment? I don't. I have no idea how I could get close to the man without attracting his notice. And second, if I were to shoot, the sound of rifle fire would set the crowd into a panic."

All the while Holmes was speaking, his brother listened attentively. Now Mycroft gestured to one of his men and spoke in quiet tones. The man walked round the wooden crate, examining it closely. Then he glanced back at Mycroft and nodded. It was an unmistakable signal of approval.

Another one of Mycroft's men stepped forward. This one was holding a long flat leather case. Mycroft took the item from the man's arms. The older Holmes called for his brother, "Sherlock?"

My friend and I walked over to Mycroft, who had already opened the leather container.

"What is that?" I asked, pointing to the unusually sleek-looking black rifle and scope that sat embedded in some sort of rubber sarcophagus.

"I was under the impression Tuscano still had the rifle," said my friend, understanding what he was seeing.

"He does have a rifle, but he doesn't have them all," Mycroft said, smiling.

Holmes shook his head in disgust. "Will you never learn, my brother? You are tampering with things that will have untold repercussions should the wrong kind of person gain possession of these weapons of destruction. What else have you risked to bring forward your questionable agenda?"

"We will discuss my politics at some future date, Brother, but right now we have Tuscano to deal with. My man is already modifying the crate to suit my desired purpose. Will you take on the responsibility of eliminating Toscano?"

"What a practical word you have chosen, *eliminate*." Sherlock Holmes shook his head. "It connotes a sense of resolution without violence."

"Sherlock... Will you?" Mycroft looked both tired and old. His voice was pleading.

"Yes." Holmes sighed. "What is it you have in mind?"

As we watched Mycroft's man make the necessary alterations to the crate, Holmes' brother told of us his plan.

"It's as I said, Sherlock. It's a Trojan horse. With you inside, my men will wheel the dollies up the platform until the crate is directly opposite Brewer's window. My men will stop the dollies whilst pretending to check on a faulty wheel or something of that sort. When the time is right, you will search for Tuscano using the scope on the rifle, and then shoot him. I will act as the bait. I will walk a few feet in front of you so he will not be paying any attention to the crate. I believe that he will not pass up such an inviting a target as I am. He won't wait for me to reach the signal box."

"And what will I be doing all this time?" I asked. I felt slighted.

Mycroft looked annoyed at my intrusion, but Holmes had a ready response, "Watson, my task is the easy one. I merely have to kill a man. Yours is the most crucial element of this entire affair—"

"Holmes," I interrupted, annoyed by his condescending manner, "I do not need to be coddled—"

"Watson! Will you be quiet for one minute! I am stating a fact! You're the most important cog in this scheme. You must go to the far end of the platform and discover who the other assassins are."

"Other assassins?" I echoed.

"Yes. Obviously Philadelphia wasn't one of them. Look at his clothes. He's not in a constable's uniform. And if you recall, Brewer took both of our constable costumes. Now, counting Brewer as one of the disguised officers, that leaves us with one remaining. But we don't know who he is!"

Mycroft joined in on the conversation. Sounding peevish, he said, "All right, Sherlock, let's suppose that you are correct. Why must the doctor go to the far end of the platform?"

Sherlock Holmes smiled. He was filled with pride by the recognition that his brother hadn't grasped the full circumstances of the case. "To answer your question, Mycroft, first I need an answer to one of my own. Who decided to have Tuscano practice his killing shot from such a distance?"

"I did," Mycroft responded, speaking slowly. "And why would that be important?" He paused to collect his thoughts, and then finished by adding, "Because that is where I am to be..."

"Right!" said Sherlock Holmes. "That is the spot where you are to be murdered. Now, am I correct in assuming that you brought Tuscano into the matter only after you had seen your own murder—and were unable to deduce the identity of the shooter?"

"Correct." Mycroft shifted his bulk uncomfortably. He didn't like where this was going. Nor did he like admitting to his younger brother that he, Sherlock, was right.

"I thought as much. And Tuscano, utilising the precise geometries of his profession, correctly deduced the location of the assassin."

"Yes—yes," Mycroft said impatiently. "What of it? What are you driving at?"

I suddenly realised that I understood Holmes' theory. That left me ready to put his brother in the dock for not having gleaned its implications.

"Tuscano didn't know about the assassination until you brought him into it," I offered, my voice hot with indignation. "The other assassin is positioned forward. He's far out of sight of Tuscano's perch. The second shooter was hired by you to take down the man nearest the signal box, because that was the likely spot for the assassin. But another gunman lies in wait. He plans to murder you, Mycroft. The man nearest the signal box is nothing more than a sacrifice."

"Tuscano was employed by me." Mycroft said stiffly. "One must assume he has been turned. He offers his services to the highest bidder. If you wish to be of use, Doctor, you must help my brother ferret out the other assassins. We'll join you after we have disposed of Tuscano. Uh, killed him."

Sherlock nodded and then turned to me. "Watson, do you want some of my men to accompany you?"

After pondering the problem, I responded, "No. I do not need the appearance of a parade warning off the assassins. I can best operate anonymously by being a wandering citizen."

"Very good," said my friend. Seeing the results of the man's carpentry efforts on the crate, he added, "Excellent work! Truly excellent!"

Picking up the gun, Sherlock Holmes turned to his brother. "How does this rifle work?"

Mycroft explained the operation of the weapon, and as he spoke his brother nodded that he understood. At last, Sherlock Holmes said, "Right. Will you gentlemen excuse us? Watson and I have some matters to discuss."

Holmes led us away from the men, stopping on the opposite side of the shed. "Thank you," he said.

"For what?"

"For being a true and loyal friend and not exposing my men to Mycroft. I have them posted all over the area, so if you run into any trouble... well, someone will always be nearby to assist you. And before you question me, they are not here because of a lack of faith in your capabilities. They are here because I can no longer trust Mycroft or his men. Do you understand?"

"Yes." Sadly, I did.

"Fine. Watson, you must stop those assassins. Everything depends on it."

"I will," I said. A subtle shift inside me sent me back to my days as a soldier. A coldness came over me. My sense of duty to God and country gave me newfound energy and purpose. Then, of course there was also my friendship with Sherlock Holmes. That, too, imbued me with the desire to do my bit.

Sherlock Holmes' eyes narrowed. If he noticed a change in my demeanor, he wisely said nothing. Instead, he said, "Good. Now head off for the other end of the platform and keep your eyes open."

"All right, Holmes." I was about to comment further, but the shrill sound of the train's whistle told me that it was pulling into the station.

※ 46 ※

Sherlock Holmes spun round on his heel and returned to his brother. I watched as he climbed into the open crate. The rifle was handed in and my friend grabbed it. The end of the crate was hammered shut.

Mycroft gave a final tap on the side of the crate and motioned for his men to transfer it. They slowly pushed the dollies forward. I turned and made my way to the other end of the platform.

The Queen's Band struck up a rousing rendition of *Rule, Britannia!* as the swell and tempo of the crowd reached a deafening crescendo. I glanced over my shoulder and saw the two actors who were portraying us as they moved forward. The Royal train squealed to a stop. The engine pinged ominously as the metal cooled. But I kept moving, too, fighting the current of the excited masses.

I cast a sideways glance to my left, scanning the window of Brewer's shop, and thought I saw a movement of the curtains as I went by. I turned my head to the right and saw Mycroft Holmes leading the way as the men behind him struggled with the dollies.

Unable to help myself, I ducked into a doorway and watched as the men toiling with the crate stopped to inspect a wheel on the cart.

Mycroft had drifted a few feet in front of them and stood nervously watching their endeavors.

Recalling my friend's earlier words about the importance of completing my mission, I hurriedly pushed away from the wall and continued my journey. But just as I began to move away, I thought I observed a small puff of smoke coming out of the side of the crate.

I reached the far end of the platform and studied all those who passed by. I paid particular attention to the constabulary and the small white Xs painted on their batons. Within minutes, the crowd had moved on. The reason was suddenly clear to me. The delighted squeals of British citizens warned me that Prince Edward was making his way down the steps of the train. I suddenly realised that my end of the platform was now virtually empty of people. With the exception of a number of weary constables, I was alone.

I gazed back across the rails and saw Mycroft leading his men. They were labouring mightily with their load.

Back at my end, the Royal entourage were already heading my way. But I had yet to discover the assassins. My head swiveled left, then right. My obvious search for a target brought me under the scrutiny of two curious constables. They made their way towards me, walking in a way that promised harsh treatment.

Nervously, I tried to locate the Xs on their batons, but from my vantage point, I couldn't see if their batons were marked or not. My hand closed round my revolver as they drew nearer. The nose of my gun jutted out from the slit in my coat.

One of the policemen called out to me. "Look here, mister." His hand was wrapped tightly round his baton. "You'll have to get going. There's no one allowed in this area till the Royals have departed."

The man who was speaking let his baton bounce repeatedly off the palm of his hand. The other officer stepped away from his associate and widened the distance between them. He, too, held a baton in his hand and slapped his palm with it.

"You heard him!" the second policeman barked at me. His eyes were dark and menacing. "Move along or you'll be tastin' a lick from my blackjack here."

"Listen to me, my good fellows!" I shouted. My frustration was mounting. I had to find the assassin, but these two buffoons were making my job impossible. "You have no call to threaten me. And if you continue..."

"You'll do what?" spat the man nearest me. "We have the authority to knock your head off if we wish it. Now leave here this instant or..." He raised the baton over his head. That's when I spotted the small X on its handle.

"Wait! You work for Mycroft Holmes!" I shouted as if chanting a talisman. "So do I!"

It was not exactly the truth, but it did stop them in the tracks. Their reactions were instantaneous. Both men lowered their batons and stared warily at me.

One asked, "You know him? What about him?"

"The Xs on your batons. They are the signal Mr. Sherlock Holmes arranged with his brother, Mycroft Holmes. We're on the same side!"

"And how would you be a knowin' that?" the other one asked, testily.

I spoke as quickly as possible, "I know about the Xs because I am Dr. John H. Watson, a friend and associate of Mr. Sherlock Holmes. Mycroft Holmes' brother!"

Nervously, I turned my head to see what progress Mycroft and his men had made. I became alarmed when I saw that they were farther down the platform. They were nearing the security gauntlet that all of the Royals had to pass through before entering onto the dock.

"How do we know you're who you say you are? I saw Mr. Holmes once at the station, and the man with him was this doctor that you mentioned. You don't look at all like I remember. What's your game? How do we know you ain't here to harm the Prince?"

The officers were again suspicious of me and moved closer.

"Because, my good man," I retorted, pushing my pistol through the slit in my coat so that the barrel showed clearly, "had I wished to, I could have shot you both dead." I cocked the hammer to make my position more clearly defined. "And if you continue to keep me from my task, I may do just that!"

The officers stood there, wondering how to best extricate themselves from their current dilemma. As they pondered their predicament, I decided to risk a glance to see where Mycroft and his men were. As I turned my head, I noticed that my confrontation with these two constables had caught the attention of the two officers standing by the security area.

Oh, no, I thought to myself, believing that I would have to explain my status all over again. But surprisingly, the two officers in the security area just stood there and watched. They were good men who couldn't leave their post, I surmised.

❧ 47 ❧

I turned back round to face my tormentors. It was clear that they were truly frightened. I spoke to them in soothing tones, "It's all right, men. I am here on special detail. You both know the purpose of the Xs on your batons, I take it?"

"Sure we do. It's so we can identify each other. We're under orders to flash them whenever we come in contact with another officer."

"Then the markings have done their jobs. I recognized them, and you know I have recognized them." Keeping one eye on the two constables, I moved forward of them. I saw where Mycroft was positioned. The crate was now crossing the end of the tracks.

"I'm sorry, men," I said, "I do not have time to explain, but you have to stop the crowd from moving any closer. Hold them back! It's a matter of national security. Mycroft Holmes is about to be assassinated. Unless I can get down there to stop it. If you don't act quickly, innocent people will be hurt and perhaps killed."

I saw the panic in the officers' eyes, but thankfully, they didn't question me further. It was now obvious that the mass of onlookers was staggering in both its size and unruly manner. Hoping for a glimpse of the Royals, England's citizens had become a dangerous and desperate mob. And they were heading our way!

Feeling that at any moment we could be trampled, I knew that I had to act. The two constables came to the same conclusion. They wheeled about and trotted towards the mob. The strident voices of the constables collided with the tumultuous roar of the crowd. "Stop!" they yelled, raising their batons and spreading their arms wide. Believing that it would be impossible to stop the press of bodies, I prayed that their intervention would at the very least, delay the forward march of unruly humanity. That might afford me enough time to warn Mycroft and Holmes that I had failed to identify the assassins.

❧ 48 ❧

As I backed away from the courageous officers, I noticed they held their batons with the leather halyard entwined round their wrists. This allowed the wood of the baton to rest against their forearms. Surprisingly, I recalled from my days in the army that they were taking a defensive posture.

I turned and ran in the direction of Mycroft and saw that my friend Sherlock Holmes was being assisted out of the crate by his brother's men.

"Holmes!" I called, over the din of the echoing crowd. "Holmes!"

Upon hearing his name, my friend looked up and saw me running. He smiled wearily, and waved. Mycroft saw my wild gestures and understood immediately. He ducked behind the crate just as the wood splintered round the spot where his head had been silhouetted a second ago.

Tuscano! I thought. He missed Tuscano!

But when I noticed my friend's head swiveling in an entirely different direction, I knew that he had hit his target. The shot had to have come from somewhere else. But where?

I called to the two constables standing at the gauntlet and motioned for them to assist my friends. Having already unbuttoned my coat, I was waving my revolver around frantically. I turned my head in time to see another shot tear into the wood.

"Holmes! Are you all right?"

My chest constricted as the desperateness of the moment began to take its toll on my exertions. I glanced at the security constables again and noticed that one of them had just brought his baton down to his side. He made an unusual snapping movement with his hand, and I recalled seeing that exact motion before. Holmes had made that very same move when he loaded my bullet into the baton that I had assembled.

Shock drilled its way into my brain, and I stumbled to the ground. I fell and suffered a burning abrasion to my scalp and face. Horrified by my clumsiness, I shakily rose to my knees and wiped the blood from my eyes.

At that very instant, Holmes peered round the corner of the crate and saw me struggling to rise. I must have been a terrifying sight, for his eyes went wide and he immediately began to abandon his position to come and assist me.

"Watson's been shot!" cried my friend, standing erect. "My God, what have we done!?"

Mycroft came out of his crouch and began moving forward.

"Stay where you are!" I shouted, trying to be heard over the tumult of the crowd, but realising my efforts had failed. I angrily watched them continue their advance. Their distraction was so complete that they didn't notice the two security constables falling in behind them.

Gasping for air, and willing myself to remain calm, I rested on one knee and raised my pistol. I chose the taller of the two, the man nearest Mycroft, as my first target. I knew that I was aiming at Brewer. Sighting down the barrel of my revolver, I cocked the hammer. From Mycroft's point of view, it must have appeared that I was aiming at him, as the assassin was a mere three feet to his right and behind him.

49

Holding my breath, I slowly squeezed the trigger. Brewer, letting out a yelp, fell suddenly forward onto Mycroft's back. Directing my attention to the constable heading for Holmes, I saw that he had already lowered his baton to the horizontal position and was about to fire.

Seeing his brother falling forward, Sherlock Holmes looked confused. I squinted, sighting my next target, and pulled the trigger. The force of the shot caused the man's arm to fly in the air, and the small puff of smoke escaping his weapon pointed directly skyward. The man crumpled at my friend's feet.

Holmes' face was full of astonishment as he suddenly realised what had happened. He looked down at the body and rolled it over with the toe of his boot. A perfectly placed dot of red was centered between the man's eyes. My friend glanced at me and nodded. He then went to his brother's side and examined the corpse at Mycroft's feet. It, too, had a similar scar in the center of the man's forehead.

As I rose shakily to my feet, the brothers conferred for a moment. With a nod of unity, they dragged the two bodies over to the crate and stuffed them in it before nailing it shut.

Staggering to their side, I arrived in time to see how deeply affected the brothers were regarding their near brush with death, as they leaned against the crate. Mycroft's normally ruddy face was white as flour.

"My God, Watson," said Sherlock Holmes, hoarsely, "how can we ever repay you?"

"Hear, hear," Mycroft Holmes chimed in. "That was an outstanding display of courage and determination under the most trying circumstances. You are to be congratulated, Dr. Watson. I now know why my brother values you so highly."

I felt uncomfortable as the brothers continued to heap praise upon me, but Mycroft's face suddenly clouded when he turned to see the Royal entourage nearing.

"Oh no!" he groaned. "I need two officers to stand and receive the Prince at the security entrance. He will have my head if all does not go smoothly." Mycroft glanced round for inspiration, but I could tell that he could find no solution.

I ran up to the two officers whom I had confronted earlier and told them of Mycroft's wishes. Thankfully, and quite remarkably, these two lone police constables were able to hold the crowd at bay until additional officers arrived. They were disheveled and weary, but they were up for their new assignment. I introduced them to the two brothers and told them of the officers' incredible exploits. Mycroft nodded approvingly and promoted them on the spot to captains. The shocked officers were led away by Mycroft as he gave them their instructions.

Holmes, leaning against the crate, made no pretense of hiding his scrutiny of me. He shook his head in wonder, as I stood calmly by, blotting the blood from my face.

"Incredible, Watson. Simply incredible."

We watched in silence as the Prince and his entourage passed and marched to the awaiting barge that was to take them out to the Royal yacht, The Victoria and Albert II.

Holmes stooped to retrieve the two batons the assassins had dropped and walked to my side. He glanced back over his shoulder and watched his brother receive the first of the Royals. Mycroft, sensing his brother's eyes, waved and followed the Prince down to the gangplank.

"What say we tend to your wounds, then make our way back to Baker Street? Or would you rather stay the night and take in the celebration?"

❧ 50 ❧

"I'm too tired," I said. "Besides, I am in no mood to celebrate."

"Why so foul a mood?" Sherlock Holmes asked me. "The Prince and my brother are safe. We've done our duty and all's well."

"Holmes, how you can stand there and say that all is well? We were nearly killed! And for what? Glory and duty? I think not," I said.

"You were so involved with the case you failed to realise what your brother had done is a crime. He stole the time machine from a private citizen. His actions have caused the deaths of four men, and who knows how many more lives have been forfeit? He shrouds his actions under the veil of national security and tramples on everyone's rights as if they are his to do with what he will."

"I offer no excuses for my brother. He is who he is. However, if it is of any comfort, I am extremely disappointed in him also. I will have a word with him in the near future."

"Which one?" I asked, nodding to the men standing in the doorway of Brewer's shop.

"Pardon?"

"Which future, I mean? How are we ever to know again what time we are in? For all I know, we may have already had this conversation many times before."

Holmes chuckled as we headed up the stairs, but his humour quickly faded upon our seeing the slumped figure of Tuscano, half slouched in a chair, the rifle lying at his feet.

I tilted the corpse back in the chair and saw the single wound in the center of the man's chest. Tuscano's dead eyes stared up at the ceiling, and his face, forever frozen in death, carried a look of confusion.

"Leave him," ordered Holmes. "Mycroft's men will take care of it."

I pulled a blanket from the cot and tossed it over the body. As we toiled with the removal of our disguises, Holmes went about his task with uncommon slowness.

"What's the matter, Holmes?" I asked with growing concern.

"Your words earlier," he responded, while morosely plucking the opaque lens from his eye.

"Forgive me, Holmes. I never should have gone off like that."

"No, old friend. It is I who should apologise. Your observations were correct. If it weren't for you, Watson, I would have failed miserably on this case. You have remained a beacon of truth. I am as much disappointed in my brother as I am with myself. I allowed my personal relationship with my brother to cloud my judgment. 'll deal with Mycroft, but not now, not yet. It would be disloyal and poorly timed. At long last our Queen is stepping back into her public role after mourning the death of her husband. Yes, I am not happy with my brother's actions, but I must wait to confront him."

My friend slouched his shoulders and went to the window. Though I agreed with him wholeheartedly, I knew that it pained him deeply to criticise his brother. I went to stand by my friend's side, hoping to bring him out of his mood, but I could not think of anything to say that would brighten him.

Feeling helpless, I stuffed my hands in my pockets and smiled.

"Dinner is on me." I laughed and pulled out the wad of pound sterling notes, my earnings from the souvenir table.

Holmes turned and looked at my overflowing hands.

"Good old Watson!" he laughed.

— THE END —

ABOUT THE AUTHOR...

CJ LUTTON

CJ (Carl John) Lutton was a Renaissance man, "a person who has wide interests and is expert in several areas." In addition to serving in the US Army for four years in Germany, CJ worked many jobs throughout his life: digging graves at cemeteries, running a print shop, owning an advertising agency, teaching at a correctional institution, and working at a high school. He even tried out for a position as quarterback for the New York Jets! Throughout his life, he wrote. Among other works, he completed four books and had notes for others that featured Sherlock Holmes and his sidekick, Dr. John Watson.

For more information, go to
www.thesherlockstories.com